The

Dishonourable

Groom

A Very British Murder Mystery

Angela Hartley

October 2024

ISBN: 9798339757627

Acknowledgements

Special thanks to all those who have supported me throughout the process of writing and publishing The Dishonourable Groom, and to Sophie Hartley for the design of the cover.

Also to Carol Marriott-Clayton and Roisin Robertson for their invaluable support in the editing process, and especially to Roisin for setting me the challenge of writing a murder mystery in the first place. As my first Murder Mystery novel it has certainly been an interesting experience. Roisin, I hope it lives up to your expectations.

Also by Angela Hartley

Finding Home	Published June 2022
Forever Home	Published October 2022
After the Rain	Published March 2023
The Godmothers	Published October 2023

Available to purchase or download from Amazon

The Dishonourable Groom

A Very British Murder Mystery

Angela Hartley

Chapter 1
The day of the wedding.......

It was Sunday and the perfect day for a wedding. The early morning sun was rising high in an almost cloudless sky, the forecast was for a dry warm day, with the promise of a gentle breeze to keep temperatures manageable. A British summer's day at its very best. It was almost too perfect to be true.

At 0600 hours the team of caterers arrived, parking at the rear of the Old Manor House, ready to offload the contents of their white vans. The florists would be arriving at 0630 hours, leaving them precisely thirty minutes to unload and remove their vans from the driveway before the next team arrived. The wedding was not scheduled to take place until 1500 hours, but there was no time to lose. Guests had been invited to arrive no earlier than 1415 hours, and by then everything had to be perfect, with the driveway and adjacent field cleared to enable guest parking, or taxi drop-offs. Preparations had been managed like a military exercise and there was no doubt today would go like clockwork. The officious wedding planner, Eduardo, who had been employed at great expense to ensure nothing was left to chance, had been quick to point this out to anyone who was not working strictly to the schedule he had prepared.

The week leading up to the wedding day had been frantic with activity. The household at the Old Manor House had been taken over. Mrs Cuthbert, the live-in housekeeper, made almost redundant as a constant stream of workmen came and went through the house and gardens, tutting and sighing at the size of the job at hand. A huge marquee had been erected in the grounds, where the meal and the evening's entertainment would be held. Industrial sized generators had been installed to provide the electricity necessary to keep the air-conditioning running and the marquee cooled, as well as brightly lit. Additionally, the outside terrace, which would be used for welcome drinks, had been decked out with a series of comfortable deckchairs and low tables. Guests would be encouraged to relax in the sun and chat with friends, or cool off outside as the evening progressed. Strings of fairy lights had been put up to provide a romantic ambiance and they were set to automatically come on as the evening fell.

A pop-up bar had also been installed, adjacent to the terrace and the marquee, from where the champagne would flow, with wine waiters in attendance throughout the day. The marquee had seating for the one or so hundred guests who had been invited, with a dance floor laid for later in the evening, when a small jazz band would play a selection of lively music. A series of round matching tables and chairs had been rented for the occasion, all trimmed in tablecloths and chair covers befitting of the occasion. There was even a bank of executive toilets – posh portaloos – installed behind the garages for the guests' convenience. "Put them close enough, but not too close," Eduardo had instructed the company when their engineers arrived to install them earlier that week.

The inside of the house had not gone untouched either, with Eduardo and Mrs Cuthbert almost coming to blows after he insisted the house needed a serious declutter, with any excess furniture being promptly moved into storage, or relocated. A transit van had arrived to cart off several pieces of furniture, with some of the smaller items retired to other parts of the house.

"The house needs room for people to flow through it, without bumping into that antique desk, or those overstuffed chairs," he had insisted, pointing disparagingly at some of the older pieces of furniture that filled the main reception rooms. "And how would his lordship feel, madam, if someone knocked over that priceless vase, or damaged his lordship's artwork?" he had added to emphasise his point, to say nothing of upselling his fees. No, it was an expensive business getting married.

The big day had finally arrived. Today was all about those last-minute touches, to say nothing of the actual wedding ceremony itself, with the celebrant due to arrive at 1430 hours. The morning suits had been collected the previous day from the gentlemen's outfitters in the town, the hair and makeup team was scheduled to arrive at 1030 hours to attend the bridal party and the wedding cake would be delivered at 1300 hours and set up in the marquee. The remainder of the food for the main wedding breakfast and the evening buffet would arrive at 1330 hours. It had already been prepared off site and would be kept warm, or chilled, ahead of service, which was to begin promptly at 1630 hours, before the evening celebrations which would begin at 2000 hours. With taxis, or carriages as Eduardo was prone to saying, to be booked for 0100 hours the following morning.

As the caterers approached the back of the Old Manor House, carefully carrying the first of the trays of canapés that needed to be kept chilled, they were whistling in tune with the birds chirping away in the distance. Despite the early hour they were happy to be working the wedding. It was going to be a long day, but the overtime alone was not to be sniffed at, and with so many dignitaries attending, they might even get tips.

As Joe, the designated catering manager for the event, went to unlock the back door with the key he'd been entrusted, he was surprised to notice it already unlocked. Nevertheless, he pushed it open and stepped back.

"It looks like we're not the first here. After you, milady." He smiled and winked, allowing Suki, his young kitchen assistant, to go ahead of him. She laughed. Obviously working at the Old Manor House was giving him airs and graces, she thought.

"Of course, kind sir. Your wish is my command." She liked working with Joe and enjoyed his banter.

"Why don't you walk these trays straight through to the chiller in the utility room, and I'll go and fetch the next two." He put his tray down as he turned back towards the van and started walking out.

"Ahh…" screamed the kitchen assistant, as she switched on the main light with her elbow, immediately dropping her tray of neatly laid out canapés. The clang of the stainless-steel platter crashing to the ground did nothing to drown out her cries.

"What on earth is the matter? Is everything okay?" Joe questioned on hearing the clattering of the plate and Suki's screams. The mix of prawn and mushroom vol-au-vents littering the stone floor suggested all was not as it should be as he re-entered the kitchen a few moments later.

As Suki stood motionless, simply pointing at the floor and unable to utter a single word, Joe just about managed to make out the scene in front of her. The sight of a dead body, lying in a pool of what looked like its own congealed blood, behind the island in the centre of the kitchen, seemed somewhat incongruous to the rest of the wedding paraphernalia that was already scattered around the kitchen.

He had the strangest feeling a dead body had not been in Eduardo's plan.

Angela Hartley

On hearing the screams, Nanny Tilbury opened her bedroom window in the annex building above the garage. It was where she had called home for the last thirty years. As the children's old nanny, at seventy-three she no longer had a formal role in the household. She simply lived out her time in the grace-and-favour apartment provided to her, courtesy of Lady Susan, the late lady of the manor. Nanny Tilbury was a light sleeper and at her age rarely got a decent night's sleep.

From her vantage point, she could just about make out the kitchen door and had heard the caterers' vans arrive a few minutes earlier. In fact, she had discreetly watched all manner of comings and goings from her windows over the years, often laughing at the thought of keeping a diary as she recalled some of the sights she had seen. Nowadays her eyesight was not quite what it had been, but even so, she still did not like to miss anything.

Quickly putting on a jacket over her lilac nightdress and slipping her feet into her outdoor shoes, she made her way across the courtyard to see what all the commotion was about. She knew the household had a busy day planned with all the final preparations for the wedding, so even if the others were not already awake, she imagined from the sheer volume of the screams it would not be too long before they too came downstairs, to investigate what was going on.

"Oh dear," she whispered as she entered the kitchen and saw the body of his lordship splayed out on the floor, a puddle of congealed blood around his head, with the caterers looking on. "Is he dead?" she asked, then quickly added, "has anyone phoned the police, or called the family down yet?"

She tried to recall how many people had planned to stay over the previous evening, and therefore who was actually sleeping in the house. From memory, there were three or four of his lordship's children, with their partners and their children, as well as the bride-to-be. In terms of other friends or relatives, she had no idea. Having not been invited to the party herself, there was no way she could say for certain either how it had ended, or who might be there. The house boasted eight double bedrooms, so had friends decided to stay over there would have been plenty of space. In addition, there was the annex at the rear of the property where Mrs Cuthbert, the current housekeeper, lived with her husband, Wilf. He did the general maintenance around the place and was a handy man to know, at times.

Neither Joe nor Suki uttered a word in response to her questions. They simply continued to stare at the body, shaking their heads.

"Come here, dear, I imagine you're in shock," Nanny said, putting her arm gently around Suki so as not to startle her further. "Shall I pop the kettle on and make you both a cup of sweet tea, before I go and call Mrs Cuthbert and the rest of the family? I imagine once the police arrive, they'll need to speak to you both."

"Today of all days," she tutted to herself, as she left the kitchen to climb the stairs to wake the rest of the household, surprised no one had already come down. "It looks like there won't be a wedding after all. Not, I imagine, with the groom dead on the kitchen floor."

Chapter 2

A month or so earlier......

Frank Paulson ran a rather unorthodox business. Well, more precisely, he ran a traditional business, just in an unorthodox manner. The business was quite simply a construction firm, which, on the surface, built homes of distinction. Its clientele were those who could afford to pay the inflated prices it charged, mainly due to the value of the land on which the prestigious homes were sited. Nothing was done cheaply. Quality and service were the main watchwords of the company, with a Paulson home something to be desired, even envied.

Beneath the marketing blurb, though, all was not as it seemed. There were secrets and agreements hidden among the dated metal filing cabinets, locked away from prying eyes, and should they ever see the light of day, Frank was sure they would not stand up to scrutiny. Deals had been done that were not necessarily above board, or in some cases even legitimate. Deals that only Frank knew about. Well, Frank and the shady characters with whom he had struck them. Deals that were coming back to haunt him.

His priority now was to think how he could protect himself and his business, and do it quickly, as the vultures were already circling.

The business had been established for over thirty years. In the early days it had benefitted from a significant capital injection from his in-laws, Lord and Lady Whinchcliffe, the original Lord and Lady of the Old Manor House. They settled a large sum of money, and a sizeable piece of land, onto their son-in-law after his marriage to their only daughter Susan. Their intention was clear, Frank would have the wherewithal to support her in the lifestyle to which she had become accustomed, and he needed to work at making it a success.

As the only daughter of landed gentry, Susan had been brought up to expect a good standard of living, the best life had to offer. Frank was not perhaps the titled son-in-law they would have hoped their daughter would marry, but they respected her choice in husband. And with their aristocratic connections and some financial backing, what could possibly go wrong?

As Frank sat back in his worn leather chair in his office, staring out of the window and surveying the depot, he wondered, not for the first time, where it had all started to unravel. His in-laws would no doubt be turning in their graves if they could see the pickle he had got himself into. At sixty-four, he should be reaping the benefits of his years of hard work, planning a long and happy retirement for himself, with a nice little nest egg to leave his children. He should even be looking forward to jetting off on honeymoon with his soon to be bride. Whereas, in reality he was dreading the next few months. The uncertainty he was facing from all directions was mounting up, his anxiety levels increasing daily. He had no clear plan how he was going to get through it this time, or even what his options were, assuming he had any. And with no one to turn to for advice, he was at his wit's end.

"Dad, some of the materials we've ordered for the new housing development have not been delivered, again." Jimmy was fuming as he stormed into his father's office, clearly looking for a resolution. He had teams of guys on standby, and every day's waiting time was costing the business money. "I've just been onto some of the suppliers, and the recurring theme appears to be that deliveries are being held, due to payment issues. I've already spoken to Si and he's no idea what's going on, so do you know what's happening?"

James, or Jimmy as his friends called him, was Frank's eldest son. He had joined his father in the building trade nearly twenty years previously, after leaving school at sixteen. He was a reasonably bright young man, although not at all academic. He had seen no benefit in wasting his time studying any longer than was necessary, or even going onto sixth form. So, with a clutch of mediocre grades in his GCSEs he had left school and turned up at the building site the following day, looking for work. He was a strapping lad and at over six feet tall, with a muscular frame, as well as being someone who liked to make himself useful, Frank was happy his son had wanted to follow him into the building trade.

Nowadays, Jimmy oversaw most of the development projects, and was not averse to getting stuck in, if needed, regularly helping out if they were a man or two down. By trade he was an electrician, having eventually gone back to college to complete his City and Guilds, but over the years he had learnt to turn his hand to almost anything. He had a powerful reach and was as happy swinging a hammer or digging a trench as he was with a screwdriver. He had a strong work ethic, and had no problem getting his hands dirty.

"Let me have a look into it, Son. I've got a lot on at the moment."

"Well, this can't wait, Dad."

Frank was still staring out of the window, failing to engage with his son. Jimmy was getting more frustrated with his father's attitude.

"Are you going to tell me what the problem is, or not? As I said, I've already spoken to Si and he's no idea what's going on either. As far as he's concerned, there should be sufficient funds in the account. And, he doesn't believe our position as a creditor has worsened, so he can't see what the issue is."

Over recent years, Jimmy and Frank were not as close as they had been, and as grown men they tended not to confide in each other on a business or a personal level. Jimmy was much closer to Simon, Frank's son-in-law and his brother-in-law. They were as thick as thieves and had been ever since their schooldays. Over the years the family joke had always been that Simon provided the brains whilst Jimmy provided the brawn in their friendship. Now, working together in the family's business, they were a formidable pairing. Almost brothers, although Frank was never slow to slap either of them down, should they ever overstep the mark.

Simon, now responsible for managing the administration and sales side of the business, was a great asset. Having married Frank's daughter, Judy, over fifteen years ago, he had entered the business after graduating in Economics. He knew his way around facts and figures, and although a job in the city had beckoned, Judy was desperate to stay close to home. At the time, her mum had not long since died, and she wanted to be there to support her father. She was clearly the apple of his eye, his favourite child, able to twist him around her little finger without any problem. So, getting a plum job for her future husband in the family business had been an easy ask, and had not even caused her to break sweat, with the beauty of it that Frank thought it was his idea.

Family and friends had rallied around Frank after Susan's untimely death. It was nearly twenty years since a drunk driver had crashed into their vehicle and killed her outright when returning from a night out. The four children were distraught, but they were strong as a unit and tried to provide their father with the support and comfort he needed as he grieved. In fact, as a family they became reliant on each other to get through.

Well, at least until Frank found he needed more than the support of his children, and started looking around for more female company.

That was over ten years ago, when he met and married his second wife, Alison. Alison was nice enough, they thought. She appeared to make their father happy, and as she did not try to replace their mother, Frank's children could handle her. After all, Nanny Tilbury was there to do that job. She was the constant in their lives, the one they turned to for affection. In time, they even warmed to their half-brother, Mason, when he came along. As a baby he was delightful.

What none of them could warm to, though, was their father's string of affairs, which started barely two years into the marriage. Or the way he treated Alison when he eventually divorced her, trying to get away with the most basic settlement his expensive lawyers could engineer. They were also furious that Alison and Mason had effectively been wiped from their lives too, their father making it clear that they were no longer welcome at the Old Manor House. To the children's knowledge, they had done nothing to warrant such treatment, and after all, Mason was their half-brother, so why should they be banned from seeing him?

Since then, James and his dad had barely seen eye to eye. James was not only furious with his dad for cheating on his ex-wife, but also for creating a reputation for himself that reflected badly on the family's name. And now he was planning on marrying the latest scheming little bitch in just over a month's time, due to the fact he had managed to get her pregnant too. In his view, that was a step too far.

James and his siblings had little, if any, patience for the next Mrs Paulson. A woman they believed had wormed her way into their father's life, her sights clearly set on the prize of becoming the next lady of the manor. Miranda Swann was a true gold digger; someone they would need to keep their eyes on.

"Not now, James. Can't you just get on with it, and leave me to think, in peace? Shut the door on your way out. I don't want disturbing."

Money was the root of all evil, and the distinct lack of it was causing Frank more issues than he cared to realise.

Chapter 3

"Make sure mine's an extra-large one, please Si. In fact, after the day I've had, why not just order me a bottle." Judy was fuming. She made her way over to join the others at the table while her husband went to the bar. She and Simon had arranged to meet her brother, Jimmy, and his wife, Katie, at seven o'clock in the Three Pheasants and they were already thirty minutes late. Tonight was not going at all to plan.

As she walked towards the table, she noticed Mrs Cuthbert and her husband, Wilf, sitting quietly in the corner, heads down and talking quietly to one another. They appeared not to have noticed her, so she moved on quickly before they looked up. Mrs Cuthbert was a bit of an enigma to Judy. She had worked at the Old Manor House for nearly five years, and Judy could honestly say she knew as much about her now as she did on the day she first arrived. Wilf, on the other hand, was chatty and very pleasant. Whenever she bumped into him around the house or gardens, he was always happy to stop and pass the time of day. "Mrs Cuthbert, Ana-Maria, is Romanian," Wilf had advised, in an attempt to excuse the fact his wife rarely spoke unless spoken to. "Her English isn't the best, but she's a hard worker," he had gone on to explain.

"Is everything okay?" enquired Katie, as her sister-in-law sat down at the table, obviously distressed by something. "You're late and you look stressed. Have the boys been playing up again?"

"No, the boys are fine. I've left them watching TV with Rosie. She offered to sit with them for me for a couple of hours. I think what she really needed was a night out of the house, and I can't blame her. That woman is the pits."

"I think I'll leave you two to your plotting and go and help Si." Jimmy, sensing where the conversation was going, picked up his pint and walked over to the bar. As much as he loved his sister, experience told him that when she was in that type of mood it was worth steering well clear. Something, or more likely someone, had rattled her cage and he did not need to stay around to hear about it. He had enough on his own mind to deal with, without adding her troubles too.

"I presume you're referring to Miranda? What's she done this time?" It was no secret that Judy and her future step-mother did not see eye to eye. Of the siblings, Judy had always been the closest to their father, and after their mum had died, in her view no woman was ever going to be good enough for her dad.

Judy had been fifteen when the accident happened. It hit her hard and as well as dealing with her own grief she found she was the shoulder her dad cried on, as well as the one he turned to for help with the younger children. She loved her dad, so was happy to be there for him.

Well, at least until he rediscovered women. Judy soon noticed a pattern beginning to form, of her father sneaking women back to the house, late at night, when he thought everyone was tucked up in bed or fast asleep. Or him staying out until the early hours, bedding down someplace else and not returning until the following morning. He sought comfort wherever, and with whomever, he could find. Before eventually deciding to remarry, arguing he was feeling lonely. At which point, they were all palmed off to Nanny, their father's sympathies and attention diverted elsewhere.

Alison, his second wife, had been bearable. She had never attempted to replace their mother, or put too hard a stamp on their house or family life. She largely settled into the household, almost like a family guest, happy to go along with whatever Frank wanted. In time, even Mason, their son, had felt part of the family, although Judy was concerned it gave their old nanny more work to do, at a time when she should be winding down, not having the extra responsibility of a newborn heaped upon her.

Miranda, though, was something else. From the first instance she had entered the house she had been manipulative, almost divisive in coming between Frank and his children. She had clearly attempted to lord it over the family, and was never shy to point out how much Frank wanted her there, especially once she had become pregnant and was expecting their child. They were his future, making everyone else feel like their time had passed.

"I've spent the day at the manor being talked at by her. All her plans for the wedding. Seating plans, table designs, floral displays, to name but a few of her current list of moans. Nothing is ever going to be quite right for her, is it? You'd think it was the celebrity event of the century the way she's going on. Not a small country do in the gardens of a family home. And the money she's spending is obscene. Those wedding planners and caterers alone must be costing a fortune, looking at what she's ordered. God only knows how much Dad's having to fork out to satisfy that little bitch's whims this time, assuming he has any idea what she's charging to his card. You'd think he'd know when to say No, enough's enough!"

"I tend to agree, but perhaps keep your voice down a bit." Katie had noticed Mrs Cuthbert at the table behind them, so did not want word getting out, or gossip spreading, about family discord. Katie was tactful, generally managing to keep her distance when it came to discussing family matters, careful to avoid the politics it sometimes engendered. This time, though, even she had been drawn unwittingly into the charade.

"I had to take Maia yesterday for her final dress fitting and it was painful. The dress is nice enough, although not what I'd have chosen myself. It's just all the fuss that's accompanying it. And her manner is awful - the way she spoke to the lady in the bridal shop was embarrassing. I didn't know where to look. You'd think she'd be happy about getting married, wouldn't you? No, something doesn't add up. Not in my view, at least."

"I know what you mean." Judy made an extra effort to keep her voice down. "I'd happily swing for her. What she's putting Dad through is simply criminal. The pressure he's under to get married, at such speed before her bump's showing too much, is incredible. How vain is she? Wouldn't you think, in this day and age, she could have avoided getting herself pregnant in the first place, or at least be proud enough to celebrate it? Why we're under some sort of moratorium to keep quiet baffles me. Unless she set out to trap him, that is? I wouldn't put it past her. God, to think she's about to produce a child, who could be just like her, it's frightening."

"I presume you're still talking about Miranda?" Jimmy and Si were walking back from the bar, carrying a bottle of chardonnay, as instructed.

"Yes, I was just saying I could almost kill her." Judy, took a huge glug of the wine in an attempt to calm herself down.

"Well, if you deal with her, I'll deal with Dad," added Jimmy. "The way he spoke to me today wasn't just rude, it was insulting. He was treating me like a nobody, not like his son or a partner in the business. He's been off with everyone recently, hasn't he Si? I don't know what's come over him."

"Yeah, there's definitely something not right. I get the distinct impression he's hiding something from both of us, and I can't work it out. There's something wrong with the numbers, and the accounts aren't adding up the way they should either.

When I approached him on it yesterday and asked him to explain a couple of transactions, I got a real flea in the ear. He told me to mind my own business and just get on with my job. I know he's family, and he's got a lot going on at the moment, but I'm not prepared to be spoken to like that by anyone, especially when I was only doing my job. I seriously felt like punching his lights out."

"Violence, that's not like you, Si." Judy laughed in an attempt to lighten the mood. "I don't think I've ever seen you punch your way out of a paper bag, let alone suggest fighting anyone before. He's really gotten to you this time, hasn't he?"

Judy had known Si for most of his life and had never witnessed anything of this side of his nature before. Nor had she ever sensed her brother, or husband, were unhappy with the way the business was being run. As junior partners Jimmy and Si had always worked harmoniously with Frank, to her knowledge at least. There was obviously some undercurrent that she was unaware of between them and her father. The knowledge of which made her feel distinctly uncomfortable.

"Yeah, the sooner he retires or gets out of the picture, the better it'll be for all of us. We can then get on and run the business, the way we want, can't we Jimmy?"

"I'll drink to that, Si." Jimmy raised his now empty pint glass. "Well, I will once I've got the next round in. Ladies, I presume you're alright for another drink? Si, do you want to come to the bar with me, and we'll leave them to continue their moaning?"

Chapter 4

Ana-Maria had noticed the others in the bar and had chosen to keep her head down, instead of risking the chance they might try to engage in conversation with her, or Wilf for that matter. She had noticed James and his wife Katie come in earlier. They both looked reasonably chirpy and Katie looked very pretty in her summer dress, with the handbag she was carrying having a designer label, last season's range she would hazard a guess. Ana-Maria appreciated nice things and could tell quality when she saw it. Access to that world was one of the things she missed most about her new life in England.

They were followed shortly by Judy and her husband Simon. Ana-Maria liked Simon. He was very good looking and reminded her of the boys at home in Romania. His height and his dark looks, with those pronounced features, made him appear striking, if not traditionally good looking. In fact, he looked similar to James, although James had a much stockier build. Judy, by comparison was diminutive, and her fair complexion made them look like an odd couple. In fact, Judy did not look like the rest of the family at all. Ana-Maria had seen pictures of their dead mother, Susan, around the house, and it was obvious Judy took after her side of the family. The aristocratic side, if what Nanny Tilbury said could be relied upon.

Wilf had suggested they go over and say hello. Ana-Maria gave him one of her looks, and in no uncertain terms told him what she thought of that idea. She'd had enough of that family recently, and on her one night off she had no intention of socialising with them too. No, a quiet drink and some time to think was what she needed.

"What's wrong with you today, Ana? I was only going to say hello, not invite them over for dinner. I was only being friendly." He had noticed his wife's body language when they had first walked in. It had almost stiffened at the sight of them. And there was something else, her eyes portrayed a sense of fear, or foreboding. Something he could not quite fathom.

"I don't need friends and I don't feel comfortable anymore. I think it's time to move on." As she spoke quietly, she kept her face down towards the table, failing to meet Wilf's eyes. He struggled hard to hear what she was saying, and even harder to understand where the sentiment was coming from.

"Whatever's the matter with you tonight, love? Where's that come from? You've got a good job at the manor, and there's plenty there for me to do. We've got a roof over our heads and we're together. We don't want for anything, so what more do you need?"

"I don't feel comfortable, I've told you. I don't feel safe. I've overheard things and some things are not right. We need to think what to do next, where to move to."

Wilf had met Ana-Maria online six years previously. At the time, she was in her early thirties and at fifty-five he was over twenty years her senior. He was retired, widowed, and looking for companionship, even a new relationship if he could find the right woman. After his wife had died suddenly, and without any children or grandchildren to his name, he was lonely. He was outgoing and loved the company of people around him.

She, on the other hand, and unbeknown to Wilf, was looking for a passport to England, an escape from Romania and the chance for a new start. She was young, attractive and had her whole life ahead of her, a life that would allow her to find true love. Wilf was her ticket to finding that life.

After several months of online messaging, Wilf had paid for her to come over to England for a visit, a short holiday to get to know each other better. Messaging and the occasional video call was useful, but how would they get to know each other seriously if she did not come over, Ana-Maria had argued? Wilf agreed and sorted her paperwork out, enabling her to arrive shortly thereafter. He met her at the airport and watched as she carried a small suitcase containing her life's possessions.

The sob story of the impoverished life in Romania she had led flowed effortlessly from her pretty lips. She painted herself as a vulnerable young woman, raised in a poor country, whose life was limited by the opportunities the country presented her. She was unmarried, only thirty-one with both parents recently dead, and she was left with nothing. She yearned for a new life in a country with opportunity, and to spend it with someone she loved. She had no one left to care for her, and Wilf had become special to her over the months, his messages keeping her going through her darkest days. She also spoke so warmly about England, marvelling at everything she saw, as she looked lovingly at Wilf, fluttering her eyelashes in the process.

Wilf listened, but cared little about the girl's background, only how he could help her. As a widower, in his mid-fifties, with little chance of developing a new relationship before had Ana-Maria turned up, what did it matter if some of her story was being laid on a little too thickly, as he sensed was the case? He could cope with that, and was sure in time the truth would become clearer.

Unbeknown to Wilf, her story was a complete fabrication, and rather than teasing out any vestige of truth over the years Ana-Maria had never wavered from her version.

The pretence had been maintained ever since, to the point where at times she believed in the new person she had created.

Nevertheless, Wilf fell for it, hook, line and sinker and they married within a few months of that first visit in a small service at the local registry office, a couple of passers-by acting as their witnesses. If anyone wondered what an attractive young woman was doing with a man, old enough to be her father, dressed in a pretty white dress and carrying a small bouquet, then at least they had the decency not to enquire. She had never returned to Romania thereafter. From that point her background and her history became a closed book.

Ana-Maria had moved into Wilf's family home in the large town where he lived on the outskirts of Birmingham. It was a nice little semi-detached house with a small garden and three bedrooms, and above all the mortgage was all paid off. It was more than sufficient for their needs and she marvelled at all the facilities it had, and how comfortable she felt being there.

Wilf and his first wife had bought the house when they had initially married in the 1990s. His wife had been very houseproud and in her memory he had maintained everything just the way she had liked it, which meant rather than comfortable the house was dated, the furniture old-fashioned and worn.

After the initial honeymoon period, Ana-Maria started making it clear that she could not settle there. The town was too busy for her, with too many people around and she felt uncomfortable, almost claustrophobic. She also argued that not being able to speak the language as well as she had hoped did not help, with people being intolerant of her accent whenever she went out simply adding to her discomfort.

When she spotted an advert in the local newspaper, less than twelve months after their wedding, inviting applications for a housekeeper at a private family home, in a small town in the Oxfordshire countryside, it sounded perfect. The salary was not huge, but once they sold the house they would not need much, she had argued. After all, their living expenses would be met at the Old Manor House, so what else did they want?

Importantly for Ana-Maria, it was a place where she could lie low with the chances of being recognised, or anyone asking questions about her homeland, remote. Wilf had gone along with her plan, selling the house and banking the proceeds from the sale somewhere safe, should they ever need it again.

"So, what have you overheard that's spooked you this time? Whatever it is, I'm sure it's not something to fret over, or anything we can't resolve, one way or another."

Wilf felt protective towards his wife. He had long since resigned himself to the fact that there would never be love, or the type of relationship he had hoped for. Nevertheless, he felt a need to keep her safe and honour the commitments he had made to her on their wedding day. In terms of what she felt towards him, well, that was a separate question. Her vulnerability was still there, and he sensed she needed him, although almost like a favoured uncle, a protector, rather than a lover.

"Come on, tell me what the matter is, love," he beseeched.

"As you wish, but try to keep your voice down. I can see them over there, watching us." She was starting to feel a little paranoid as her eyes roamed around the pub. "I overheard that woman say as soon as they marry we are out. She wants a new start and a new housekeeper."

"Who do you mean, Miranda?" He had looked around and could not see who she was referring to otherwise. "Don't you want to work for her and his lordship anymore?

Because I'm sure what you overheard was probably just a misunderstanding, don't you think?"

"He's not 'his lordship'. He just pretends to be. Nanny says he's a bad-apple. His dead wife's parents were Lord and Lady, but he's nothing more than a builder. He just likes to think he's important."

"Well, that's as may be. He's our employer, though, so we have to give him some respect, don't we?" Wilf did not doubt what his wife said. He had heard talk around the town that Frank had all but insisted the locals adopt the formal title for him, once his father-in-law had passed away. His wife, Susan, had not thought anything of it. The household already called her Lady, so if Frank wanted to call himself Lord, then she was not going to fight him over it. What did it matter anyway, was her view. It was only an honorary title, after all, although at the time it had obviously grated on some of the older inhabitants of the town, and by the sounds of it, still did.

"I did not misunderstand, and I don't like him either. Not anymore. I know when things are not good, and I tell you, they are not good." Ana-Maria had noticed a few of the associates Frank had invited into the house recently. People he was in business with, or trying to impress from the way he had instructed her to serve them. Some of the looks they gave her had spooked her; their names ones she recognised as Eastern European, their mannerisms familiar. She had seen men like that before, had dealings with them, dealings that had left her fleeing her homeland for safety. Experiences she had never explained, or shared with Wilf, on any level. She was in no hurry to cross paths with them again, and if her employer had got himself mixed up in something dodgy, as she suspected, she wanted nothing to do with it.

As much as she may have wanted, Ana-Maria could not explain any of that to Wilf, so preferred to simply lay the blame at Miranda's door. "I think if she wants me out, then I should probably start to think about where we could move to. I will start to look for other positions. We do not want, how do you say, to be booted out, do we?"

"Well, no we don't. But I don't think it'll come to that. I'm sure it will all die down once they're married, and you might actually grow to like her." Wilf tried to console his wife. He was not ready to move on yet. He quite liked the Old Manor House and the pottering around he did there. It was just enough to keep him busy and out of mischief, and he even felt like he had made a few friends. Apart from which, where would they go? They may have a little money left in the bank, but not enough to get by in the long term. "Let's not try to be too hasty, shall we? Let's see how the land lies, once the dust has settled. Now, do you want another drink, or is it time for us to be heading home?"

Ana-Maria gave her husband a look that clearly said the discussion was not over; resigning herself to wait for another day to bring it back up again. The last thing she needed was for someone to go digging into her past, and the longer they stayed in one place, the higher that risk became. Neither her old life nor her new life was as it appeared, and if she was to work towards establishing the new life she wanted, any skeletons were best left well and truly hidden.

Chapter 5

Rosie pulled the car slowly into the driveway around eleven o'clock later that evening. She had enjoyed a couple of hours of mindless fun with her young nephews and was in no hurry to get home. She had chilled on her sister's couch, eaten popcorn and looked after the two boys as they watched a couple of superhero movies. They insisted on giving her a running commentary throughout each film, competing between themselves to see who could explain the characters and the plots best. Who were the goodies and who were the baddies, screaming in delight whenever a baddie got blasted by whatever good force was working against him. She nodded in all the right places, but they were not her type of films at all, and when bedtime arrived she happily switched channels for the latest instalment of the Netflix series she was currently absorbed in.

Rosie was up to series three of *How to get away with Murder*, and was fascinated. A friend at the dress agency that she ran had recommended it, and Rosie was in catch-up mode, anxious to understand how Annalise and her students would navigate their way through the latest drama. It was full of plots and twists and kept her on the edge of her seat, guessing about whether they would get away with the crimes that had been committed.

Judy and Simon had arrived home around ten o'clock – Judy a little worse for wear by the way she staggered up the drive, to say nothing of the way she slurred her words as she came into the house. "We're home," she announced, for all to hear. The fresh air had done nothing to sober her up.

"Shush, you'll wake the boys," Rosie had counselled, raising a finger to her lips as they entered the lounge and pressed hold on the episode she was watching. "They only went up about forty minutes ago, so knowing those two they're probably not asleep yet."

"Thanks, Rosie. I'll go and check them," Simon offered. "Judy, why don't you put the kettle on and make yourself a strong black coffee?" The look he gave his wife clearly indicated she needed it.

"Are you staying for a drink, Rosie, or do you need to get off?"

"I'm in no rush, so yeah a coffee would be great, thanks."

"So, how's everything up at the manor? I was telling Katie earlier that it all got a little heated this afternoon when I was there. I was so glad to escape. Miranda's being a real cow at the moment, isn't she? She's so demanding. I don't know what Dad sees in her."

"Well, after you left it didn't get any easier. I went upstairs, but I could hear them talking, well arguing really. And from the sounds of what I overheard, I think both Richard and I are on borrowed time. We're going to need to look for somewhere else to live shortly, as I got the distinct impression we're not going to be welcome there once they're married."

"Why do you say that? It's your home and Dad wouldn't throw you out, surely?"

"Miranda's planning all sorts of changes, apparently. She was even talking about converting the annex above the garage into a gym or a studio for her. Somewhere she can have private Pilates sessions, or whatever it is she's into, rather than having to drive five miles down the road to the leisure centre. It's absurd. I dread to think what Nanny would say if she ever got wind of what they were thinking of doing to her home. Because by the sounds of it, she'll be homeless too.

And my bedroom is to become the nursery, with a playroom attached to it. Why they need to do that is anyone's guess, especially as Mason's room was the nursery, and it could easily be repapered if they have a girl. Why can't they use that, and why's it my room that's being targeted, when there are so many other rooms to choose from? It's a mystery. The message was clear, though. We're not part of their scheme."

"What did Dad say? Surely he didn't agree to it?"

"He didn't say much. He lets her get away with murder, though, doesn't he? Whatever Miranda wants, Miranda gets. He's beginning to really wind me up too, almost as much as she does."

"Well, I don't think either of them are going out of their way to win friends at the moment. They're both so selfish and self-centred, and I don't think I'd have ever said that about Dad. He's changed since he met her, and not for the better."

Simon caught the tail end of the woes Rosie had been recounting. Layered on top of their earlier discussions in the pub, he was starting to get increasingly worried. Unless Frank had access to significant private funds he was unaware of, or doing deals on the side that he and Jimmy were not party to, something did not stack up. The financial implications of Frank's behaviour was almost irrational and completely out of character. Frank was normally risk averse in business matters, careful with his money.

Managing the company's finances meant Simon had access to numbers that the others didn't see, but from what he did see, he feared that unless the spending was reined in significantly, Frank's actions could be putting the financial security of the business, and the family's home, into jeopardy.

As Rosie re-entered the house, a degree of calm appeared to have fallen on the Old Manor House since she had left it several hours previously. It was eerily quiet. A brief lull before the next storm, she imagined, realising one would not be too far off, not if tonight's argument was anything to go by. Tensions were clearly running high prior to the wedding day.

Other than the kitchen light shining in the distance, the rest of the downstairs rooms were in darkness. Her dad and Miranda were either already in bed, or still out, Rosie presumed. She had overheard Miranda earlier mentioning that she wanted Frank to take her out for dinner to celebrate the pregnancy, now that her appetite was starting to return, and before she got too big to enjoy it, or fit into any of her designer dresses. At almost ten weeks pregnant the bouts of morning sickness had still not passed and for now at least there was no sign of any bump. Her stomach was still flat; her strong abdominal muscle remaining taut, thanks to her rigorous Pilates routine. Rosie might not like the woman, but she could do nothing to hide her envy towards her future step-mother's figure.

Making her way to the kitchen to get a glass of water to take upstairs, Rosie was surprised to see Richard and Nanny sitting at the breakfast table, enjoying a cup of hot chocolate and a bowl of ice cream, chatting away to each other. They both stopped talking as she entered, almost giving the impression she had disturbed their conversation.

"Oh hello, dear." Nanny smiled over at her. "Richard was just telling me a little about the wedding plans. I believe there's a marquee planned, and caterers. I'm sure it will be lovely. Only three weeks left to go, I understand." Nanny was not blind to the fact the children did not like Miranda. She had eyes and ears, and missed little of what went on in the house.

"Anyway, enough of that. Did you have a nice evening with the boys? I thought I'd wait up for you. You know I don't sleep too well until I know you're all safely home. I'll make you a nice warm drink, shall I?"

At twenty-eight and twenty-seven respectively, it had been a long time since either Rosie or Richard needed a nanny, or anyone else, to wait up for them, but that never stopped Nanny Tilbury from fussing. She had nursed them both as babies, and without children of her own, it was clear she loved them as if they were her own.

"Yes, I've had a lovely evening, thanks, and you didn't need to wait up for me. I just came in for a glass of water before going upstairs." Rosie yawned - it had been a long day and she was tired and ready for her bed.

"That's nice. While you're here, though, why don't I make you a mug of hot chocolate, just the way you like it, with plenty of milk? That will help you sleep. I don't imagine you'll want a bowl of ice cream, too?" For years, Nanny and Richard had sneaked down to the kitchen to indulge in their shared passion; a passion no one else could explain or choose to join them in. "Then you can sit and talk for a few minutes while you drink it, can't you? It seems ages since we've had a proper chat, just the three of us, and I do so miss them."

She smiled over at Nanny Tilbury, noticing for the first time how much she had aged in the last few years, how her clothes had begun to sag, the increasing number of wrinkles around her greying eyes. She had once been sprightly, running around after four children, before Mason arrived, making it five. She never complained, she just got on with her business without any fuss. To look at her now, as she slowly rose to boil some milk, Rosie felt sorry for her. The mere thought of her being thrown out of her home, after all her years of loyal service, simply to make way for an exercise studio, was intolerable. She was not prepared to let her father do it. She would be having strong words with him in the morning.

"Alright then, you win. But no to the ice-cream. That's gross." She exchanged a wry smile with Richard as she sat down, both fully aware how much Nanny liked to talk. And, since she no longer had a real role in the household, and little life beyond her front door, they felt duty bound to humour her. "Just, please don't ask me anything about the movies I've just watched with the boys, as I'm clueless."

Chapter 6

Present day………

Detective Sergeant Ruth Jacobs arrived at the Old Manor House within an hour of the police receiving the call to the emergency 999 line, driving her police car up to the front gates of the property and pressing the buzzer to gain access. The call had been patched directly through to her office as the incident had been reported at an address that was in her vicinity, with the request that one of her officers follow up on the report. She was advised a body had been discovered on the property, and to expect an ambulance to be arriving on the scene in due course. It was not being treated as an emergency, as the body was already dead. Time of death could not be accounted for, but the corpse was cold, according to eyewitness reports at the scene.

It was a quiet Sunday morning, with little prospect of much else happening for the remainder of the day, so for DS Jacobs the call at least provided something to get excited by; a break from the normal monotony that passed for a weekend in Chidlington. "It's not every day a dead body's discovered, is it? Something meaty to get stuck into," she thought to herself, allowing her dark humour to take hold. It certainly made a welcome change to the usual call outs her officers had to deal with.

Chidlington was a relatively sleepy hollow, nestled in and around pretty farmland in the Oxfordshire countryside. It was a small town, with less than ten thousand permanent residents, although there was a growing number of second home owners and landlords who were intent on buying up property for the purpose of rentals or holiday lets. The locals were none too happy about this. Disgruntled residents were regularly complaining, even protesting at the increasing number of properties being lost to the disease of capitalism, as they saw it. Properties being snapped up by greedy developers as soon as they came onto the market. The practice was not only driving house prices further out of the reach of local young families, already struggling to get their feet on the first rung of the property ladder, but it was also changing the dynamic and profile of their town. Weekend travellers, holiday makers or people simply visiting to use the increasing number of shops, bars or restaurants that were springing up to service the growing trade, were not always welcomed by the stalwarts of the town. No, their peace was being shattered and something needed to be done about it.

Crime rates were also starting to creep up. Nothing too spicy, just an increased volume. There were the typical neighbour quarrels, usually over something or nothing, or complaints about traffic or illegal parking when visitors descended during the summer months, abandoning their cars wherever they could. Whilst some visitors stayed over in the town, most usually passed through, en route to, or from, the south coast. Chidlington was seen as a convenient place to break their journey. It was a chance to stop and have an afternoon tea, or a bite to eat, or simply somewhere to exercise the dog. There was a local park, as well as surrounding fields, with a host of popular country walks and bike trails to explore. The roads soon became logjammed, with parking at a premium. There had even been a spate of burglaries and petty thefts recently, to say nothing of the increase in the number of complaints about noise and disturbance, especially in the evenings with reports of drunkenness and other unwelcomed rowdiness. The locals did not appreciate it and they were not shy in letting the authorities know.

It was a long time, though, since a dead body had turned up in this manner. Deaths were a common enough occurrence, especially with an aging population, but rarely did they warrant a police presence. And this was not just any body, it was reportedly the body of a respected local businessman, and, if Ruth got her facts correct, someone who had been due to be married that very day. The force had been alerted to the forthcoming nuptials the previous week, even asked to be on standby should it require any additional support. Ruth had been unimpressed by the request. With a limited budget, and enough trivia already to deal with, why on earth would she want to call in extra resource, simply to support a wedding? Strange that the family was now getting the extra support they had requested. Perhaps just not for the right reason. Bizarre.

So, as it was a property Ruth was familiar with, rather than allocate it to one of the team, she decided to attend the incident in person. As it was a Sunday morning, with nothing much else happening, she would quickly finish her cup of tea and bacon butty and drive straight over. After all, she could do with some excitement.

"Put that sausage butty down and grab your notebook, Dickson. You're coming with me," she shouted over, deciding at the last minute to take PC Neil Dickson with her. With less than twelve months in the police force he needed all the experience he could get, as well as something to spice up his weekend too – to say nothing of justifying all the overtime she was paying him.

Living in the sleepy hollow that amounted to their beat, juicy crimes were few and far between. And, still in his early twenties, PC Dickson was very much wet behind the ears. "It'll do him good to see his first corpse," Ruth thought ruefully to herself, wondering at the same time if he had the stomach for it, or more worryingly, if he'd be able to manage to keep the contents of it down. Perhaps she should stand close by, in case he suddenly keeled over and she needed to catch him, although not too close in case he did vomit. The last thing she needed was two dead bodies or more casualties on her hands.

Gossip was always rife in the town around the Paulson name, with the actions of Frank, his family at the Old Manor house, or his dubious associates regularly open to speculation. For Ruth, though, as well as his name being raised in relation to his high-profile wedding, more surprisingly it had recently come up in connection with a separate investigation in which she was involved. That investigation was connected with an anonymous complaint concerning bribery and corruption, involving some notorious names in the area. It was a complaint that was being taken very seriously, so her interest had therefore been well and truly piqued when she heard the victim's name.

As she drove, whilst PC Dickson attempted to finish off the sausage sandwich he had decided to bring with him, she filled him in.

"So, Neil, according to the 999 report the body was found in the kitchen, lying in a pool of congealed blood. The son called it in, James Paulson. The identity of the body is understood to be the owner of the house, Frank Paulson. I'm not sure if you've come across Frank before?" Neil shook his head, continuing to focus on his sandwich and the road ahead of him.

"Well, he and his family are well known in the area, they've been around for decades. He was a local business man. You've heard of *Paulson's Homes*, the company that's building that new development on the outskirts of the village? Well, that's him." Neil continued to stare blankly at his DS, as he chewed. He was not from the area and as yet was unfamiliar with the comings and goings of the town.

"He's also landlord to some of the townsfolk, people who are tenant farmers on various properties on the family's land." Still no reaction.

"Well, what I'd like you to do is speak to the family and try to establish what happened. Ask around and note down anything they say in your book. It may have been a simple accident, so I don't want us jumping to any conclusions, or sparking an MIT enquiry, just yet." She smiled across at him, attempting to lighten the mood. Seeing Neil's blank face at the mention of a Major Investigation Team enquiry, Ruth wondered whether it was his inexperience as a PC, his fear of seeing his first dead body, or simply she was flogging a dead horse trying to get him interested.

"Right, now you've finished that sandwich, let's go. Keep your notebook at the ready, and follow my lead." Straightening her hat as she rang the doorbell, Ruth realised it was going to be a long day.

Chapter 7

"Detective Sergeant Ruth Jacobs and PC Neil Dickson." They both showed their warrant cards to the elderly woman who answered the door. "We're responding to a call that was made earlier this morning. May we come in please?"

"Oh yes. Come in, dear. I'm Nanny Tilbury. The family are through there, in the sitting room. You'll be wanting to speak to me. I was the one to alert the family in the first place when I found his lordship in the kitchen. Blood everywhere, I might add." Ruth smiled as the woman rambled on. She appeared to be in her late sixties or early seventies, and was somewhat doddery on her feet, almost overbalancing on the doorstep as she walked backwards to allow them to enter the house.

"Thank you, my dear. I'm not as nimble as I was," she smiled, as PC Dickson reached forward, putting his arm out to break her stumble.

"You're very welcome, Ma'am. Happy to help." She reminded him of his grandma, even down to her thick black spectacles, reminiscent of ones Mr Magoo had worn in the comedies he had enjoyed watching as a boy. His grandma's sight was failing her too. Over the years the lenses had got thicker as each new prescription recorded her worsening vision. By the look of the lenses this lady was wearing, her eyesight was not much better.

"You're a handsome young chap, aren't you? And what lovely manners you have. I bet your mother is very proud of you." Nanny Tilbury observed, taking her time to give the young man a closer inspection. He looked a little like a young

Sidney Poitier, all dark and brooding. She might be getting older, and was well past her best, but she could still appreciate a good-looking man when she saw one. He appeared to blush as she continued to stare at him, unsure which way to look. He was also conscious his sergeant was watching him out of the corner of her eye, straining to stifle a giggle at the thought of him being propositioned by an elderly witness.

"My PC here will be talking to everyone in due course, madam, so please bear with him. I'm sure he will love to hear what you have to say, Mrs Tilbury. Now where did you say the family was?"

"It's Nanny Tilbury, actually. I've never married." As she replied she continued to smile over at PC Dickson. "Oh, yes, follow me, the family is through here. I'll arrange for a cup of tea too, if you'd like. Milk and sugar?" Ruth smiled at the thought of their visit being treated almost as if it was a social call, rather than a serious police investigation.

The family was gathered in the sitting room. It was a relatively large room, running almost the full length of the property, and at this time of the morning it was bathed in sunlight. The central part of the room looked oddly strange, though, given it was completely bare of furniture, with some of the family almost perched on a series of formal chairs positioned against the back wall. Ruth could see the huge marquee through the patio doors at the rear of the property, and people milling around outside, both of which acted as stark reminders that a wedding should have taken place here later that day.

As she and PC Dickson followed Nanny Tilbury into the room the conversation went quiet as everyone turned to stare at them.

"Good morning, Sergeant." Simon, recognising the police officer from a previous meeting, moved forward to shake her hand. "Thank you for coming over at such short notice." He remembered her from an incident a few weeks ago, when she had called in at the building site looking to speak to one of their employees. He could not recall what the incident was about, but did remember the officer as she was striking in her appearance. She was tall for a woman and very slender, almost athletic in her build, with very distinctive angular features. He would put her somewhere in her early forties, if he was to hazard a guess.

"Ah, good morning." It felt unusual for him to shake her hand, but people acted strangely where death was concerned, so Ruth let it pass. "I'm Detective Sergeant Jacobs, and this is PC Dickson. We're here because there was a report of a body being found, who I understand is Frank Paulson, the owner of this house. Is that correct?"

"Yes, that's correct." Simon appeared to be acting as spokesperson for the group as none of the others attempted to say a word. "I'm Simon, by the way. Simon Goodman. Frank's son-in-law, and Judy's husband." As he spoke, he pointed to a small blonde lady who was sitting on one of the chairs. Ruth took in the scene.

There were four young women and three young men, all she would suggest in their twenties, or thirties at a push. The women still wore their dressing gowns, no doubt having come straight downstairs at the news of the discovery. There was a gentle sound of sobbing, but otherwise the women appeared composed. The men were casually dressed in jeans and T-shirts. None of them looked to be too distressed. Quite calm and collected, Ruth perceived. She was good at observing body language, and all that non-verbal claptrap the management courses spouted, which was a useful attribute in her line of work.

"Would someone please show me where the body is, and then I'd like to understand what's happened and have the chance to speak with you all, if that's okay?"

"Yes certainly, Officer. Please follow me." Simon led the way into the kitchen, followed by Richard, leaving the others in the sitting room. Nanny was standing by the kettle and close to the body, busying herself making cups of tea for the police when they entered the room.

"Madam, can I ask you to please leave that, immediately. This is a potential crime scene and you could be destroying vital evidence." There was a pool of blood around the body, which had already started to congeal, and for some unexplained reason Ruth noticed food strewn all over the floor. "I would request that no one comes back into this room until after the police have notified you that it's clear. We will need to get SOCO over here," she said directing her comments at Simon and Richard.

"Oh dear, I was just tidying away some dirty dishes whilst making your drinks. Are you sure I can't finish them for you? I only need to add a splash of milk."

"No, that's fine. Please can I ask you to leave."

"Yes, dear, I'm so sorry. I'll go back to my apartment and leave you with the family. Richard, please call me if you need anything. Otherwise, I might try to get some sleep. It's been a busy morning and I'm feeling a little weary now." With that, she exited the house via the back door, before crossing the courtyard and climbing the stairs to her apartment.

"Sorry about Nanny. She's completely scatty, but harmless. She's sometimes too helpful for her own good." Simon laughed, relieving a little of the tension resulting from standing within two feet of his dead father-in-law's body. He had never been very good around blood, so had to focus his mind away from what he was actually seeing.

"No problem." Ruth was relieved Nanny Tilbury had finally left them to it. It looked like she was going to have her work cut out dealing with that little old lady. "So, since you made the 999 call, has anyone touched the body, or interfered with the scene in any way? Or, is it just as you found it?"

"Technically, I didn't make the call, or find the body. That was Jimmy, James Paulson, Frank's son. He was the first on the scene after Nanny came upstairs to wake the family, to break the news to them."

"So, let me be clear. Are you saying Nanny Tilbury found the body?"

"No. The caterers found the body when they came to the house around six o'clock this morning. They'd arranged to arrive early, to start the food preparations and get things finalised for the wedding. I believe, Miranda, Frank's fiancée, arranged for them to have a key, and arranged for the alarm to be left off, to save anyone being disturbed earlier than was necessary. Miranda likes her sleep, so wouldn't have wanted to be woken up, just to let them in. It was quite a late night last night, and we'd all been drinking, so there's a few sore heads this morning." Simon watched as the young PC scribbled down notes in his notebook. "Although, thinking about it, I don't know why it was necessary. Frank doesn't sleep much these days. He's usually awake by six. He always said he'd got too much going on to waste his time in bed. I don't think his mind ever really switched off, not these last few years, at least."

Ruth could almost see the cogs going around as Simon struggled to reconcile what had happened to his father-in-law.

"Apart from which, Mrs Cuthbert should have been around, so it baffles me why they'd need a key," he continued.

"Sorry, Mrs Cuthbert?" questioned Ruth.

"Oh, she's the housekeeper. I think she's from somewhere like Romania, or one of those Eastern European countries. I'm not entirely sure. Anyway, I think it was the young girl who discovered Frank's body. And, as you can see, she promptly dropped the tray of canapés she was carrying all over the floor. I think the shock was too much for her."

"Understandable. Well, at least that explains the food." Ruth could also see a broken glass on the floor. "So, are the caterers still here? We will need to speak with them and take their statements. And perhaps talk to Mrs Cuthbert, if she's around."

"Yes. I believe the caterers are around the back of the house. Tidying away the marquee. Mrs Cuthbert is milling around somewhere too. Her husband, Wilf, is helping them to sort things out. As you can imagine, with the wedding planned for later today, the house is in complete turmoil, so we've got a lot on. We've also got to let people know what's happened. Otherwise, we'll soon have people arriving in their finery, and I'm sure you don't want that, do you?"

"Well, I appreciate that. I imagine there'll be a lot to sort out as well as people to notify. However, until SOCO has completed an assessment, I will need to insist that everything is left as it was. That includes the gardens and the front and rear of the property. Can you please inform everyone to hold off doing whatever they are doing, until they get clearance. We'll try not to take too long. Also, will you ask the two who discovered the body to be on standby for me. We'll need to speak to them as soon as we get the chance, as well as the housekeeper, Mrs Cuthbert, did you say, and her husband?"

"Yes, I'll go straight away. Just bear with me a moment and I'll come straight back."

"There's no need. I'll meet you both back next door, with the others in a short while. I want to leave the kitchen sealed for the time being."

As Simon and Richard left the room, Ruth looked over at Neil, who she was pleased to report was holding up remarkably well against the sight of his first bloody corpse. He was carefully walking around the room, assessing the scene, his pencil poised to make notes in his little black notebook if anything untoward jumped out at him.

"What on earth d'you think's gone on here, then?" she asked him eventually, noting the puzzled look on her PC's face.

"I'm not sure, Sarg. Should we suspect foul play, or do you think he may have had a heart attack, or some sort of medical incident, and just collapsed?"

"I don't know. Looking at the scene, though, with the exception of the food on the floor, blood from what looks like a head wound and the broken glass that possibly smashed when he fell, nothing else in the room appears to be out of place, or looks suspicious. There's no sign of a struggle, or a break in – although it's strange what he said about the alarm not being on and the caterers having a key. In theory, anyone could have got in. And, there's no sign of any murder weapon, if it was a murder, that is. Also, as Frank's wearing nothing but a flimsy dressing gown, he obviously wasn't planning on meeting anyone down here, was he? No, that's something we need to keep an open mind on, at least until we have the autopsy report detailing the cause of death. It may, like you suspect, just be an unfortunate accident. Bad timing. I'll admit I'm baffled for the time being."

"Yes, Sarg."

"Well then, why don't you make your way back to the sitting room and you can start talking to the family and the caterers. We need to find out who knows what, and where they all were last night. By the sounds of it there was some sort of drinks party going on. Pre-wedding celebrations, no doubt, that may have got out of hand. I'll make a couple of quick calls to get some support down here, and have that body moved, as soon as the pathologist has given his clearance and the ambulance has arrived. Then I'll come and join you."

PC Dickson felt excited at the prospect of taking witness statements and checking alibis. It was something he had always wanted to do, ever since he had watched Chief Inspector Morse as a young boy on television with his grandma. He would marvel at the way his hero and his sidekick, Lewis, solved some of the most obscure crimes. Living in Oxford, though, he did worry why the crime rate was so high, and why so many people got murdered. His grandma had laughed as she reassured him it wasn't real, adding that not everyone who was associated with Oxford university was doomed to die. No, for the first time since he had qualified, Neil felt like a proper policeman. His grandma would be so proud when he told her how he had spent his weekend.

As her PC was about to leave, Ruth walked around the kitchen, taking in the scene one more time. Her mind, for once, struggling to piece together a scenario based on what she had seen and heard so far. It was still early days, although, mindful of the shady world Frank inhabited and some of the unsavoury characters he dealt with, she was resisting accepting her colleague's innocent explanation.

"I have to say, Neil, those canapés look like they would have been tasty. And that nice cup of tea Miss Marple was making us, would have gone down a treat. I'm parched after my bacon butty, and I do hate to see good food go to waste."

"Me too, Sarg, I can't resist a good vol-au-vent and I'm starved. My sausage sandwich hardly touched the sides."

Chapter 8

Some weeks earlier…...

Miranda was fuming. It was early Monday morning and she was sitting in the car park outside Chidlington leisure centre, ahead of her Pilates class. She had driven at breakneck speed down the country lanes, her heart pumping. Her car, a distinctive bright red Mazda MX-5 convertible, was great at handling the winding bends and she enjoyed the sensation of the wind rushing through her hair when the top was down. Miranda loved to pose around town, driving along and waving at the locals, almost as if she was passing royalty. The thought of having to swap it for a more practical model once the baby arrived was something she was definitely not looking forward to. But there was no way a pram or a pushchair would fit into the boot, or a baby seat into the passenger side's leather bucket seat. And with only two-seats, how would she cope if she ever had passengers?

For now, she just needed to calm down. It was not good in her condition to get so worked up, or become too anxious. How could she not, though, after what Frank had done at breakfast, after what he had said to her?

The class did not start for another hour, so she had plenty of time to compose herself. She was desperate to speak to her instructor, Leo, before class began. She was just unsure exactly what she wanted to say to him, or importantly what she wanted him to do about it. She rang his number, leaving a voice message when it went to answerphone.

"Leo, it's me, Miranda. I need to talk to you, it's urgent. Can you meet me in the car park in 5 mins, usual place? Thanks."

Clutching her bags to her, Miranda got out of the car and made her way towards the back of the leisure centre, to where the staff parked their cars, adjacent to the smoking shelter and the bins. At this time of day, it was quiet and there was no one around to observe them. She waited, nibbling away at the loose skin around her nails as she did. It was a habit she was fighting hard to break, especially with her wedding in less than a month and an expensive manicure booked. She needed to be able to show off her rings, didn't she? She would need to choose the right colour, one that would best show off the flashy diamond and emerald engagement ring Frank had presented her with.

Five minutes later, Leo arrived, looking relaxed and without a care in the world. He was dressed in a navy-blue track suit with white reflector stripes down the arms and legs, the colour setting off his tanned complexion. Miranda smiled as she saw him approach. He looked hot, the tracksuit doing nothing to hide his muscles, nor his tight backside, of which she was particularly taken with.

"What's the problem, babe? You sounded stressed from your message. Is everything okay?" He leaned towards her, giving her a quick peck on the cheek.

"No, it bloody well isn't!" She wanted to scream, but managed to keep her voice down. You never knew who might be listening. "Frank's bloody gone and presented me with a pre-nuptial agreement this morning over my muesli, so it's not been the best start to the week." She thrusted an envelope at him. "It was completely out of the blue, and he says he wants me to sign it before the wedding. Apparently, his ex-wife, Alison, tried to take him to the cleaners after their divorce, and he's not going there again. So, he asked his lawyers to draw it up. I don't know what to do, or what to say. Or whether it's still worth going ahead with this blasted wedding after all."

"Do you think he suspects anything?" Leo was worried that even though they had taken every precaution to hide their affair, Frank might have somehow found out, or someone might have seen them together and said something to him. Leo did not want to mess with Frank, or more's the point have Frank mess with him. Although Leo was handy, and could hold his own if it came to a fight, he knew of Frank's reputation around the area, especially how he could play dirty. By all accounts he was no Mother Theresa.

"I don't think so, otherwise he'd have said something, or at least dropped some hints. No, there's been no signs that he's suspicious." Miranda thought about Frank's behaviour over recent weeks, specifically the times they had argued, or she had done something to annoy him, which was not difficult at the moment. He appeared to be on edge most of the time, like a coiled spring ready to let rip if anything, or anyone, upset him. "I know he's not too happy with me at the moment, especially about me spending so much money on the wedding, but he's got it, so why shouldn't I? We had an almighty row over the weekend when the invoice for the caterers came in. He was already in a foul mood about something that had happened in the office on Friday, that spilled over once he got home. Jimmy and Simon had been on his back about something, and they'd really wound him up this time."

"Well, don't start getting cold feet now. Let's have a think about our options. You don't want to be too hasty, do you?" Leo put his arms out to soothe Miranda, but dropped them as soon as he saw another car pulling into the car park. He was not normally so cautious about being seen together, as he and Miranda were old friends from their days at high school, so had every right to be friendly. They had known each other for over twenty years, even dated in their teens, before they had lost touch. However, being caught alone in the car park before class could easily be misconstrued, especially if someone wanted to cause mischief.

"What does the agreement say about the baby? I presume there's no question mark hanging over that, is there? Once you're married, he or she will be a rightful heir to the estate, I presume, even if you were to divorce him at some later stage and get cut off?"

"Yes, but that doesn't help us, does it? If I do divorce him, or he divorces me if he finds out about us, or the baby, then where would it leave me? Penniless and homeless, presumably? If anything, the way I look at it, my situation worsens once I marry him. At least at the moment I have a healthy allowance, a gold credit card and a manor house to call home. To say nothing of the child I am carrying. That at least gives me some kudos in the family. All being married does is put another ring on my finger, and if I sign this, ties me into potentially losing everything."

"Yeah, babe. I see the problem when you look at it like that." Leo was not the brightest of guys, but he could see her point.

As a personal trainer and Pilates coach, Miranda knew that Leo was certainly not earning the type of salary that could keep her and a child in the lifestyle to which she had become accustomed since she had taken up with Frank. That was over five years ago now, five years of having everything she wanted, materially at least. There was a lot at stake.

When they had originally got together, Frank had still been married to his second wife, Alison, and their son, Mason, was a toddler, barely eighteen months old. Rather than being the doting new father, staying at home looking after his young son with his new bride, he had taken to going out a few nights a week, usually to the pub for a couple of pints. Mason was not an easy baby and Frank needed a break after his day at the office. Mason's crying was constant and Frank did not have the same patience he'd had when his older children were that age. He had been much younger then, and both Susan and Nanny had done most of the heavy lifting in terms of rearing the children. He had rarely got his hands dirty, and he certainly did not intend starting now.

Alison was more hands on and insisted on spending her time with the baby, only reluctantly handing him over to Nanny when Frank insisted he needed her, or there was a function he wanted them both to attend. Over time, Frank's insistence for Alison to be close to him waned, as he began to seek his company elsewhere. Then in his late fifties, constant talk of babies every night when he got home, no longer excited him. Alison was nice enough, but motherhood had made her dull.

Miranda, at the time worked behind the bar at the local pub, the Three Pheasants. She was a bubbly barmaid, lively and good company. She was happy to listen to his occasional moans and always ready to laugh at his jokes or join in with the banter. Above all, she was single and available and responded to the flattery he sent her way. Their affair started and Frank lavished attention on her. Gifts and treats, the occasional nights away in swanky hotels and meals out at fancy restaurants. Always in neighbouring towns, away from prying eyes. After all, he was lord of the manor, and had his reputation to consider.

However, being his bit on the side was not enough for Miranda and it was not long before she manipulated a situation that ensured Alison found out about their affair. Miranda had always been scheming, so on seeing an opportunity to be with Frank she wasted no time in putting her plan into place. The receipt for a dinner in a Michelin star restaurant in Oxford, attached to the hotel bill for a double room at the Randolph Hotel, casually sneaked into the inside pocket of Frank's jacket as he left her apartment late one evening after closing time, was enough to get Alison asking questions the following day.

Frank and Alison's divorce was inevitable. Alison had no intention of staying around to play second fiddle to a trumped-up barmaid who had somehow managed to get her claws into her husband. No, she had more self-respect than that. She was sad to leave the Old Manor House, and Frank's older children, to whom she had become remarkably close, given the circumstances. Her divorce lawyer went into battle against Frank's and eventually negotiated a healthy settlement, one that allowed her and Mason to move to a small three-bedroom house on a new development at the other end of the town. It also provided for a small trust fund, effectively creating a nest egg for Mason for when he turned twenty-one. It was a massive come down from living in the Old Manor House, but it was hers and she could make it into a home. That chapter of her life was over, and if she did not see Frank again, provided he continued to pay his child support for Mason, she was comfortable with that arrangement.

Within a month of the divorce being finalised, Miranda swooped in, convincing Frank that if she moved into the Old Manor House with him it would be good for them as a couple. After all it was no longer a secret around town, so what was the harm? She quickly handed in her notice at the Three Pheasants and concentrated on building up her role as lady of the manor. Frank's children were appalled, not least because she was younger than some of them. Miranda was not fazed. She would handle them, in time at least.

Life continued quite comfortably for Miranda for nearly three years. She was enjoying the luxury her new lifestyle allowed, and had even grown fond of Frank in a quirky sort of way. At fifty-eight, he was nearly thirty years her senior, an age gap that had taken her some getting used to once she became a permanent fixture around the house. The jovial man with whom she had started an affair, was not the same man when he was at home. He had his routines, his habits and a way of doing things that at times she struggled to accept.

He could also become moody, often irritated by the smallest of things, with any desire to party long since behind him. No, he was no longer the fun guy who had lavished champagne on her to get her into bed in those early days, sending flowers and presents to woo her. But he was not all bad, even though their relationship had mellowed, particularly in the bedroom department. She was frequently left wondering where her life was going, as she balanced the pros against the cons of any future together.

That was until the day Leo turned up at the leisure centre to take her Pilates class. He had been employed as a personal trainer and Pilates coach, having recently moved back to the area from Kent. They instantly recognised each other from their school days, laughing as they commented on how the years had been favourable to them. Gone were the two spotty teenagers who had met at the local comprehensive school, both of whom at the time had carried more weight than was fashionable. Fast forward twelve or so years, to two very attractive young people. Leo had continued to grow and was now six feet tall, all his puppy fat replaced by a body that Miranda believed any man would envy; his washboard stomach clearly visible through his tight-fitting lycra top. Miranda in turn had outgrown her acne and braces and now had a clear complexion and straight teeth. Her breasts had also filled out, much to Leo's delight, and her slender waist promised a very shapely figure under her designer joggers, he thought to himself as he allowed his mind to wander.

After their first class they had gone to the café in the leisure centre for a drink and reminisced about their school days. Leo, at thirty-two was a year older than Miranda. They had initially become friends whilst travelling on the bus together, to and from school each day. Their school was a thirty to forty minutes bus ride away, and as there were few pupils who travelled that route, they would talk and keep each other company. They had even dated for a few months, going to the cinema together or having a pizza after school, whatever their pocket money allowed. It was all very innocent. After Leo's GCSE year, at sixteen he was forced to leave the area when his parents moved to Kent for his father's work. They promised to keep in touch, but somehow life got in the way and they drifted apart.

Leo had recently moved back to the area. His ex-fiancée had broken off their engagement and he was looking for a fresh start. Kent had been okay, but he missed Oxfordshire, so had looked to find a job and an apartment in and around the area he'd been raised. Having qualified as a fitness instructor, there were various options available to him, leaving him unconcerned about finding employment. Also, an insurance pay-out, after a motorcycle accident some years earlier, meant he had enough money to buy a small one-bedroom property. So, with his job at the leisure centre paying enough to cover his day-to-day bills, he was comfortable. Beyond that, he had no real plans.

Miranda explained her position too, clarifying she had never been married, but was currently in a relationship with a much older man, going on to describe him as a bit of a sugar daddy. She explained that it was still early days, and although they were reasonably happy, in the longer term she did not know where it might lead. The age difference specifically was something she had started to get concerned about.

Their talks and drinks after classes soon became a habit, each looking forward to spending their time together. Leo did not know many young people in the town – most of the lads he used to knock about with had moved away, or had married and had families of their own. He found Miranda fun, someone to whom he could relate. Miranda in turn had cut herself off from a lot of her friends since moving into the Old Manor House. None of them had seemed particularly pleased for her, or her relationship, so she had chosen to give them a wide berth. They were not the type of people Frank would want around the house anyway. It was at times like this, talking to Leo, that she realised how much she missed people her own age.

They would laugh and joke about others in the classes, imagining all nature of scenarios for what their lives were like, once they had returned home and stripped off their sportswear. They had a wicked sense of humour too, even a degree of black humour, as they imagined some of the old dears croaking after doing a particular move - a swan dive or a plank perhaps, then collapsing on their mat in a heap, a heart attack in full swing. They would laugh at the thought of Leo rushing to administer first aid, even, heaven forbid, the kiss of life, whilst someone rang for an ambulance.

Leo was having such a good time with Miranda that he even started to allocate time in his schedule for their chats, ensuring they were not rushed, or that he would need to run off between classes without time for their catch up. It was nice to see a friendly face, someone who was on his wavelength.

Drinks after class soon developed into lunch dates, even the occasional trip out if Leo could swing an afternoon off. He was looking to furnish his apartment and suggested that if Miranda had time one afternoon, he would welcome her advice on some things he had seen at the local IKEA store. He was looking for a few items that would add a softer touch to his space, admitting he had got bored of living out of boxes and suitcases. Their friendship was all quite innocent and platonic, until it wasn't.

The inevitable affair began, both unable to fight the growing attraction between them any longer, with Leo's new king-size bed suddenly seeing more action than even he had imagined possible. Miranda had a healthy sexual appetite, but not for the type of servicing she had been getting from Frank, which invariably left her frustrated and unfulfilled. She was bored with a quick fumble, before he eventually rolled over, fell asleep and began snoring.

Leo's athleticism brought a whole new dimension to her sex life, igniting a passion and desire in her that she realised, in her relationship with Frank, she had compromised on for too long. No, she could not get enough of Leo, increasing the number of Pilates classes she took to five times a week. After all, she needed to keep her fitness up, especially if she stood any chance of matching Leo's stamina.

Getting pregnant had not been part of her plan, with both concerned that the reality of it, once it became common knowledge, would put paid to any relationship they could have. Sneaking around was fun, the element of risk adding a certain frisson to their lives. Miranda had made it clear, though, that as much as she cared for Leo, she cared more for the lifestyle Frank's money provided her. Leo's home might be perfectly fine for a bit of afternoon delight, but he could not seriously expect her to live out of a one-bedroom apartment, could he? Her handbags alone would fill the space, to say nothing of all the paraphernalia a baby would generate, or the costs involved. She had no income or savings to speak of and no job. And she had no intention of returning to the Three Pheasants, begging for a few shifts behind the bar. Her life had moved on. No, she had to get married to Frank in order to secure hers and the baby's rights. And do it as soon as possible, before anyone became suspicious.

Frank had not been too enamoured at the thought of another wedding when Miranda raised the subject, or another baby for that matter when she announced her news. He did care for her, though, and liked to be seen around town with her on his arm; a trophy young bride would do something to enhance his image and his ego. So, he agreed to her suggestion to get married, and saw nothing untoward about the haste. Neither of them was getting any younger, after all, so why wait around? Better to have a legitimate child than not, was her view, as he slipped the engagement ring onto her finger.

Leo knew in his heart that the baby was his, although he could see no alternative, other than going along with Miranda's plan for the time being. He was unhappy at the thought of another man raising his child. At the same time he was at a complete loss to come up with a better option. Miranda had been adamant, until now at least, the only way forward was for her to marry Frank and continue the pretence. Although, with a pre-nuptial agreement on the table, that now appeared to be clouding her thinking.

"So, what do you suggest we do?" Leo had to take his lead from Miranda. Life would be so much easier if it was just the two of them together, preparing for their baby's arrival, without either a sham wedding or an agreement hanging over them. He was beginning to develop real feelings for her, and he knew beneath her bluster, she had feelings for him too. Once the baby arrived he was excited about the life they could lead, if only they could be together. God, if only that man was not around, Leo thought to himself. What dastardly deed did he need to do to get him out of their lives for good? His black humour was never too far from the surface.

"I don't know, but with only three weeks away before the happy day, I've got some serious thinking to do, haven't I?" There was a wry smile on her face at the thought of happiness being a key ingredient to her wedding day. Since meeting Leo, and seeing the type of relationship she could have, under the right circumstances, marriage to Frank had simply become a means to an end. And it was certainly unlike any happy ever after she had read about in the Bride magazine, that was for sure.

Chapter 9

Present Day……..

"So, can I just go over your stories, one more time? And please correct me if I've misunderstood anything you've said, or you think of anything else as I run through what we have so far."

There was a general nod around the room as Ruth and Neil addressed them from the centre of the sitting room, their notebooks in hand. They had spent the morning individually talking to members of the family, using the small study adjacent to the kitchen to take them to one side and go through their accounts of what may have happened. It was only preliminary questions to determine the basics facts. Ruth knew further work would be needed by herself and her colleagues, once they got back to the station and more information became available from the coroner's office, the pathologist, or even the SOCO team, all of whom had attended the scene.

The private ambulance had collected the body around an hour ago, with the driver and his wing man obviously in no rush to transport the corpse to the mortuary. It was Sunday morning and they were operating on a skeleton staff. The SOCO team had almost completed its assessment of the kitchen and the surrounding areas, taking enough blood samples, fingerprints and photos as they felt necessary. Neil had been fascinated to watch the forensic teams in action, eager to compare some of the things they were doing to things he had seen on Silent Witness. Admittedly, he was a little disappointed to realise that in real life it was nowhere near as exciting. After Morse, Silent Witness had to be his next favourite TV crime series, although in truth he would happily sit down and watch any of them.

Ruth had to wait until the official report came back with anything concrete, but in the meantime the pathologist had shared with her that, in his view at least, there was no evidence of foul play. His best guess in terms of what had happened, was that the deceased had somehow fallen backwards, banged the back of his head on the marble worktops as he fell, effectively knocking himself unconscious. He believed his head wound, created when he fell against the corner of the unit, where some evidence of blood had been found, had simply bled out as he lay on the stone floor, unattended for what he suspected may have been several hours. The time of death was put at some time between two and four o'clock in the morning, according to the pathologist.

Ruth was tired, and as she looked around the room suspected she was not the only one. She was hungry too, her lunchtime had come and gone with nothing more than a cup of tea and a custard cream. Today, this house had been preparing for a wedding, and by the end of the day it would be planning for a funeral.   Over and above what the forensics had already hinted at, she was struggling to make any sense of what might have happened.

"Now, to summarise. There was a pre-wedding party yesterday evening, that ended around midnight." Ruth looked down at her notebook. "In addition to yourselves, there were about forty or so more people in the house, some of whom were expected to be attending today's event also, with most being either locals, or staying in hotels nearby. I understand three of the cars outside were left by visitors who got taxis home, is that correct?"

"Yes," replied Judy, her voice reflecting the weariness she was obviously feeling. "I know two of the owners, and they should have walked over to collect them by now. I rang them earlier to ask them to hang on, until the forensic team had finished, as you'd asked. I've no idea who the third car belongs to. One of Dad's business associates, I presume. There were a few faces here that I didn't recognise last night, as I mentioned earlier."

Miranda had not been able to shed any light on that either, even though it was her wedding, her guest list.

"Thank you. In time I'd like a list of the names of the people who attended, and the contact details for the drivers of those cars, and anything else any of you might remember about the mystery driver. I'll run his plates through the system, so at least we'll have his name." Ruth noticed a few odd looks exchanged between the siblings at the mention of their father's potential business associate, and the complete blank look on the bride-to-be's face. For someone whose special day had been ruined, waking to find her fiancé dead in the kitchen, she was holding up remarkably well.

"So, once the party broke up, I understand it was just you who remained in the house?" Ruth continued.

"Yes, as far as I'm aware. Apart from our children, that is," replied James. "Katie and I have a daughter, Maia, who's upstairs, and Judy and Si have their two boys. They all shared the attic nursery last night and were put to bed before the party got started."

"And Rosie and myself, we live here anyway. Our rooms are on the first floor, just down the corridor from Dad's room. Rosie's is next door to Dad's, and mine is directly opposite from hers. The other two guest rooms, where Judy and Si, and James and Katie were staying are at the other side of the house. Effectively over the kitchen." Richard, until this point had remained quietly in the corner, taking it all in. He was not one who liked the sound of his own voice, just for the sake of it.

"Oh, and Mrs Cuthbert and her husband, Wilf. Their rooms are out through the door at the rear of the kitchen," chipped in Rosie. "I haven't seen either of them around much this morning, but it may be worth talking to them as their bedroom is the closest, so if there was any noise or disturbance they should have heard it. Like I said, though, I didn't hear a thing. My room's perhaps the furthest away."

"Thank you. And from what I understand, none of you heard anything strange, from the point you went upstairs," Ruth looked down at her book, "around midnight, until Mrs Tilbury knocked on your bedroom doors shortly after six o'clock."

"Actually, it was my door. I then knocked on all the rest," James was quick to clarify. As the eldest he felt a need to take the lead. Until now, Simon had stepped in. "You're correct, though, none of us heard a thing." More nods around the room.

"And Miss Swann," Ruth directed her question at Miranda, "you said you'd no idea why Mr Paulson went downstairs in the middle of the night. Was this something he was in a habit of doing?"

"No, I'm sorry. I was feeling a little woozy from all the drink, so as soon as my head hit the pillow I was dead to the world." Miranda regretted her turn of phrase as soon as it left her lips, as well as the lie that came out before she had time to correct herself. Other than the family, news of her pregnancy was still a relatively closely guarded secret, and she could not see the bearing of that on this investigation. No, she had been stone-cold sober, as befitted a woman in her predicament, and clearly remembered Frank lying in bed next to her, snoring away for at least an hour before she eventually drifted off. His snoring was so loud she was surprised none of the others had commented on it. He had certainly had a drink or two too many, that was for sure.

"Well, thank you for your time. I'll be in touch when we have some more information. We'll show ourselves out." Ruth closed her book and moved to the door, closely followed by PC Dickson. "Oh, by the way, I'll need someone to come down to the morgue later to do a formal identification of the body. There's no hurry, at some stage in the next forty-eight hours would be fine. Please ring through and let someone know you're on your way, so that I can let them know to expect you."

Once they were back in the car, Neil, from behind the wheel turned to Ruth. "Looks like an open and shut case to me, Sarg. An unfortunate accident, where the timing couldn't have been worse. Imagine, dying on what should have been the happiest day of your life."

"Mmm, I'm not so sure, Neil. Something doesn't add up to me, and in terms of it being the happiest day of her life, the bride-to-be didn't look overly upset, did she? And why did she lie about being drunk, when I know she's pregnant. The eldest daughter, Judy, mentioned as much when I spoke to her. No, I think there's someone in that house who knows more about this than is letting on at the moment. Right, as you're driving put your foot down. I'm ready for my lunch."

"Yes, Boss. I suppose, you don't need me to put the blue lights on, so that I can get us back to the station even faster, do you?" He didn't often get to drive the police car, and in his short career had yet to experience driving with the sirens on.

The look on his sergeant's face told him everything he needed to know. He wondered what Chief Inspector Morse would have said had Lewis suggested using the sirens on his iconic Mark 2 Jaguar, if he had ever been allowed to drive it, and presumed he'd have received a similar response.

Chapter 10

Whilst the police had been at the Old Manor House carrying out their preliminary investigation, Ana-Maria had done her best to keep herself out of the way, keeping any contact with anyone, especially the police, to the minimum. Wilf, on the other hand, had been keen to get involved, even making warm drinks and carrying them through from the small kitchen they had in their suite of rooms at the rear of the house. It was a comfy enough set up; a small kitchen, the bedroom, a bathroom and somewhere to sit and watch television on an evening. He was a simple man with simple tastes, and by nature he was a helpful chap, so could see nothing wrong in what he was doing.

"Wilf, will you please put that down and leave them to it," his wife had requested as she saw him carrying a tray of drinks and biscuits. "Let them do their job, and keep out of the way." What she meant, was don't do anything to attract their attention, or give them cause to ask any unnecessary questions. Ana-Maria already had enough experience of the Romanian police, and she did not want to add to that.

"What's your problem? As you're the housekeeper, if we don't help, or offer them some refreshments, won't it look odd? We've got nothing to hide, so I don't understand what you're so worried about, my dear."

He had noticed his wife's strange behaviour from the moment the police car had pulled into the drive, even surprised to hear her ask Nanny to open the door to them, rather than do so herself, or ask him. In fact, thinking about it, he had noticed her behaviour had not been the same for a good few weeks now, certainly not from the time when they had been at the Three Pheasants and had that odd conversation, where she had first admitted to feeling uncomfortable, even unsafe at the house. She had obviously been upset about something, although whatever it was she was not prepared to share, no matter how many times he had tried to dig a little deeper or cajole it out of her.

"Well, if you want to help you can, but I'm going out for some fresh air. I'll be back in a couple of hours."

Before Wilf had time to ask her where she was going, Ana-Maria had applied her lipstick, put on her jacket, picked up her handbag and left through the side door, careful to avoid attracting attention.

"Oh look, darling, there's that nice housekeeper from the Old Manor House, Mrs Cuthbert I think her name is. She's just walking past our house and appears to be in a bit of a hurry. I wonder where she's going. Do you think I should pop out and ask her what's been happening? After all, it's a couple of hours now since we received that call from Judy."

Marjorie Dent was prone to watching passers-by from her front bay window. Whilst others might believe she was nosy, in her view she was simply curious by nature. She saw no harm in engaging in the odd bit of gossip either, even guilty of elaborating it on occasion when she felt it lacked that certain oomph it needed. She also loved to daydream, imagining all nature of scenarios happening in other people's lives. She often thought '*Things people get up to behind closed doors*' could easily be her specialist subject, if she ever went on Mastermind. She quite liked that new presenter and imagined he had a few stories to tell, the twinkle in his eye often leaving her convinced there were some secrets buried in his past.

"No, I don't. I'm sure when there's anything to report we'll be informed. I imagine all the guests will have been told by now, one way or another, that the wedding's off. Rum business, in my view. I can't imagine what must have happened to poor Frank," her husband replied.

Gregory Dent was a councillor on the Chidlington borough council, with special responsibilities on the planning committee. His and Frank's paths had crossed on numerous occasions, with many a cross word between them, although it was the first occasion he had felt a need to refer to him as 'poor Frank'. He would never have referred to him as a particularly close friend either, rather an acquaintance or an associate, someone to whom he felt a need to keep close and remain on the right side of. Frank's reputation did not win him friends easily, so the ones he did have were a rare breed.

At last night's drinks party, Gregory had exchanged some quiet words with a couple of the other councillors, people he believed Frank had always had in his pocket, with the nature of their discussions leading him to believe their relationships were not as sound as they had been. Rumours were that Frank had perhaps got himself into a bit of financial trouble, trouble that was deeper that anything he had experienced in the past. He was known to cut a dodgy deal on occasion, even sail close to the wind legally speaking, but he had always appeared to have the golden touch. Everything had worked out in the end and he had generally profited well from whatever it was that he had been involved in.

Talk this time was that perhaps he had gone too far, and might never come back from his latest escapades. His reputation was under threat and if the rumours were to be believed, his business was on the brink of collapse.

"Well, if you won't let me ask her, then I'll have to let my mind wander. Do you think he's taken an overdose and committed suicide? Or maybe he disturbed a burglar, trying to abscond with the family silver. There are some interesting pieces at the Old Manor House after all, perhaps some are quite valuable. Or, perhaps he's been bumped off by a disgruntled customer who didn't like the way the bricks had been laid in their new house, or the colour of the front door. I'd say all of those are feasible motives, especially given the motley crew he's had around the house these last few weeks, wouldn't you? Anyone could have found a way to access that building, or even have hidden out in one of the cupboards after everyone had left last night, don't you think? My money's on someone's been casing the joint, perhaps whilst the marquee was being put up, and has had his eye on one of the old masters in the hall. I noticed last night that all the good stuff had been put away, so I bet someone's gone looking for that." Marjorie smiled to herself, glad she had solved the mystery of Frank's demise.

"God give me strength, woman," Gregory thought to himself, as he watched the pretty housekeeper walk by, whilst his wife went off into another of her flights of fantasy. With her imagination, she should write a book.

Chapter 11

Some weeks earlier......

The Paulson family had been clients at Laycock, Mears and Campbell Solicitors for over fifty years, long before Frank joined the family. His father-in-law, Lord Winchcliff had always used them, and Frank saw no reason to break with tradition once he married Susan and joined the family. So when he eventually set up his own business and required legal support in his own right, that was where he went.

They were traditional solicitors covering the full range of legal services. In recent years, in addition to consulting them on various business and personal matters, he had sought their advice on trusts, wills, inheritance taxes and general estate planning. Most recently their advice had concerned his impending marriage, and some of the ramifications of that. Having been married twice before, and having in his view, been taken to the cleaners after his second marriage ended in divorce, he had no intentions of going there again. Miranda may have thought she had got her hooks into him, especially after news of her pregnancy, but he was wily. He was certainly a lot more attuned to what was going on than she gave him credit.

After his in-laws' deaths, their estate had automatically passed to Susan in its entirety as their only child, their heir. However, Frank had been made a trustee of the estate by Lord Winchcliff, who trusted him to manage the interests of his family. Lord Winchcliff was old school and believed a man needed to run things. Women, in his view, did not have a head for business or money.

On Susan's death, with the exception of a sum of money that Frank inherited in his own right, the remainder of the estate largely went into trust, for the benefit of their children and any grandchildren that might eventually arrive. The trust had a clear provision that the Old Manor House would remain in the family's possession, until such time at least until after Frank's death. At which point, provided the children had reached adult maturity, they could dispose of the assets as they saw fit, sharing the proceeds equally among them, with the exception of a few bequests that had been well documented.

In addition to the Old Manor House itself, the estate comprised a significant sum of money, with further income being generated through tenanted farmlands. There was also a selection of artwork and antiques, items Lady Winchcliff had been bequeathed from her own parents. Theirs was old money, and with the passage of time, and changing legal and taxation regulations, over the years it had become a complicated estate for the solicitors to deal with.

"Mr Paulson, I think you will see that I have done everything you've asked." Mr Mears Jnr. handed Frank a file containing the draft of the pre-nuptial agreement he had requested, along with an updated Last Will and Testament. "If you would like to take these documents home and look over them, before returning them to me at your earliest convenience it would be appreciated."

Frank automatically started to scan read the documents in front of him, flicking through the pages at an alarming pace. He had developed a strong business acumen, with a good eye for documents over the years, and was nobody's fool.

"You will note, given some of the other recent transactions I have dealt with on your behalf, I have made an adjustment to the estate's valuation, taking note of the sale of land and the recent mortgage positions. There's nothing to be unduly alarmed with at the moment, however I do have some concerns that would be worth a more detailed discussion, once you return from your honeymoon, that is. Perhaps you could book an appointment."

Mr Mears' officious manner and tone of voice made it obvious that his client's requests, although perfectly legal, were perhaps not in the spirit of what the trust had originally intended. However, it was not his place to question his client's instructions. Following his father's retirement, Mr Mears Jnr. had inherited Mr Paulson's portfolio, and as much as he may have had issues with some of the things he was being asked to do, he had to remain professional at all times.

"Thank you." Frank was not listening. He was too busy checking over the paperwork the solicitor had provided him. "Right, I'm happy with the will," he declared, after a few minutes time. "So, I'll sign that now and leave it with you." Handing the document back to the solicitor. "The agreement looks fine, too. I'll get that back to you once Miranda has signed it. You may need to give me a few days on that one." Getting her to sign it may not be as straightforward as he had hoped, but as always he had a plan to deal with that.

"Well, in that case. Good luck with the wedding, and I will see you on your return. In the meantime, I'll file this away for safekeeping. Good afternoon, Mr Paulson."

Nanny Tilbury was just exiting the travel agents on the high street when she saw Frank leaving the solicitors' office, next to the coffee shop. It was Thursday afternoon and traditionally her day for wandering into town to meet up with some of the ladies, for some shopping and a chat over a cup of tea and a sticky bun. Today she had feared she would be a little late, having spent longer in the travel agents than she had intended.

She had foregone shopping so only needed to cross the road to get to the café. Looking at her watch she realised she still had a few minutes to spare, so there was no need to hurry, and as she could see Mrs Dent and Mrs Hargreaves approaching from the other direction, she knew she was not late after all.

The solicitor's office was directly across the road from her, and she could tell from the way Frank was walking, and the look on his face, that he was stressed and in a hurry. He was also dressed more formally than was usual for him, wearing a suit and an open necked shirt.

"Gone are the days when men wore smart ties," Nanny thought to herself. She always felt a tie finished an outfit off nicely. Added that bit of style. Anyway, she presumed he had either had an early meeting at the solicitors, or was rushing off to one, because from the direction he was walking, he was not heading back to his office, or to his car, which she had noticed was parked further down the street.

Without a proper glance at the traffic situation, Frank stepped into the road, causing a bicycle to swerve around him. The cyclist's language was a little choice for her delicate ears, as he wobbled to retain his balance. As was Frank's, as he swore at the cyclist, accusing him of not looking where he was going.

"Oh dear, there was nearly an accident there, Mr Paulson. Are you alright?" Nanny Tilbury had never been on first name terms with her employer. Lady Susan had been more relaxed and easier to converse with, whereas her husband had always been rather standoffish, particularly towards the hired help. He hardly exchanged the time of day with Mrs Cuthbert or Wilf, and the way he did speak to them when he needed something doing was never too polite. She may be getting on a bit, but she still had eyes and ears and did not miss much around the house.

"Ah, Tilbury, I didn't see you there. Yes, I'm fine."

"Well, that's good. We wouldn't want an accident before the wedding, would we? I'm sure neither Miss Swann nor that nice wedding planner would have built that into their planning, will they?" She smiled kindly at him, keeping her thoughts and views to herself on the impending nuptials. Like the rest of the household, including Frank's children, she had serious reservations about what he was doing. "I've just been to look at booking myself a river cruise, on the River Danube. I thought after the wedding a break would be nice. It's years since I've had a proper holiday. I imagine you'll have a nice honeymoon planned too, somewhere hot and sunny?"

"Yes, quite. I hope you'll excuse me as I have somewhere I need to be in five minutes, and I'm already running late. Good afternoon, Tilbury."

Frank had neither the time nor the patience to hang around listening to her rabbiting on about holidays, or anything else for that matter. In fact, he could not understand why she still chose to live at the Old Manor House. Surely, she must have somewhere else she could go, family she could live with? After all, there were no longer any children around to occupy her time, so what did she do all day long? And it was clear Miranda saw her playing no part in raising her baby once it was born, so even more reason for showing the old nanny the door. No, the one good suggestion Miranda had made was finding a way of getting her out of that annex. Whether it became a Pilates studio, or simply a store room, was immaterial to Frank. He just needed to find a way to get around that proviso in Susan's will – the one granting her use of it as a grace and favour apartment, for as long as she wanted. What on earth had Susan been thinking? He made a mental note to discuss it with Mr Mears at their next meeting. He would surely help him to find a way around his little problem.

For now, he needed to get to his accountant's office and sort out what he needed them to do for him. Simon, his son-in-law, was starting to get too inquisitive for his own good, asking questions Frank was not prepared to answer at this stage. Simon's questions suggested his trust and reputation could be under scrutiny, the nature of them leading Frank to believe Simon was getting too close for comfort.

Frank needed to cover his tracks, or come up with a plausible story to account for what had happened to all the money that was missing from the books. Exactly what he could concoct at this stage, he was not at all sure. "There'll need to come up with some creative accounting, but isn't that what I pay my accountant for, after all?" he thought to himself, as he scurried off.

As Nanny watched him disappear from sight around a corner, she could not help but wonder what his haste had been to do with, or why he was obviously so distracted. She loved to solve a good conundrum and thought that perhaps over a sticky bun it might come to her. For now, she could see the ladies approaching, so waved over at them. It was high time for her well-deserved coffee and cake, all topped off with a good dollop of gossip. One of the highlights of her week.

Chapter 12

Councillors Gregory Dent and David Hargreaves were both on Chidlington borough council. Gregory had special responsibilities on the planning and housing committee and David's responsibilities related to the parks and recreational side of things. The town's communal areas, countryside walks and public playgrounds all had to be in good order and repair, as well as attractive to the locals and the growing number of visitors who came to their town. It was not the most taxing of council appointments, but it was one that gave David a great sense of pride, especially at this time of year as he walked around the town and saw the flowers in bloom, the litter bins empty and the graffiti cleaned off the walls of the shelter in the public park. None of that happened by magic.

Gregory's responsibilities were a little more taxing, especially given the growing number of new housing developments that were springing up in the area, or the increasing demands on the council to make better use of the space they had in the town centre. Calls to reduce the number of bars with late night licences, and increase the number of affordable shops that meant locals were not forced out of town to buy their groceries. They had multiple planning applications to consider each month at their regular committee meetings, both of a residential and a commercial nature, and had to balance each request against a specific set of guidelines, whilst endeavouring to apply a modicum of common sense at the same time.

They were both long serving committee members, totalling over fifteen years' service between them, and both now in their late sixties had been drawing their pensions for some time. "I'm happily retired from the rat race; least said about that the better," Gregory was prone to say whenever anyone asked him what he had done for a living. In truth no one really knew, he was a bit of an enigma. He and his wife had moved to the town some ten years ago, following his early retirement. He did not believe he had been living in Chidlington long enough to earn himself the right to call himself a local, however he was committed to serving the people of the town, and from the point at which he had got himself elected had done a respectable job. He was an affable chap, and made it his business to not cross swords with anyone, unless it was strictly necessary.

As Frank was hurrying off to meet his accountant, Gregory and David were sitting in the coffee shop, idling their time away while their wives were off shopping. Neither of them enjoyed being dragged around the shops, politely commenting on things they could not give two hoots about, so had got into the habit of meeting up whenever their wives' retail habits coincided. It was an arrangement that worked well for all concerned, and something they did at least once or twice a month. Mrs Dent would meet up with Mrs Hargreaves, and occasionally Nanny Tilbury from the Old Manor House, and put the world to rights whilst wandering around the shops. With their husbands doing the same over a coffee whilst reading their newspapers. The women would then rendezvous back at the café to continue their discussions and allow their husbands to treat them to a sticky bun, before carrying their bags back to the car to drive home.

"Is that Frank Paulson over there? He seems to be in a hurry, and with an expression on his face that suggests he's not overly impressed by something, or someone." David had been reading his paper and had looked up and seen Frank out of the corner of his eye, almost getting himself run over by a cyclist. "I think that's Rosemary's friend who's talking to him, isn't it? I can never remember her name, but I thought she was meeting the ladies for coffee today, or have I got that wrong? I can't always admit to listening when Rosemary goes on. Either way, he's not too happy by the looks of him."

"I think you might be right, David." Gregory put his paper down and took a sip of his latte, deciding what if anything he could say. Committee meetings were confidential, until the minutes had been published of course, at which time they became a public record. Not everything made it into the minutes though. "I imagine he's probably had notification that his latest planning application, you know the one he submitted regarding Coronation Terrace, has been delayed again. The council reviewed it last week and there were quite a few points raised. He won't be at all happy, if I know Frank."

"That's interesting. I'd heard he'd been lobbying hard on that one, and even had some of the committee members in his back pocket, so to speak. Word on the street is that he's been greasing a few palms, again."

"Well, that's as may be. I can assure you, though, that mine's not one that's been greased. He has tried to apply pressure, I will admit to that, but nothing I can't handle. Although, I think if he is greasing some palms, I've got a good idea whose they might be."

"What makes you say that?"

"Oh, the ladies are back. Is it that time already?" Gregory looked at his watch, grateful for the chance to move the conversation along. As much as he trusted his friend, it was not in his nature to spread malicious gossip. Especially not if there was any chance that at a later date it could come back to haunt him, in some shape or other. And if it was who he was thinking it might be, there was a real possibility of that.

"Look sharp and smile, David, or else they'll think we've been talking about them."

Chapter 13

Present day.........

As the news of Frank's death gradually spread throughout the town, James and Simon were hard at work trying to deal with the fall out, specifically in terms of the impact on *Paulson's Building Co.*, or the offshoot company *Paulson's Homes,* the two companies the family operated. Apart from anything else, there were building contracts that needed to be completed, houses in various phases of construction and other obligations to honour. Whatever else was happening, they could not afford to take their eyes off the ball, not if after all that had happened they wanted to keep the businesses running. If recent months were anything to go by, they knew they had to steady the ship and show some leadership, and fast, otherwise they were in danger of losing it all.

Suppliers were already banging on the door demanding to know when their bills would be paid, with some of the staff understandably wanting assurances they would get paid when the end of the month arrived. The fact their boss had died would be of little comfort when the mortgage needed paying, or the electricity bill arrived and there was no money in their bank accounts to do so, or they needed to put food on the table. James and Simon had worked around the building industry long enough to know that builders and tradesmen could be a fickle bunch, people who voted with their feet. If paid work was not secure at *Paulson's*, then they could easily find it elsewhere. There was always demand for skilled resource and hard grafters.

It was Wednesday afternoon and Simon had popped his head around Frank's office door. James had temporarily moved in there, in an attempt to sort through his father's filing cabinets and drawers, with the help of Mrs Ellington, his father's old secretary. She had been at the company almost since its inception, so if anyone knew where the skeletons were buried, then James presumed she was his best bet.

They had been working all morning, going through file after file, and so far had failed to turn up anything significant. Frank had been old school and had never trusted electronic record keeping, so everything was filed away in buff folders under lock and key. James was not finding it at all easy, especially when he had no idea exactly what he was looking for, and Mrs Ellington was not proving an easy nut to crack. Leaving him to wonder whether she was remaining loyal to Frank even after his death, or whether she too had been kept in the dark. Either way, going through the paperwork was proving much more difficult than he had imagined. It was like trying to find the proverbial needle in the haystack.

"Jimmy, I've been going over the figures again to see what flexibility we have. Now that Frank's not here to countersign documents, or make any payments, it could get difficult. If we're to continue operating legally we need to understand what we can and can't do." Simon was conscious that just because his father-in-law operated close to the edge, he did not want to emulate those practices. The last thing they needed was the authorities on their backs for something they had done. "I've arranged a meeting with the accountant later this afternoon, and then one with the bank in the morning to discuss a line of credit, should we need one. I'm struggling to get a clear picture on what money is in the account at the moment, or where it's come from." As far as money and business was concerned, Simon was as straight as a die and as honest as the day was long. "Do you want to sit in on either of those meetings with me? I think it might be useful."

Simon's earlier concerns that the numbers did not add up had not gone away. In fact, since he had first raised it with Frank, nearly a month ago, in his view the situation had worsened. There was something not quite right, with gaps in the accounting and transactions that he simply did not recognise. Large sums of money had disappeared in the last few months from an account Frank oversaw, and although Simon had questioned him about it, he had not received any answers. He was hoping the accountant might know more, or at least be able to offer some explanation.

The overall businesses, whilst a family concern, were solely in Frank's name. Over the years there had been talk of floating the company, bringing in shareholders and raising equity through investors, but Frank had always resisted that. He had never wanted shareholders, or investors involved, least of all not ones who would question his decisions. No, he wanted to manage everything himself and keep it as a small privately owned company. James and Simon had eventually been brought in as part of his management team and given day-to-day responsibilities, with access to sufficient information to keep the business operational. Control, though, was still with Frank and at no stage had he ever considered letting go of that.

"Yeah, it might be useful. I suppose we should arrange to talk to Mr Mears too, as there will be all the legal stuff to sort. I haven't a clue where to start, have you?"

"No, not really. Especially as we've not seen the will yet, so we don't know what's to happen to the business. Is it our responsibility to keep it running, or do you think we might have to shut it down? And what will be required under probate is anyone's guess. That can take months and can be a real pain, especially where there are complicated estates, which I presume your dad's is. I assume you're not an executor to his will, are you?"

"No, well at least I don't think I am, and Judy's never mentioned that she is either. And I can't imagine he'd have asked Rosie or Richard to do it, can you? So, I'd guess it's been left for the solicitors to handle. I know him and Mr Mears have become close over the years."

It was one of the many subjects James and his father had never fully discussed. He knew his father had made a will, and imagined the provisions were that it would leave everything to be shared equally between him and his siblings, but he was not certain of that. He also knew the house was held in some sort of trust, along with the farmlands, but other than that he was clueless. Perhaps he had been too naïve over the years, simply relying on the assurances his father had given him that everything was in hand, and comfortable in the knowledge that there was family money, so what did he need to worry about? He had never had a head for all that kind of stuff anyway, and as his father had never offered to share any details, James had never bothered to ask.

Perhaps as the eldest son, he should have known better than to just trust in the little he had been told, and wondered whether Judy, Rosie or Richard had any better idea of what was going on. Perhaps Rosie and Richard, given they still lived at home, may have more knowledge of what their father had been thinking about over recent years, because one thing was for sure, he had absolutely no idea how his old man ticked.

"Thinking about it, Si, it's probably worth us getting together with Judy, Rosie and Richard as soon as we can. We probably should talk through what we need to do about a few things, because it's not just the funeral that needs sorting, is it? There's a whole lot of other stuff to discuss, with the business and the house and everything."

"Yeah, you're right. The house is quite a big worry in my mind. Judy was only saying the other day that there's quite a bit of maintenance needed. Your father seemed to keep on top of the superficial stuff, but Wilf mentioned to her that there were a few bigger jobs that required to be done quite urgently. Things that had come up in discussion when Miranda started talking about all the work she wanted doing on the nursery and in the annex, you know her hairbrained idea to convert it into an exercise studio?"

Miranda's plans had not gone down well with anyone, it would appear.

"Which leads me onto wondering what you're all thinking of doing about Miranda. It is, after all, her home at the moment and I don't know legally what her position is in terms of having a right to stay there, do you? I imagine, with the wedding not going ahead, his death leaves her in a bit of a predicament. She'll be feeling like she's in no-man's land, without Frank there to protect her. I don't think it's any secret what you all think about her, so she'll be feeling quite vulnerable, I'd imagine."

"Yeah, you're right. In fact, I wonder if Dad's will makes any provision for her and their child, or even if it's been updated since they started seeing each other. You never know, if he's not updated it for a while, it could even still have Alison benefitting in some way. I know she was pissed off with her divorce settlement, so he may have promised her more when he goes. It might not all be coming our way, after all."

Simon could see where James was coming from, but the look he gave his friend demonstrated he seriously doubted that. Knowing the old bugger, Frank had not done much for anyone whilst he was alive, so it was highly unlikely he would change his spots once he was dead, he thought, rather unkindly to himself. His father-in-law's death might have been a huge shock to everyone, resulting in one almighty mess, but they would get through it, somehow. They were a strong family unit and Simon truly believed that whatever pain they needed to go through, once they emerged on the other side, they would all be much better off for it. Of that he was sure.

"And vulnerable or otherwise, in terms of Miranda, over my dead body will that conniving little bitch get another penny from Dad. I'll fight it all the way, even through the courts if I have to. These last few years, she's done nothing but bleed him dry, spending his money and throwing it around, without a care in the world. I wouldn't be at all surprised if his death, or at least the state of the finances, has got something to do with her. I have to admit, though, that I've been scratching my head to see what she'd gain by him being dead, if that was the case. And as far as Alison's concerned, if there's nothing in the will for her, at least he should have provided for Mason. He is after all his legitimate child. God, it's a mess. I think I need a drink."

"I'd like to join you, but I think we'd probably best refrain until this evening, if we're to keep a clear head and meet with the accountants, that is. How about I ring Judy and ask her to summon the troops together for a pow-wow later tonight? Is the Three Pheasants okay with you, say seven o'clock? In fact, why don't you drop Maia off at ours on the way, and I'll ask Mum if she can babysit? She's overdue a cuddle with her grandsons, so one more won't harm her."

Chapter 14

No sooner had Simon returned to his own office than the phone rang. Mrs Ellington, having just returned from her lunch break, answered it. It was Mr Mears, Frank's solicitor.

"Yes, certainly, Mr Mears. Mr Paulson is here. We're both in the office, as we speak. We're going through some papers and files of the late Mr Paulson," she offered by way of explanation, her tone both polite and officious. "I'll put him on the line for you. Hang on one moment, please." Putting her hand over the mouthpiece, "James, I have Mr Mears for you. Would you like to take the call here, or should I transfer it through to your own office?"

"No, here's fine, Mrs Ellington, thank you. Would you please leave me for a few moments and we'll resume this when I've finished. Oh, and can you close the door?"

He suspected even with the door shut Mrs Ellington would have a way of listening into the call, should she so want. Over the years of working for his father, she had guarded his office fiercely, like her life depended on it. She was famous for never letting anyone over the threshold, unless Frank had summoned them in or they had made an appointment. She was certainly the eyes and ears of the business, and Jimmy suspected nothing ever got past her.

After taking the handset from her, Jimmy sat down in his father's chair, behind the desk Frank had occupied for many years. It was an old traditional wooden desk, with keys to every individual drawer, all of which had been locked when he and Mrs Ellington had started their search the previous day. She held spare keys for most of the drawers, but there was one that even she could not open, so they had arranged for a locksmith to come in later that week with the purpose of gaining them access.

"Mr Paulson, thank you for taking my call," Mr Mears began. "I'd like to start by offering you and your family my deepest condolences on the recent death of your father, on behalf of Laycock, Mears and Campbell. I might add it was a massive shock to me personally, and such awful timing. I'd only spoken to your father a few days ago and he was in good spirits."

"Thank you. Yes, it's been a shock."

"I didn't know if you would be working, or at home with the family, given it's only a couple of days since his death. I know times like this can be quite stressful, and people need to take the time to process what's happened, especially when the passing has been so unexpected. There's so much to organise, and people to tell. No one ever knows what to say, or do for the best at times like these, do they?" Mr Mears voice was dour, and had he not been a solicitor, Jimmy felt an undertaker may have been more his calling.

"No. I think that we're all just trying to muddle through, the best we can. Si and I decided to come in to work to let the team know it's business as usual for the foreseeable future, unless you have something to tell me to the contrary, Mr Mears? Si and I had intended making an appointment to come into your office later this week, to understand how things stood. I presume you've got more of an idea about the legal position of my father's affairs, than I have. As you can imagine, all of us have been left a little blindsided by his death."

"Quite. It's a difficult time when anyone passes away, but with your father, and his affairs, I can only imagine it could easily become quite complicated. That's why I rang, to assure you that we are here to help, and to let you know that as your father made me executor of his will, I'll need to speak to the family quite soon, to go through its contents and implications with all of the beneficiaries. And as Mr Paulson did not get married, due to the unfortunate timing of his death, you James, as the eldest son, are legally his next of kin. As such, I would like to go over a few points with you as a matter of urgency, before the formal will is read. Would now be convenient, or would you like to make an appointment for later in the week? As some of what I need to say pertains to his funeral arrangements, I don't want to leave it too long."

"Now's fine, although there's no hurry as the police haven't released his body yet, so we're unable to make any funeral arrangements, even if we wanted to," Jimmy offered. "Just hang on a moment while I get a pen and paper so that I don't miss anything."

Mr Mears waited a moment then continued.

"Right, well here goes. Let me start by outlining what your father's funeral requirements are and we'll go from there, shall we? If you've any questions, please let me know as we go through and I'll answer to the best of my ability." Mr Mears took the two sheets of A4 paper from the plastic folder in front of him and started going through the long list of points Frank had left in his safe keeping, to be read in the event of his untimely death.

Mr Mears had observed at the time of noting these down, some weeks previously, that his requests were a lot more detailed than most of his clients'. But then again, most of his clients had not died in mysterious circumstances soon after, had they? Leaving Mr Mears to wonder whether Frank had perhaps had more foresight than he'd previously given him credit.

Chapter 15

Richard and Rosie had already arrived, long before the others got to the Three Pheasants, and had grabbed one of the larger tables in the corner of the bar. It was Wednesday evening with mid-weeks never being too busy.

Richard, at twenty-seven was the baby of the household and like Rosie, who was only twelve months older than him, still lived at home. Over the years, he had occasionally toyed with the idea of moving out and finding a small place to rent. At one stage he had even considered sharing an apartment with a couple of old friends from university, who had found work in the Oxfordshire area, but at the last minute it had all got complicated and seemed a bit too much like hard work. Apart from the fact it would eat into his allowance, and as he was not paid very much he could not really afford it.

Richard was the typical youngest child, completely spoiled by everyone and happy to let others do the running around after him, including picking up the tab if it came to that. He was also quite savvy and could not see any significant advantage in moving out of a comfy family home, where a housekeeper did all his cooking, cleaning and laundry. In order to move into a small apartment, where he would have to fend for himself, or worse still have to deal with people. And as his father had always been so preoccupied with Miranda, or with his business, he had never bothered to check if his son was around, which effectively resulted in Richard having the free run of the house. Being left to his own devices suited Richard perfectly. Father and son had barely seen each other, and on those odd occasions when they had bumped into each other, conversation had usually been kept to a minimum, and had certainly never ventured towards anything personal.

Richard had rarely felt close to his father growing up, and as adults their worlds were so far apart it was almost laughable. He often wondered if they were even from the same gene pool. They'd had little, if anything, in common. The father, an extrovert, go-getting businessman, intent on making his next deal, whatever that might involve. The son, the thoughtful laid-back introvert, happy in his own world and careful to avoid conflict at any cost.

Laid back he may be, but stupid he most certainly was not. He had studied philosophy at the University of Brighton and had been awarded a Bachelor in Philosophy degree, gaining first class honours. Studying critical thinking and being able to analyse situations and the meaning of life was all very well on paper, however converting those skills to real life, or the concept of earning a living, was not as easy. Currently he was registered with a local employment agency, picking up random jobs whenever they were able to match his CV and interests to any vacancies that became available. In reality, though, that did not keep him fully occupied, or fulfilled, meaning his days were spent reading, or driving out to galleries or exhibitions, or events that piqued his interest.

Richard had no clear idea of what he wanted to do with his life, or if he did, any real impetus to get on and do it. He was a drifter, happy to go with the flow, until the point at which the flow was no longer going in his direction. At which point he would no doubt up and leave, and try his hand at something else.

That philosophy applied to his love life too. He was a good-looking man, tall with blond curly hair and an innocent boyish charm, with enough charisma for attracting almost any woman he wanted into bed. Keeping them interested thereafter was neither his problem nor his style. If they stayed, he was fine with that. If they wanted more than he was prepared to offer and decided to leave, then so be it. It was the fate of the gods and he did not let it faze him either way. His longest relationship to date had been ten months with a student on the same course as him at Brighton. As they were both similar personalities, when the summer term ended after his second year and they all headed home for the holidays, their relationship simply fizzled out. She lived just outside Newcastle and he was near Oxford, and for both of them it was too far to make the effort. Since then, other than the occasional casual relationship, there had been no one serious in his life.

"Do you think we should order some food whilst we're waiting, Rosie? I imagine the rest will have eaten already and I'm starving."

"That's probably not a bad idea." Rosie had not eaten either. She had returned home from work at the usual time and found the kitchen deserted, with no sign of anything being prepared for their dinner. "I'm not sure if since Dad died Mrs Cuthbert's gone into mourning, or is just on strike, because I've hardly seen her around recently. Have you?"

"No, I heard her yesterday morning, I think. Today, though, I don't think I've had any sight of her, or Wilf, come to think of it. Then again, I've had my headphones on most of the day. You don't think I should go through to their rooms in the morning and check they're not dead on the floor too, do you?"

"Richard, that's not funny." Rosie chided her brother. "I don't know what it is about your morbid fascinations recently. You're getting worse."

Richard was showing no outward signs of any distress or grief following the death of their father. In fact, Rosie thought he was finding it all quite amusing, in a macabre sort of way. He had even made a flippant comment the day after the murder, whilst they were in the kitchen having a drink with Nanny Tilbury, questioning whether it had been Miss Scarlet with the candlestick, or Colonel Mustard with the lead pipe that had done the dastardly deed. Neither she nor Nanny Tilbury had known where to look, or what to say, both exchanging a glance that assumed everyone processed grief in their own way.

Richard studied the menu one more time. "Right, well I'm going to order the steak and kidney pie and get another pint before they arrive. What do you want?" He stood, ready to walk over to the bar to order the food, then started to fiddle in his pockets.

"I'll have the scampi and chips please. And can you get me another glass of white wine when you're at the bar. I think we're going to be in for a long evening, so I'll need a top up."

"No probs, Sis. Although, can you lend me thirty quid, or give me your card. I've just realised I've left my wallet at home," he added, proffering her one of his best smiles.

Handing over her debit card, with the clear realisation that was the last she would see of the money, Rosie smiled at her younger brother. At times she worried about him, particularly how streetwise he was, but as she watched him amble over to the bar she knew he was certainly not stupid.

Chapter 16

By the time the others eventually arrived at the Three Pheasants, Rosie and Richard were both tucking heartily into their food. They waved them over, and Judy and Katie made their way to join them, as James and Simon headed towards the bar.

Rosie had been at work all day in the dress agency she ran with her friend, Vanessa, in the neighbouring town. It specialised in pre-loved outfits, mainly designer ball gowns and dresses that people had either tired of, outgrown or simply wanted to raise some money by selling. As an agency it had become well known, earning a reputation for offering a good price to anyone who traded an outfit in, but also a place where there was always a wealth of new items to choose from. Rosie spent most of her time at the front of the shop, dealing with customers, or on the road looking out for stock, with Vanessa concentrating on tailoring and adjusting outfits to suit their clients. A small nip or tuck here or there, a hem raising or lowering, even a bust line adjusting, or the addition of a small accessory. Anything to make the outfit feel that bit more personal.

The number of mother-of-the-bride outfits they stocked was staggering. Outfits, including shoes, hats and bags that had cost thousands of pounds originally, and had only been worn once still looked new. They also stocked a phenomenal selection of dresses suitable for Ascot, or royal garden parties, or other such events, as well as a growing number of prom dresses, attracting the younger clientele. Throughout the year there was a constant stream of society events and even if people could not afford the latest fashion, they still wanted something designer, or at least something timeless that fitted them well and did not look like it was second hand.

Rosie advertised widely for items and always kept her eye out for anything that was brought in that would suit either her sister or sister-in-law, neither of whom were precious where their designer wardrobe came from, or whether their handbags were this season's or last's. In fact, all three had got their wedding outfits from the shop, with no one wanting to spend too much on an outfit, for an occasion they did not believe in. No doubt they would be asking her to buy them back, no longer having a need for them; maybe even look to trade them in for a little black number, suitable for the funeral.

Rosie often wondered about all the talk of the country being in recession, the regular news reports of how people were struggling. In her experience she was not seeing it. For women to be spending that amount of money in the first place, on clothes and accessories to attend functions and events, meant that whatever hardships there were, some people were feeling the pinch a lot more than others.

"You two look like you've not been fed in ages, the way you're eating those meals. I hope you leave the patterns on the plates," Judy observed light-heartedly when she and Katie arrived and sat down next to them at the table. "The food's good in here, isn't it?"

"Yes, and I was starving." Rosie replaced her knife and fork and sat back. "I didn't have time for lunch today. Vanessa and I have been run off our feet all day, and then when Si rang, just before I was leaving, with a three-line whip to get here by seven, I didn't have time to make anything at home."

"Yes. Sorry about that. Si's mother was a little late coming around to ours to babysit. I think she'd made plans for tonight, ones she didn't appear too happy about having to rearrange. I left Si to deal with her. Never mind, we're here now." Judy smiled over.

"And Mrs Cuthbert has, we think, gone on strike since Dad died," Richard added, scraping the remains of his steak and kidney pie onto his fork. "She's nowhere to be seen. She's effectively gone into hiding and I get the feeling cooking's the last thing on her mind, although what she's got to worry about I've yet to determine. It's certainly not overwork as she's not rushed off her feet, is she? Which means I could die, too, if I waited around for her to feed me."

Being in the house most of the day, Richard was attuned to movement, or lack of movements around the place. And as far as Mrs Cuthbert was concerned there was a distinct lack of movement. The last time he recalled seeing her was late Sunday evening, walking back up the driveway looking quite flustered. He had seen her leave the house earlier that day, shortly after the police arrived, and had absolutely no idea where she had gone. Wilf was around, busying himself as usual, but there was no sight nor sound of his wife.

"Oh Richard, my heart bleeds for you, and your poor stomach. I do hope, for your sake, Mrs Cuthbert resurfaces soon," Judy laughed at how dramatic her brother was being. She knew how healthy an appetite he had, and also knew how much he enjoyed Mrs Cuthbert's Romanian cooking; the names of some of the dishes she could not even begin to pronounce. The number of times as a young boy he would finish off his meal and then go straight for seconds, or would eat his dessert whilst waiting for the rest to finish their main course, was legendary. Nanny used to say of all the children she had ever looked after, Richard was the hungriest by far. Where he put all the food he ate no one knew as there was hardly an ounce of fat on him, and it wasn't as if he was running around all day, burning it off, was it?

"Perhaps being a laid-back good-for-nothing burns off more calories than I'd realised," Judy pondered lovingly as she smiled over at her brother.

James had already shared the highlights of his discussion with Mr Mears with Simon, and as both of them had spoken to the accountant earlier that afternoon they were starting to get a good idea of the dire straits in which the company had been left. So, as they finally joined the group, with a tray of drinks, it was not to impart good tidings.

"So, Jimmy, what's this all about?" Rosie questioned as soon as they sat down. "How bad is it, because I can tell from both of your expressions that it's not good news, is it?"

"No, I'm afraid it's not, Rosie. There's quite a lot of detail, which I won't bore you with, and it's not all straightforward, but the bottom line is that neither the legal nor the financial position is anywhere near as healthy as Dad led us to believe." Jimmy took a gulp of his pint before continuing. "Mr Mears wants to go through the will with us all together, which I've pencilled in for ten o'clock on Friday morning at the house, if you're all okay with that?" They all nodded.

Simon, picking up from where James had left off, continued. "The highlights are that once probate has been cleared, which could take several months, and any death taxes have been paid, there may not be anywhere near enough money left over to keep the business and the house going."

"The house, I don't understand?" Rosie questioned, looking over to her brother. "I thought that was neatly locked up in a trust fund, or something, along with the farmland, and all that was safe. I thought we knew that after Mum died, didn't we? Wasn't it a trust our grandparents set up before we were born?"

"Yes, you're right, Rosie. That's exactly what I thought, too," Judy chipped in. Simon had already briefed her on the highlights, so she was not hearing this for the first time. "From what I understand, though, Dad apparently took out a loan, a kind of mortgage against the trust, which, from what Mr Mears told Jimmy earlier, he was legally entitled to do as the trustee. Even though, under normal circumstances he was ill-advised to do."

"Judy's right. Mr Mears cautioned Dad against it, but Dad said he needed to raise capital for the business, so went ahead and did it anyway. Mr Mears has copies of all the paperwork. As the business has not been faring so well in recent months, it appears he'd been robbing Peter to pay Paul for some time."

"Which is the problem I'm still struggling to reconcile." Simon remained a little non-plussed by it all. "I do the accounts and see the orders, so from an order book perspective we've been doing well. Like everyone, the company had its problems during lockdown, and prices have gone up recently in almost all areas, so everything is costing more for labour and materials. However, we've bounced back a lot faster than most businesses, so in reality we should be in a healthy position." He took a drink of his pint to allow that to sink in, before adding, "I've suspected for a while there was a discrepancy in the books, even questioned Frank as you all know, but he wouldn't acknowledge it. Nor would he give me any explanation in terms of what had happened. He always got so defensive on the subject, which is understandable if what he's been doing has been dodgy."

"So, you think what he's been doing is dodgy then, even illegal?" Rosie knew her father liked to duck and dive and make out he was a skilled negotiator. She had never suspected whatever he was doing, though, was not above board.

"I don't know, Rosie.   And it's not up to me to speculate on whether it's legal, or not. I think we all recognised your father was not always squeaky clean, but I never suspected anything illegal either. Anyway, the top and bottom of it is that I've absolutely no idea where the money's gone, or how we're going to carry on at this rate unless we can trace it."

Simon sighed. He hated not knowing the answers, or worse still finding discrepancies in his own accounting systems. The meeting with the accountant had not gone well either, the accountant unable to give him or James any reassurance they could weather this, or that they would have sufficient money in their trading account to pay their creditors if they came knocking.

"The next couple of months are going to be critical whilst we go through the process of trying to understand where it might have gone, and with probate running in parallel that could become awkward. I think we'll need to go to the bank and see what support they can provide, although how good an investment we are at the moment is anyone's guess."

"Well, in terms of where all the money's gone, I think we've all got a good idea who's been helping Dad spend it, haven't we?" Judy had made no secret of how much she hated Miranda, or objected to the way she had been spending her father's money these last few years. The money he had lavished on her with fancy cars, expensive jewellery, designer clothes and eating out at posh restaurants was obscene, and all by the sound of it money he did not have to spend. "As I've said previously, that woman is dangerous. I get the impression she's been taking Dad to the cleaners these last few years and has effectively wiped his bank account clean, even blowing an absolute fortune on a wedding that didn't happen. To think how much that alone must have cost him. I bet he's turning in his grave."

"Yes, and it's not as though she's even a grieving widow, is she?" Rosie chipped in, no fan of Miranda's either.

"What does that mean?" Judy asked, surprised at Rosie's comment. "Are you saying she's not upset by Dad's death? I know she's in shock, but aren't we all?" They all nodded, unconvincingly and without comment.

On reflection, it was true that none of them had shed many tears since the body was found, although as the bride-to-be Judy had been surprised by Miranda's reaction, or more precisely her lack of reaction at Frank's death. She had taken the discovery of his body in her stride, her emotions completely unreadable. Even when the police asked their initial questions, she had been circumspect in the manner in which she had answered them, almost as if she was withholding a piece of the jigsaw. And since Sunday she had hardly spoken or engaged with any of them, not even as far as offering to get involved in preparing the funeral, or letting people know what had happened. Judy had just presumed she had locked herself away, and until now had never questioned any other motive. Miranda was a cold fish, that was for sure.

"Well, I saw her yesterday, near the shop. She was talking to another guy, someone I vaguely recognised from the pub, or around town. I'm not sure exactly where, but his face was familiar. And from what I was seeing, they were old friends, not casual acquaintances. Their body language gave them away. They were talking for quite a while, and at one stage it looked to be getting quite heated, before they went into the café across the road from my shop. I didn't see them leave as I was dealing with a customer, but I was in two minds about going over and seeing what they were up to, or at least asking Glynis behind the counter if she'd overheard anything. It looked suspicious to me, like they were planning something. It certainly wasn't a chance encounter, I'm sure of that." Rosie was adamant that something was not right.

"Dad's only been dead a matter of days. You can't be suggesting she's found someone else already, can you? That would be fast work, even by her standards." Judy was surprised at what her sister was suggesting.

"I'm not saying that, no. But whatever it is that I saw looked very suspicious, even as you say by her standards. And another thing, why did she lie to the police and say she'd been drinking the night before the wedding, implying she couldn't remember because she was drunk? When all the time, she was the most sober of the lot of us. She hadn't touched a drop all night."

"Yes, I'd almost forgotten about that. I did wonder why she said that at the time. And for the life of me I can't think why I didn't question it when she said it. I think we were all in shock. In fact, I don't know why the police didn't pick her up on it either, as I'm sure I told them about it when they spoke to me. Although how that would have any bearing on Dad's death baffles me." Judy was annoyed with herself for not picking it up earlier. "I'll remind the police when I next speak to them."

Katie had sat back drinking her wine, quietly listening as the siblings exchanged their views on Miranda. She was not at all surprised by what Rosie had observed, not in the slightest. In fact, it supported something she had suspected for a while and had kept to herself. Gossip in the hairdressers never went unnoticed, especially when it related to a member of the family, although that did not mean she needed to spread it, or pass it on. After all, what was said in the salon stayed in the salon.

However, if the gossips could be relied upon, then the chances of Miranda having another fella on the go, at the same time as being engaged to Frank, was not as far-fetched as Judy assumed. Sightings of her with the Pilates instructor from the leisure centre had been hinted at, with reports of them even being seen together in IKEA, of all places, picking out lampshades. Katie had not paid much heed at the time, believing there to be an innocent explanation. But when she had seen with her own eyes Miranda with another man, driving in her distinctive red Mazda down the high street a few days later, it did leave her wondering what on earth could be going on. He looked distinctly like the guy she regularly saw jogging around the park in a morning, at the same time she went out for her run. And if he was the same guy, she had to admit he was not at all bad looking, with his well-honed abs a huge contrast to Frank's ever growing beer belly, to say nothing of his greying hair with his receding forehead. Given the choice, she knew which direction she'd be looking in.

"Well, whatever it was, we do need to have a discussion about Miranda, and the house, because from what Mr Mears said, she has no legal right to remain there – and that from our perspective is good news. However, there is still the matter of the baby, so we do need to discuss how we broach the subject of getting her out, and when. I suggest we leave it a couple of weeks, at least until after the will's been read and the funeral's out of the way, then do it. We can discuss with Mr Mears perhaps the best approach nearer the time."

"I'll go with the flow in terms of timing, although I could happily suggest a 'how' if you'd like, or Mr Mears doesn't offer a good enough solution for getting rid of her," Rosie added mischievously.

"Does it involve Professor Plumb, with a revolver in the billiard room, by any chance?" Richard suggested in an attempt to lighten the mood as he stood up. "I'm going to the gents, then I'll get another round in, if someone can lend me the money, that is? Or should I just tap your card again, Rosie?"

As Richard walked off, there was a collective sigh in the direction of their little brother.

Chapter 17

That same evening......

It was Wednesday evening and Miranda had been left in the house all alone. The others had gone to the pub about an hour previously. She had overheard Richard and Rosie talking about everyone meeting up earlier as she had been in the kitchen, preparing herself a warm drink and a snack for her dinner. The thought of the warm pub, the congenial atmosphere of chatting with friends over a glass of wine and some good pub grub, instead of a microwave meal for one, washed down with a cup of tea, sounded very appealing. She could not describe what she would give to be opening a bottle of wine, rather than putting the kettle on. The idea of getting completely plastered and telling them all where to go, was something she could only dream of at the moment. What a time to be pregnant!

If only being pregnant was the worst of her current predicament, she could probably deal with that. However, assuming she was reading the mood language around the house correctly, she would soon be penniless and homeless too. Her emotions were all over the place, and sadly grief was not among them. No matter how much she tried to act the grieving widow, she sensed Frank's children had seen straight through her.

She had obviously been looking forward to the wedding, and the reassurances being Mrs Paulson would have given her, even recognising that blasted pre-nuptial agreement Frank had insisted upon her signing. He had assured her it was simply a technicality, due to the legalities around the trust and the estate, none of which she had bought. They had argued and exchanged words, but the bottom line was he had left her without an option. Failure to sign would have marked her out as money-grabbing and without signing it she risked the wedding not going ahead. Signing had been the lesser of two evils.

Over the last couple of days, she had mulled over the events of the weekend, barely seventy-two hours since her life had fallen apart. The party the night before the wedding, and all the excitement of the day ahead. Then going to bed late and tired, after being on her feet for most of the evening, sober whilst all around were drinking with abandon. After all, it was a free bar, so no one was holding back. She remembered telling the police she'd had a few drinks and felt woozy, when in reality she had not touched a drop, as much as she may have wanted to. Why had she said that, because although the pregnancy was being kept quiet outside of the family, everyone else in the room at the time of the police asking the question had known, so why had she felt the need to lie? She needed to get her story straight before it came back to haunt her.

Then going up to bed, watching as he undressed and collapsed on the mattress, barely conscious, his socks the only item of clothing still on. Thinking, was she in her right mind going ahead with the wedding, or was it too late to call it off? Questioning what she was letting herself in for if she did go ahead with it, whilst asking was this the type of duplicitous life she wanted to lead, or what she wanted for her unborn child? She would always have lived in fear of Frank finding out about the baby, or Leo making a claim.

Then waking up on the Sunday morning to the knock at the bedroom door, with James telling her there had been an accident in the kitchen involving Frank. She knew Frank had gone downstairs around two in the morning; she knew he had gone to take a phone call. She was a light sleeper and the sound of his phone beeping, as well as disturbing him, had woken her up too. She remembered reaching over to look at her own phone to establish the time, before getting out of bed and going to the bathroom. She had then stood at the top of the stairs, listening.

It was not unusual behaviour for Frank to take calls late into the evening, or in the early hours of the morning, and she had long since stopped asking him who was on the phone, or enquiring what they wanted at that time of night. And, on the basis of the times the messages generally came in, they were unlikely to be from another woman. So, knowing her fiancé dealt with some very shady characters, Miranda had not wanted to ask too much. Frank would not have told her anyway, although that did not stop her from being inquisitive. They never spoke about his business, nor his personal or family life, outside of what they did together. He had always been private and mysterious, neither quality particularly attractive, she now realised, in hindsight.

Then seeing him sprawled out on the kitchen floor, lying in a pool of his own blood, still wearing his socks, with his modesty barely preserved by the silk dressing gown he had obviously pulled on before leaving the bedroom. It was not a pretty picture, not by any stretch of the imagination, with the sight of all that congealed blood, coupled with her morning sickness, sending her darting to the downstairs bathroom to throw up.

Had he died the day after the wedding then all would have been well and good. She would have had the best of both worlds, with legal rights as his widow; someone who was carrying his unborn child, at least as far as the world was concerned. No one would ever have questioned that, or suspected otherwise. And most of all, she would no longer be married to a man to whom she was not in love. She would have been free to start a new life with Leo eventually, or anyone else for that matter. As a beautiful, young and rich widow, she would have had the pick of the crop.

Now though, she had little if any rights and where she stood in terms of maintaining the charade of the baby being Frank's, well, that was anyone's guess. For the time being she would keep that nugget to herself, if only until the contents of his will had been communicated and her position was better understood.

For now, Miranda had more pressing concerns. Leo was a great distraction, and amazing between the sheets, but he was far from marriage material. He might own his own house, have a job and an amazing body, otherwise what did he have going for him? He had nothing, at least not in terms of a career, or the earning potential to keep her in the lifestyle to which she had become accustomed as Frank's fiancée. No, she needed to consider her options, and keep her eyes focussed on what she needed to do to get out of this fiasco. Otherwise she might find she did not even have enough money to pay her bus fare back to her parents' house.

As she considered the depressing thought of going home, weighed against the prospect of moving into Leo's one-bedroom apartment, her phone rang. It was Leo. Did she want to speak to him, or should she let it go to voicemail? They had not been in touch since Sunday morning. Miranda had messaged him to let him know Frank was dead, and stated the obvious that the wedding was off.

He'd replied briefly, "Right – hope you're OK."

It left her wondering what he meant, his message showing neither any sign of shock nor surprise, which in turn led to her questioning what his knowledge of Frank's death was, before she'd let him know. He could not have had anything to do with it, surely? She knew he was unhappy at the prospect of Frank bringing up his child and the risk of their affair coming to an end, if and when Frank ever found out about what they were getting up to behind his back. Added to that, the fear of what Frank could do to him, or more likely arrange for someone else to do on his behalf, had worried him. Frank did not like to get his own hands dirty, or implicate himself, but that did not reduce the risk as far as Leo was concerned.

Could Leo have tried to take matters into his own hands, even possibly confronted Frank the night of the party about the affair, with the intent of getting it called off, and things had gone wrong? Had he been lying in wait after the rest of the guests had left? She now tried to recall whether she had seen him leave, or not. She had definitely seen them chatting during the evening, which at the time had led her to question the sense of inviting him along with the group of people from the leisure centre in the first place. Maybe Leo had said something out of turn and later they had got into a fight, which given the amount Frank had been drinking would have put him at an immediate disadvantage. Although regardless of the drink, Leo's age and physical strength alone would have been more than enough to knock Frank out, if he had wanted to. Her mind did not want to contemplate what could have happened. At the same time, she could not completely dismiss the idea either. She needed to know, so answered the phone.

"Hi, can you talk?"

"Yes. I'm alone. Everyone's left to go to the pub." It was lovely to hear from him and the lightness of his voice automatically made Miranda feel relaxed, any suspicions she may have had parked for the time being.

"What are you doing?"

"I've just eaten dinner and I'm in the sitting room, watching television. I'll probably go up for a shower soon, before everyone returns. I'm trying to keep out of their way. It's all got a little awkward."

"Shall I come over and scrub your back? You know how good I am at that."

"Mmm, nice thought, but I don't think you coming over here is perhaps your brightest idea, do you?" she had laughed.

"Perhaps not, but it would be a good distraction and I could help with your relaxation techniques. After all, there's our baby's welfare to consider in all this. I can't have you getting all stressed out, can I?"

"I'll bear that in mind for another day, for now, though, I think we'd best keep our distance. I don't want anyone suspecting anything about you or the baby, do you?"

"Spoil sport. Just don't leave it too long though. I'm missing you in my bed and I need to see you again, soon."

"Missing you, too." Deciding she needed to know, she added, "Leo, I have to ask, did you have anything to do with what happened on Sunday, you know Frank's death? It's just you didn't sound at all surprised when I messaged the other day to let you know, and it's left me confused."

"Me, I don't know what you mean?" Miranda could not tell from his surprised tone whether he was being serious or not.

Either way, it did not answer her question, or the questions that were being raised in the mind of the person standing in the hallway. The person who had happened to overhear at least one side of the conversation as they had been passing on the way back to the kitchen. That person was left in no doubt what the conversation had been about, although remained at a complete loss to know who had been on the other end of the line. The name Leo meant nothing to them, not yet at least.

Chapter 18

A few weeks previously.....

The small lock-up was on the outskirts of Chidlington, located down a disused side street behind Coronation Terrace. There were several garages, most of which looked like they had been abandoned over time, the doors damaged and in some cases the hinges hanging off, rusty from years of neglect. No one ever visited them and there were rarely any cars or people around to witness what was going on.

It was in an area of town that was ripe for development, an area Frank had had his eyes on for some time now. If he could get planning permission to demolish the terrace he could build the apartment block he had set his heart on. The views over the river that meandered in front of Coronation Terrace were pretty and for the right price they would sell. Perhaps not as second homes, or holiday rentals where the real money was, but for much needed homes for local people. There was a shortage of them at the moment, and whilst it was not where he made big money, if he could buy the land at the right price and build within his budget there would still be a good profit in it for him.

He would also be doing something for the town. It was crying out for properties like this. It might even help improve his reputation with the council and the local community. He was savvy enough to know it had taken a real hit in recent months, when the luxury development at the other end of town encountered problems and had to be put on hold whilst they sorted it out, at great cost to himself, he might add. Several of the buyers had pulled out, using a clause in their contract as ammunition to recover their deposits. That had hit him hard, especially as that money had been committed elsewhere. Other bills needed to be paid and for a while the business had effectively been living hand to mouth, operating on a system that meant he was moving money between his projects in a less than orthodox manner. If he could not find a way to resolve it before the accountants came to prepare the end of year accounts it would raise serious concerns, with cries of fraud being a real risk. A project like Coronation Terrace might help turn his fortunes around.

The problem was that a small number of the houses on the street were still occupied, the owners unprepared to leave them, regardless of the incentives the council was prepared to offer, backed by Frank underwriting their offers. Some had moved without much pressure, enticed by alternative housing or grants towards improvements to other properties.

There had even been the offer of help with residential care in the case of one particularly elderly resident. He continued to remain stubbornly in situ, threatening to chain himself to the railings, if necessary. He maintained he had lived in that house, man and boy, for over eighty years and was not prepared to go willingly, and certainly not at the whim of some trumped-up developer. He still had all his marbles, with all his home comforts around him, and, at his time of life, what need did he have for the money they were offering for him anyway?

And as far as his health was concerned, in his view, he had no need for anyone to look after him, thank you very much. "You'll have to carry me out, feet first in a coffin, before I give way to any developers." His scream, through his letter box at the last council official who had dared to knock at his door, could be heard several doors down the street. No, there had been various offers made, and some had been taken, but a few resolute characters continued to put up a fight.

Frank had been lobbying certain members of the council for some time, even requesting they apply for a Compulsory Purchase Order, and although there was some support to his proposal, there was insufficient backing to get it off the ground. The hard-line councillors were using excuses that it did not reach the threshold of being in the public interest, arguing it would be thrown out once it was submitted to the Secretary of State. It was not worth their time and effort in preparing the paperwork, and no matter how much Frank lobbied for it, or offered to sweeten their pockets, they were unwilling to risk it. In the council's view, other projects were more deserving.

So, as far as Coronation Terrace was concerned, it was simply a waiting game. They would continue with the approach they were taking, sure in the knowledge that it would not be too long before all the properties were vacant, and they could then reassess their development opportunities. Frank was not convinced the "slowly, slowly catchy monkey" approach was in his interests, but for the time being he was running out of other ideas.

Talk of the potential for the terrace to be demolished had been bandying around town for some time now, and according to insider reports it was a regular agenda item at the Planning Council's monthly meetings, with heated debates each time it was raised. Some of the councillors and locals were happy with the vision Frank was offering; the idea of new affordable housing was something the town desperately needed. Others were less supportive, believing Coronation Terrace was of historic significance. Having been built at the turn of the twentieth century and completed around the time of Edward VII's coronation in 1902, the terrace had been named in his honour, with the royalists in the town unwilling to let that fact be lost. Granted it was in need of repair, but it was certainly not the eyesore some people were suggesting.

The arguments were set to rumble on for some time, and as interesting as that might be, as the lock was secured at garage number 46, the person turning the key was relieved with that fact. They were happy as long as the council maintained its position, content for the decision to be kicked into the long grass for as long as possible. After all, they needed the space to store items. Items that for various reasons could not be stored anywhere else, and needed to be protected from prying eyes.

For the time being they were safe, but should Frank Paulson ever get his way, then that might not always be the case. It was definitely a development they needed to stay close to, and be ready to act should circumstances dictate the gear needed to be moved, or disposed of, more quickly than had been planned.

Chapter 19

Present day.......

As arranged, at ten o'clock on Friday morning Mr Mears pulled into the driveway of the Old Manor House, parking his car under the shade of the oak trees. It was a hot day and the short drive from his office to his client's home had given him little time to think. He was here to share the contents of Frank Paulson's Last Will and Testament with his family and a couple of other beneficiaries who he had arranged to be present.

Reading the will was one of the formal aspects of his role as an executor that he did not particularly enjoy, and certainly not when he was charged with imparting bad news to a family. A family that was already going through the grieving process. He much preferred the more straightforward estates where any money or property was simply left to the spouse, or divided equally between the children. Those cases were not too difficult to handle as the contents of the will were usually well known, and had probably been discussed beforehand. There were generally no surprises, no histrionics, and certainly no ill feelings between the parties, or towards the deceased.

Mr Mears had no expectation that today's reading would go that way and whilst he had provided the headlines to Mr Paulson's son, James, the devil could often be found in the detail, and that so far had not been discussed. He girded his loins as he approached the front door and rang the bell.

"Good morning, Mr Mears. The family is waiting for you in the sitting room. Would you like me to show you through?"

"Thank you, Mrs Cuthbert, that would be most kind." He had met the housekeeper on a couple of occasions previously, so offered her a smile. He found her an interesting character, but as Frank had not left any bequest to her, she had not been required to join them.

"Very well, follow me."

As Mr Mears entered the sitting room, the conversation went quiet. He was used to having that effect on people so took no offence by it, he was just pleased that everyone was already assembled and they could get on with the reading without undue delay. He had another appointment back at his office at noon, so really did not want to waste any time waiting around, or engaging in small talk. It was not his style.

"Good morning, Mr Mears. Would you like me to introduce everyone to you before we begin? And shall I ask Mrs Cuthbert to bring you a cup of tea, or coffee perhaps."

"No, thank you. That should not be necessary, although a glass of water would be most welcome."

He knew the siblings from various dealings over the years and smiled awkwardly at them. From the way the others were positioned in the room he could easily work out who they all were. He had spoken to Mr Goodman on the phone on a couple of occasions, but had never met him in person. Apart from the four adult children from Frank's first marriage, and their spouses, and Mr Paulson's fiancée, Miss Swann, who was seated alone on one of the sofas, nervously biting her nails, the only other person in the room was the old nanny, Mrs Tilbury, he believed her name to be. She was sitting primly between Richard and Rosie, on the sofa directly opposite Miss Swann, holding Richard's hand. Mr Mears was unclear who was benefiting the most from this simple action, as neither looked to be grieving, nor appeared particularly upset. It was a relatively small and intimate gathering and the atmosphere felt most unusual.

"Now, as you know, I have already outlined the main points of your father's will to James, and I trust he has briefed you? However, I am duty bound to read the full document to all beneficiaries, so I will do that when you are happy for me to begin." A quick look around the room indicated they were all eager for him to commence. "I will start by saying that your father only updated his will a matter of a few short weeks ago, during a regular meeting at my office. I will add that at the time there was nothing to alarm me regarding his health or his state of mind. As you know, I have represented your father and his company's interests for some time, so I have got to know him quite well. In terms of its contents, I know that it reflects his recent thoughts and particularly his views leading up to the wedding, which due to his untimely death did not in fact take place."

He felt by stating that at the outset, any questions later regarding contesting the will might be more easily addressed. Frank was of sound mind, even if his solicitor felt that his actions were perhaps a little unbalanced.

Mr Mears then proceeded to go through the document, word by word, pausing occasionally to gauge the reaction of his audience. Throughout the process, he noticed that Miss Swann kept her eyes down, staring at her hands that remained clasped in her lap. She barely engaged with the rest of the family as they looked from one to another as each of the points was raised.

After he had finished reading, Mr Mears looked up. "Does anyone have any specific comments before we proceed to what needs to take place next?"

"Yes, I do." Rosie was the first to speak up. "What you have said, if I understand it correctly, is that the estate, which includes the house and his business is split between myself,

James, Judy and Richard in equal proportions, and that my father has not provided for his youngest son, Mason, in any respect. Is that correct?"

"Yes, technically that is correct." Mr Mears had prepared for this question as he was sure it would be raised, although he was surprised it was their first question. "What you may not be aware of, though, is that at the time of his divorce from Mrs Alison Paulson, the terms of their settlement dealt with that, through the establishment of a trust in Mason's name."

They all exchanged a glance. This was something they had never discussed nor been made aware of. They knew Alison had done reasonably well out of the divorce, after having in fact lobbied their father to ensure Mason was provided for, but the terms of what had been agreed were never something he had talked to them about.

"Your father made it clear that their son, Mason, would not go on to inherit any part of the estate, and his argument was clear, that he wanted to retain any control within the direct descendants of the Winchcliff family, whose estate it had originally been. After some prolonged debate, Mrs Paulson was happy with that arrangement. She sought a clean break between Mason and your father, so this helped, in terms of the financial provisions at least. It also avoided any future ambiguity. The quid pro quo was that a trust would be set up with a financial settlement that Mason could access once he turned twenty-one, so not for some years yet. A separate firm of solicitors handles that trust on behalf of Mrs Paulson and her son, and as such it is no longer of any concern to Laycock, Mears and Campbell, or yourselves. Her only other stipulation with regards to Mason was that she had full custody, and received a monthly allowance for his expenses, until he turned eighteen, at which point that would stop being paid. This always assumed your father would still be around to pay it, I might add. You may also be interested to learn that now that your father has died, there is no surviving obligation on the estate, or anyone within the family, to continue that arrangement."

"Thank you." Rosie was happy at least that was clear. "I suppose that explains why Alison is not here today, if Mason does not inherit anything. I had been wondering."

"Quite." Mr Mears maintained his formal tone throughout.

"So, do you mind me asking, in terms of the trust that was put in place for this house and the farmlands by our grandparents, am I correct in assuming that's still in place, or has that gone? I'm not sure what happens to the trust, now that Dad's not here. Or what the implications are on it, given the loans Dad took out against it. Loans for the business, I presume?" Judy had still not got her mind completely around what it all meant.

"Well, Mrs Goodman, I can assure you that the trust is still very much in place, for the time being at least. I, acting through Laycock, Mears and Campbell am one of the trustees and have overseen the transactions your father has made in recent years to release money against the equity in the properties. He was within his legal rights to do so, although in the coming weeks, I suggest I spend some time to help you to understand that a little more. We may also want to discuss whether now is an appropriate time for the trust to be dissolved, now that your father is no longer here. Or, potentially it could take on a different form, for the benefit of your children perhaps. It's early days, but whichever way you decide to go the debts on the house will still need to be repaid. That is a decision between you all, which I will support you on, of course." By all, he was careful to avoid Miss Swann's eyes.

"In terms of the Old Manor House, the trust stipulated that it should remain in the family for as long as Mr Paulson survived, thereafter it was for his main beneficiaries, that is his legitimate children, to determine what became of it, and of course the farmlands that surround it. The *Paulson* businesses are outside of the trust, and as I said earlier, the operational running of those now transfers to Mr James Paulson, with each of you four children having a twenty-five percent stake in the business. How that is set up I believe also needs a separate discussion, with the appropriate legal and financial advisors. It's not my area of expertise, I'm afraid.

"Now, going back to the house and lands, with his passing you will be entitled to sell all or any of that off, should you determine as a family that is what you would like to do, once probate has been cleared, of course. That is clearly your decision, and there is no pressure on you to decide anything immediately. The one question that will need addressing, though, is how much the estate is worth, or more correctly how much the proceeds would be once the mortgages and debts against the assets have been taken into consideration, along with any death taxes due. That will all be a matter for probate, which I will steer you through once we are in a position to apply for it. Sadly, the process is unlikely to be straightforward and may take some time, so we will need to be patient."

"How is Nanny impacted by all this in the meantime? The Old Manor House is her home, as well as ours. When Mum died she was given the apartment above the garage on a grace and favour basis, for as long as she needed it. If we do decide to sell, then what happens to her?" Richard had listened and had fully understood what had been said, but nowhere within his father's will had Nanny's name been mentioned. There was no legacy or gift of any description mentioned, which had led him to wonder why Mr Mears had invited her into the room in the first place.

"Oh, don't worry about me, dear. I'll be alright." She patted Richard's hand, giving him one of her genteel smiles, hoping it would give him the reassurance he needed.

"No, you're quite correct, Mr Paulson. I apologise, for I have not made that clear yet. There are a couple of further documents that pertain to the will that I need to take you through, so if there are no more questions on the main document for the moment, I will move onto those." Looking around he could sense they all had further questions, but were perhaps struggling to articulate them. There was an atmosphere, an apparent elephant in the room; a point that they had still not raised.

"So, the first of those documents relates to Mrs Tilbury. As you have correctly said, she has the right to stay in the current property for as long as the house remains in the family's possession, with the provisions of her grace and favour status dissolved once the main house is sold. However, what your mother's original will provided for, which I probably should have clarified earlier, was that in the event that the main house was sold, then Mrs Tilbury would be offered an alternative cottage on the farmland. It did not go into too much detail thereafter, as I presume there was no expectation of either of your parents passing in the manner, or timescales, that they did." He tried to choose his words carefully, not wanting to be as obvious as stating that neither had expected the old woman would outlive them both.

"Other than that, there is a small list of bequests detailed on a codicil that accompanies Mr Paulson's will. For the purposes of probate, the value of these will still need to be accounted for, but thereafter the items will go to the recipients, as indicated by your father. They mainly relate to pieces of jewellery your mother had that are currently held in the vault at the bank, which I have a full inventory of here, along with your father's watches, his golf clubs and some pieces of artwork. Here is the list." He handed over pieces of paper to each of them, including Miranda who looked down at it.

"Miss Swann, you will see that Mr Paulson has agreed to you retaining the emerald and diamond engagement ring he bought for you. The remainder of the family jewellery, which I understand on occasion you have worn, and originally belonged to Mrs Susan Paulson or her mother before her, is to be returned to the family. I trust you are happy to comply with this?" Miranda's face remained blank, although a slight nod of her head indicated her understanding.

"So, am I missing something, or is that the extent of what Miranda, or her child inherits?" Rosie had listened carefully and could see nothing other than a solitary gold engagement ring that had been a present anyway, that her father had left to his bride-to-be. That did not sound right, and as she sat there was left to wonder why it was her asking the question and not Miranda in the first place. Surely she would have expected to have something, or at least for their child to have been provided for?

"Miss Paulson, to answer your question, I can only advise that your father and Miss Swann entered into a pre-nuptial agreement some weeks ago, and although I am unable to go into the details in any way, I can assure you that neither she, nor her unborn child, has any other claim on your late father's estate." There was silence in the room as each of them turned to stare at Miranda; her demeanour giving nothing away as her head remained bent.

"Now, unless there is anything else I can help you with for the moment, I hope you will excuse me. I have another pressing appointment in town that I need to attend to. Please get in touch with my office if I can be of any further assistance, or you have any more questions once this has all sunk in. I will of course leave you a copy of the will for you to mull over." He stood and straightened his trousers that had almost stuck to his legs with the heat, before turning to Judy. "I understand you're already working through your father's list of requirements for his funeral? Should you need anything more from me, please don't hesitate to ask." Her smile saying all he needed to know about what she thought about that.

"Let me show you out, Mr Mears," Nanny volunteered, carefully lifting herself off the sofa. She had sat for too long and needed to move before cramp set in. Her legs might have started to get a little numb, but compared with the rest, who looked to have turned into stone by the solicitor's announcement, at least she could still walk.

"If you'll excuse me, too. I'm feeling a little unwell. I'm going up to my room for a rest." Miranda rose to follow Nanny Tilbury out of the room. She was unprepared to stay around with the others any longer than was necessary, simply to listen to them going over the details of the will.

Whilst she had not expected to get much, she had expected something. It was worse than she thought as she now had nothing in her own name. Her bank account had less than two thousand pounds in it, and other than the clothes she stood up in she had no other assets to her name. Apart from the diamond and emerald engagement ring, a piece of jewellery to which she no longer had any sentimental attachment. It would need to go, as soon as possible, because she needed the money and needed it fast. Thankfully, she recalled how much Frank had told her it was worth, so at least that gave her a bit of a nest egg.

She could not imagine being thrown out before the funeral, or what people would think if she turned up without it on her finger, so at least that bought her a little time. Thereafter it was anyone's guess what they would do.

God, it was a nightmare, and if Leo had anything to do with this, as she increasingly suspected he had, she was furious.   Her position, whichever way she looked at it, was not good and her options were narrowing by the day.

As Miranda was consoling herself upstairs, the others remained in the sitting room, Nanny having returned with a tray of cold drinks, before going back to her annex to leave them in peace to think through what they needed to do next.

"Well, that was a bit of a shocker, wasn't it?" Rosie was the first to break the silence. "Dad was obviously more wised up to her motives than we gave him credit, wasn't he? I can't say I'd ever thought he'd want a pre-nup, though, did you? I always got the impression he was loved-up, even if she wasn't. Although I have to say in recent weeks the atmosphere around the house has on occasion been quite toxic between them. They did seem to be arguing a lot more than was usual, but I just put that down to pre-wedding nerves."

"Yes, I was surprised, too. It leaves us in an interesting position, though, now about her, doesn't it? As well as what we do in terms of the house. Can we throw her out, with her expecting Dad's baby, and if we did where would she go? Imagine what everyone would say about that, our name would be mud, don't you think?" Judy worried most about what people thought about the family, and the need to maintain its reputation. She feared it had taken a hit recently and wanted to do whatever she could to restore their good name.

"Do you think there's any chance he thought the baby wasn't his, or that he'd heard rumours around town about her playing around? I know it's only recently that I've suspected something, but it could have been going on for quite a while. And it was interesting that when we asked Mr Mears he didn't bat an eye at the mention of the baby. Dad must have spoken to him about it, don't you think? As far as I was aware it was not being discussed outside of the family, at least not until after the wedding. Dad and Miranda had been adamant about that, hadn't they?" Rosie and Judy exchanged a glance.

Katie, as always, had kept quiet until now, although she felt it was an appropriate point to add her view. She could not sit back any longer and ignore what she had heard.

"If talk around the salon is anything to go by, then it was not as secret as you'd believe, Rosie. A couple of comments have been made, which I never react to, although I'd be lying if I said it had never been suggested or suspected. Some talked about a shotgun wedding, whereas others, once she and the Pilates instructor had been seen out together, did start to put two and two together in terms of who the father might be. And the good money wasn't on it being your dad."

"Well, that does put a different perspective on it. If Dad had his suspicions, then with the terms of his will clear that only legitimate children inherited, that's probably how he got around it. Although, if that was the case, if the baby is legitimate, why wouldn't he, or she, inherit in its own right? I'm baffled."

"You're not the only one, Jimmy." Simon too had been scratching his head in terms of where it left them all. He had not expected to inherit anything, but his wife's position was clear. "At least the position on the business is known, in terms of ownership and management, that is. If you four are now all equal owners, then we need to get together and understand how that looks, and what needs to be put in place to continue trading. As far as I'm concerned, I'd like to keep the business going, with Jimmy if we can, but that's clearly now up to you four to decide."

"Yes, Si, I agree with you. Perhaps if we keep going as we are for the moment, and allow some time for the dust to settle, then we'll have a better idea what we have to deal with, or if there's a business worth keeping going for. If by the time the debts are paid, along with any taxes that are due, we need to sell up and cut our losses, then it will be a whole different ballgame."

"I agree." Richard had been considering the whole scenario, allowing the different connotations to work their way around his mind. He liked complex conundrums and this was certainly one to which he could apply his skill set, along with the unanswered question of what actually happened to his father that he had been thinking about since Sunday. He still believed it was murder, or manslaughter at the very least, unable to buy the view the others had that their father had fallen, or suffered some form of medical condition.

Richard had been listening closely as Mr Mears detailed the contents of the will. He was looking at who benefitted financially from the death, looking for clues to a motive. There was nothing in his father's will, though, that had helped on that score. Miranda, in his view, was no longer a suspect, because in his mind she did not have anything to gain. Arguably her position was much weaker following Frank's death.

The mystery Pilates teacher did however shed a different perspective onto that. If he needed his love rival out of the way, in order to claim the prize of his baby and prevent Miranda from marrying his father, then that was motive enough, surely? And his timing could not have been better.

Richard was not convinced, though, and needed more time to think about that, and to do some digging of his own. "I don't fancy moving out yet, and I couldn't afford to anyway, so let's kick the can down the road until we know better. We can then make an informed decision. In my view, though, for what it's worth, I think Miranda has enough to contend with, without her losing her home, too. So, I don't think we should do anything too hasty. And in time, especially after what we've just heard, we might want to think about a DNA test, should she ever try to contest the will. If it's not Dad's baby, or she refuses to do one, then we'd have our answer and the issue would become a whole lot less complex, in my view."

The others nodded in his direction. Richard did not say much, but when he did what he said was usually worth listening to.

Chapter 20

Whilst the family was coming to terms with the contents of the will, the police were still interested in working their case, which was not made any easier without having a clear cause of death to work with. Ruth Jacobs did not know whether they were treating it as manslaughter, resulting from perhaps a burglary gone wrong, or a targeted murder, or simply an unfortunate and untimely accident. The evidence was sparse and while she still awaited the formal forensic report she found her hands were well and truly tied. She was not only unable to release the body, but equally unclear where she should be directing the efforts of her team. And until, or unless, it became anything more serious, Neil happened to be the best she had available to commit. A point that did not bode well, as far as Ruth was concerned.

"Neil, why don't you come through to my office when you've finished your lunch and we can work on what you've managed to pull together so far on the Paulson case." Ruth had returned from the toilets and a quick cigarette break to see Neil casually sitting at his desk, eating his sandwich and tapping away on his phone. He behaved as if he did not have a single care in the world.

"Right, Sarg, give me five minutes and I'll be straight in." Ruth returned to her desk and awaited his arrival, almost slumping into her chair.

"So, Neil, what have you got?" she asked when he eventually turned up. It was Friday afternoon, five days since the incident and importantly only two hours until the end of her shift. It had been a busy week and Ruth had been called in to investigate a number of other more pressing enquiries, leaving Neil following up with statements from various people. People who were at the house at the time of the incident, or names of people who had been brought to their attention subsequently as possibly having information that may be able to shed some light on the investigation.

"Well, I've spoken to the housekeeper, Mrs Cuthbert, and her husband. That was a strange conversation and no matter how much I tried, I got very little, and certainly nothing new. They were apparently asleep and didn't hear a thing. They'd gone to bed quite late, around one o'clock in the morning, having tidied up most of the mess from the party and stacked the dishwasher before going through to their rooms. They said they were exhausted, so nothing had disturbed them until their alarm went off at half past six; roughly the same time the rest of the family was getting up. I have to say, though, Mrs Cuthbert is a strange character. She's Romanian, and her English isn't brilliant, but every time her husband tried to say something, or clarify something she'd said, she shut him down and gave him a look. It was very weird and it was clear she was not happy having to talk to the police."

"Okay, what else?"

"Well, I spoke to the caterers, Joe Williamson and Suki Coops. They both work for *Great Food - Made Easy*. Joe works there full time and Suki is only part time and gets called in whenever there are events that require extra catering staff. Anyway, I called around to the unit the company operates from, on the Raymore industrial estate, and spoke to them there. It's quite an impressive set up, Sarg, and they let me sample some of their food. It was very tasty."

"Neil, please don't let your stomach distract you again. Every time I look over at you, you're eating. I don't know where you put it. Anyway, go on, what did they have to say?"

"Well, the only point they added, that was contrary to what the family had said, was that the back door was unlocked. So, although they had been given a key, in the end they did not need to use it. They confirmed the alarm was off, which we knew before."

"Anything else?" Ruth was starting to believe pulling teeth would be easier than getting information out of her PC.

"No, they just said the nanny turned up about five minutes after they got there and took over, going upstairs to alert the family, which corresponds to what we already know."

"I bet she did take over. She's an interfering old busy body." Ruth hated amateur sleuths trying to interfere and force their view of the world onto her, and this one in particular was being a real pain. "I'd keep Miss Marple well clear of proceedings, if I were you Neil. She's already got her fingers into too many pies, for my liking."

"Yes, Sarg," PC Dickson nodded as he consulted his notebook to see if there was anything he had missed. In his view, though, the real Miss Marple, at least in the television programmes he'd watched, had always been very helpful with the police, and usually pinpointed the answer. As such, he was unsure why his sergeant had taken such a dislike to this particular old lady. She was quite a sweet old dear.

"The only other thing I could find is the owner of that vehicle. You know, the one that was left overnight. I've tracked it down and it belongs to someone who lives locally, a Mr Carl Gilbert. I haven't been able to contact him, but I did speak to someone who knows him, a Mrs Dent. She said he'd arrived late to the party and was by himself, which wasn't surprising as he's unmarried. She couldn't remember when he left, but she did remember him having a couple of drinks, so he probably decided to walk home. The way she said it, though, was quite odd, so when I pushed her she said that Mr Gilbert and the deceased had apparently been arguing about something."

"Okay, then why not do a bit more digging on this Mr Gilbert next week and see if his movements stack up? See if you can find out what they were discussing too."

"Well, Sarg, that's the funny thing. I did try to check up on him and apparently he's not at home. A neighbour said she saw him getting into a taxi very early on Tuesday morning and she's no idea where he's gone or when he'll be returning. She thought it was odd, as he normally asks her to feed the cat if he's going to be away for any length of time. Apparently this time he went without warning."

"Well, he's definitely someone we need to speak to. At the same time, it might be worth visiting *Paulson's Builders*. Mr Paulson must have had a secretary, or someone close to him, who may be able to shed a bit of light for us while we're waiting for the forensics to come back. I can't believe it's taking them this long."

"No, Sarg, me neither." In Neil's experience it never took this long on television. Doctor Nikki Alexander on Silent Witness would have worked through the night to get her evidence together. It certainly would not have taken her nearly a week to get back to the police. No, real-life policing was a lot different to television, and it had a lot to answer for.

Chapter 21

By the following Monday, news of Frank's death was all over town and was the subject of most of the discussions on the high street, with speculation rife in terms of what had actually happened. There had still been no official line taken by the police, with reports simply confirming a body had been found at the property that they were looking into. The fact it was found by the caterers, lying in a pool of blood on the kitchen floor, were points that had been elaborated on by people in the know, people who had talked to people. Theories to what could possibly have happened were growing by the day, each getting more farcical as the news passed from person to person.

People at the pre-wedding party were thought to be one of the best sources of information. It was felt that if it was a break-in, or a burglary that had gone wrong when the intruder was disturbed, or worse still a murder, then the guests could have witnessed something untoward during the evening. Someone casing the joint, or at least acting suspiciously. After all, they were the last people to have seen Frank alive. And having been guests at the Old Manor House that not only put them in a very privileged position, but ensured they were competent to describe the scene, in among the mayhem of the wedding preparations.

Nanny Tilbury had been at home all day, tidying a few things away and sorting through her clothes. She still had her holiday to decide about and really should be thinking of contacting the travel agents to confirm or cancel her plans. She was sure the nice lady in the shop would understand if her plans had changed. Frank's death had left her reconsidering whether a holiday was still what she wanted, or whether it was the right time to be going away. Cruising down the Danube still sounded ideal, but was she required at the Old Manor House, did she need to stay around? It was creating her a real dilemma.

Although, if she was going, she should probably check what she needed to buy before it was too late, or what items in her wardrobe needed replacing. It was some years since she had last gone abroad, so fashions, if nothing else, would have changed, and as old as she was, she still wanted to look presentable. She was intending to travel in just over three weeks, her new passport now safely locked away, so the clock was ticking. She needed to decide whether to go or to stay, but either way she had so much to do and to think about.

After a light lunch she decided to go out for a short walk. It was a beautiful sunny day and the perfect temperature for a steady amble into town. She needed to collect a few items from the chemist and wanted to get some eggs for tea and perhaps some mushrooms; a simple omelette would suit her fine tonight. Since the incident with Frank, she could not seem to focus on anything and her appetite had all but deserted her. The sight of his blood kept replaying in her mind. That poor girl from the caterers, Suki she seemed to recall her name was; for her to have walked into the kitchen and witnessed that must have been very distressing, and what a waste of good food. Nanny still had images of Frank's blood-stained body, scantily clad in a silk kimono styled dressing gown, with a dragon on the back, surrounded by a selection of canapés and vol-au-vents. An odd sight by anyone's standards.

"Good afternoon, Nanny Tilbury. How can I help you today?" There were only a couple of people waiting ahead of her at the chemist when she arrived. She smiled as she was greeted by the friendly young assistant, Lucy. Nanny recognised her face but could not remember her name, and as she did not have her glasses on, she could not read her name badge too clearly.

The assistant obviously remembered her though. Nanny was quite a recognisable character around town, always prim and proper in her tidy clothes, with her grey curly hair neatly clipped back or worn under a hat. Now only five feet, three inches tall she was a couple of inches shorter than what she had been in her heyday, time and the signs of aging obviously taking their toll on her figure and her appearance. However, having lived and worked in Chidlington for over thirty years, there were few people she did not recognise, or who did not recognise her, by face if not by name.

"Oh, hello dear. I've only popped in to collect my prescription today and to get some more of those painkillers I like, those over there in the yellow box." She pointed to the locked cabinet behind the girl as she smiled. "I seem to have run out, my bones are not what they used to be, and my aches and pains are getting worse by the day. I'm finding it a real struggle getting off to sleep most nights. I really should have come in last week, but with all the confusion it must have slipped my mind. As you can imagine, it's been quite a difficult week at the Old Manor House since his lordship's death."

"Yes, I imagine it has. Now if you wouldn't mind taking a seat and waiting over there for a few moments, I'll go and check where your prescription is."

As much as Lucy would have liked to chat, and find out more about Mr Paulson's death, a queue had started to form behind Nanny Tilbury and she needed to attend to that first. Her brother, Ollie, worked for *Paulson's* as a plumber and had told her a little about what they were saying at the yard. Some were saying "he got what was coming to him," and even worse, some were saying they wished it was them that had done him in, adding they were glad to see the back of him.

Lucy knew it was not right to talk ill of the dead, yet no one appeared to have a good word to say about him. Having gone to school with Rosie, she felt for the family and imagined how difficult it would be for them to lose their father.

Yes, she was interested to learn more, and it would have been good to hear it first hand from someone who was close to the family, and who was closer than Nanny Tilbury? After all, she was almost family, having brought Rosie and her brothers and sister up after the sad loss of their mother all those years ago. Lucy could remember her waiting patiently outside the school gates each afternoon, ready to walk Richard and Rosie home, always with a smile on her face and a ready snack in her hands for them to munch on as she listened to them chatter about their day as they walked home. She would then take each by the hand and steer them safely across the road, before walking down the lane and back to the Old Manor House in time for tea.

In all the years of going to junior school, whilst other children walked home by themselves, Lucy could not recall a single day when Rosie's nanny had not been there to collect her. She often wished she'd had someone so caring waiting for her outside the school gates.

As Nanny moved to one side of the shop to wait for the assistant to return with her prescription, she noticed Mrs Naylor already sitting on one of the two chairs that had been put there for the purpose of waiting, either for a prescription or to see the pharmacist. Mrs Naylor was an old stalwart of the parish, someone who liked to get involved in everything, regardless of the topic. Whether it was the church jumble sales, charity cake bakes or social events, she was there. Even town meetings, where everyone was invited to get together to hear about developments or offer their views, she would invariably be involved, or more likely have taken charge of the arrangements in some shape or form. She liked to feel self-important and you could almost see her puffing her feathers up as she strutted down the high street, talking to anyone and everybody she felt she could bend to her way of thinking.

Nanny felt quite sorry for her really, as she sensed deep down it was loneliness that was driving her behaviour. Since her husband's death, and the fact her children had moved away, taking her grandchildren with them, Mrs Naylor had little other than her good works to fill her day. Over the years, she and Nanny had become nodding acquaintances rather than friends, people who would pass the time of day. She was not someone she would share her innermost secrets with though, or importantly the private matters that took place within the walls of the Old Manor House. However, as Nanny took the vacant chair next to her, that did not appear to stop Mrs Naylor from getting straight to the point.

"So, Nanny Tilbury, what's all this I hear about the Old Manor House, and the death of Mr Paulson? I believe you were the one who found his body, apparently naked on the kitchen floor, by all accounts."

"Yes, the sight of him was quite distressing, I must say."

"And apparently he'd been bludgeoned to death by a hammer, with blood splattered all over the place. It must have been quite frightening for you, especially if the murderer was still on the premises, as I understand he was."

"I'm not sure where you've heard that from, Mrs Naylor. I don't believe the police have established the cause of death yet, so I think perhaps that theory is a little curious."

"Well, if someone did smash their way in and murdered him, on the eve of his wedding no less, we'll know more when the truth comes out, I'm sure. I understand the police special forces were scouring the woods behind the house for hours, searching for the murder weapon, with sniffer dogs and everything."

"Oh, I'm not sure about that. It was certainly a busy day."

"Well, mark my words, I think it's one of the family that's either done it or arranged to have it done, some sort of contract killing. It could even have been that fiancée of his, she's not good news and was never right for his lordship. She's always been on the take, I understand, not that I listen to what the regulars at the Three Pheasants say, I hasten to add. No, I wouldn't put it past her at all and her behaviour has been quite odd recently, hasn't it? Although, my money is probably on one of his friends or associates being involved somehow. By all accounts, Frank had been mixing with a very odd bunch of people recently, some foreigners I believe. And if rumours are right, he owed money all over the place, leaving a few people questioning whether they'll ever see their money again, no doubt. I bet Lady Susan is turning in her grave. Mark my words, when the truth comes out, I don't imagine any of us will be surprised, will we?"

Nanny smiled, unsure what else she could add. Mrs Naylor appeared to have covered every angle imaginable.

"Prescription for Mrs Tilbury." The pharmacist poked his head around the screen and handed a small package to Lucy for passing onto their customer.

"Oh, please excuse me, Mrs Naylor. I think that was my name he called." And with that she rose from the chair and walked steadily over to collect her items, happy to escape the endless speculation. Nanny loved a good gossip as much as the next person, but sometimes it was just too farcical to listen to what people were coming up with.

As she left the chemist, Nanny Tilbury almost collided with Mrs Hargreaves, who had her head down as she was talking on the phone to her husband. She was arranging for him to collect her and give her a lift home, as was their habit. They lived in a small bungalow less than a mile from the town centre. The distance was neither far enough to justify a taxi, nor on a direct bus route, and with shopping to carry the twenty-minute walk would have been too much for Mrs Hargreaves to manage, even though Nanny believed with the weight her friend carried from her love of cream cakes, the exercise would have done her good. Mr Hargreaves did not mind acting as her chauffer.

"Oh, hang on dear, Nanny Tilbury's just here." Mr Hargreaves was left to wait whilst his wife spoke to her friend. "I'm just arranging for David to come and collect me, but as I've bumped into you, do you fancy a coffee and a cake? He can easily collect me later and perhaps drop you off too, if you'd like that?"

"Yes, I could do with a nice cup of coffee, thank you. And a lift home would be very kind. It's always easier walking into town than home I find, especially when you've got shopping to carry." Nanny was relieved to be finally out of the chemist and away from the gossips, although a drink with Mrs Hargreaves was unlikely to be without questions either, she presumed.

"Right, that's all sorted," Mrs Hargreaves announced putting her mobile safely away in her handbag. "David will come back in an hour and meet us outside the post office, he said. It's easier to pull in there as there are no yellow lines or parking restrictions to worry about, if we're a few minutes late that is. Shall we go to our usual place, I could do with a sticky bun after the afternoon I've had?" Mrs Hargreaves was quite a rotund woman, who over the years had eaten her fair share of sticky buns, if her waistline was anything to go by. Nevertheless, Nanny followed her down the high street until they reached their café. It was a quiet afternoon, so they soon found an empty table near the window, both letting out a gentle sigh as they relaxed into the comfy chairs.

Angela Hartley

After they had ordered their drinks and snacks off the pretty waitress, Mrs Hargreaves turned to Nanny Tilbury with an expectant look on her face. "So, tell me all about what happened last week. By all accounts it was very harrowing. David said there's been quite a lot of speculation within the council all week, as to whether his murder had anything to do with that failed planning application the other month. Do you remember, Coronation Terrace? It got rejected again and Frank was furious. It would appear, from what David overheard, that Frank offered one of the councillors some money to try to swing the vote in Frank's favour. Hang on, his name will come to me in a minute. Anyway, I understand it all got quite heated between them when the vote didn't go Frank's way, with Frank making all manner of accusations about how he'd taken his money. Money that Frank alleged was intended to be a donation to a local charity, not a bribe as people were suggesting. I even heard Frank had threatened him, saying there would be trouble if he didn't give him the money back. In fact, that Saturday night at the party, Marjorie says she thought she'd overheard Frank arguing with the man later on in the evening, after they'd all had too much to drink. She couldn't make out what they were saying, but both looked cross by all accounts, as if they were spoiling for a fight. Gilbert, that was his name, yes, Carl Gilbert. He's not married. And what's worse, he apparently went on his holidays, overseas I believe, the morning after the murder and no one knows where he's gone, or if he's coming back. His next-door neighbour is worried about his cat, as she normally feeds it and hasn't seen it around. The police will no doubt be wanting to talk to him, assuming he ever returns that is. Although I don't think we'll see him again, do you? It's all sounding suspiciously like he came back later that evening and murdered him, presumably after another argument, and then fled the scene, doesn't it?" For someone who was only hearing the information second hand, Mrs Hargreaves had a lot to say about it, and whilst she had been giving her monologue her coffee had not only arrived, but had almost gone cold.

"Interesting, although as far as I know the police have not said it was murder, well not yet at least. I haven't spoken to them myself, but I understand from Richard that the family is still awaiting the police's report on the cause of death. We probably should wait and see what they say, don't you think?"

Mrs Hargreaves took a large bite of her bun whilst she considered this piece of additional information. The raspberry jam oozed out of the sides as she squeezed it into her mouth; the sight of her chewing it was reminiscent of a cow chewing grass, Nanny Tilbury thought ungraciously to herself.

"Well, as far as Marjorie says, it's a cut and dried case, and the evidence is clear. She can't see any other reason, and neither can I. After all, Gregory was a good friend of Frank's, so he should know, shouldn't he?"

Realising it was a rhetorical question, Nanny Tilbury diplomatically tried to move the subject on. "Anyway, how was your bun, dear? Did it hit the spot?"

It seemed no matter where she turned, all people wanted to talk to her about was how Frank had died, yet as a trusted family retainer she did not feel it was within her remit to invent another version, simply to fuel the fire for the local gossips any further. No, by the sounds of it they already had enough hypotheses to work on.

Chapter 22

The following day was Tuesday, eight days after Frank's death, and not only was talk of his death still doing the rounds, it was now being supplemented by news that the will had been read. Prior to then, locals could only engage in speculation, but after Wilf's visit to the Three Pheasants the previous evening, for his usual game of dominoes with his cronies, details of the will had begun to emerge.

Wilf had let it slip that Mr Mears had called the family together the previous Friday afternoon to go through the contents of the will. Obviously he and his wife had not been invited to attend, although he did add that Nanny Tilbury had been included, which as an old retainer and someone who had lived with the family for over thirty years, was not found to be surprising. In fact, it would have been more surprising had she not been included, he went on to say, to which the others around the table nodded. They all knew how close she had been to the late Lady Susan and how devoted she was to the children, so it went without saying that his lordship would have left her some trinket or other, as a small token of his appreciation. Other than that, Wilf confirmed there were just the four children, their spouses and Frank's fiancée in attendance.

Wilf was not ordinarily one to gossip. He generally kept his own counsel and found little interest in talking about other people's business, and had his wife been with him he certainly would not have been allowed to get into any discussion about the will in the first place. Ana-Maria would have given him a look, or more likely a kick under the table to prevent him from talking. She certainly did not engage in gossip, or do anything to attract attention to herself or her business.

So, when a couple of the men had asked Wilf how things were going up at the Old Manor House, especially after the mysterious death, not to mention the fiasco of the cancelled wedding, he thought nothing of talking about it. After all, neither he nor his wife had anything to lose, or gain either way, so what did it matter if he said anything? The police had not asked him or anyone else to keep quiet, and as far as he knew there were no secrets in what Nanny Tilbury had told him and Ana-Maria about the contents of the will, so what was the harm?

"Well, I'll be damned," appeared to be the general consensus of opinion when Wilf let slip that Frank's fiancée had not been left anything in his will, or the fact she had signed a pre-nuptial agreement a matter of weeks before their wedding. "That old bugger must have been brighter than we all gave him credit for," one of them said, laughing as he took a slug of his beer. "We all thought when he took up with that flighty piece that he'd lost his marbles, chasing after a woman half his age. It was obvious she was just out to take him to the cleaners, from the moment you saw her swanning around town in that fancy new sports car and acting as if she'd suddenly got all airs and graces. She's only a girl from the back streets, a barmaid, so who she thought she was going to be once she married him, God only knows. It's good to see that she got her comeuppance, and didn't get away with it after all."

Wilf did not feel in a position to offer an opinion on Miranda. He already knew very well what his wife's thoughts about her were, and it was obvious, listening to his friends, that Ana-Maria was not alone in having reservations. Wilf, though, had not had many dealings with Miranda, having hardly spoken more than a dozen words to her since she had first moved in, so he was in no position to judge.

"And you say Jimmy Paulson's taking over the business, is he?" Wilf's friend's son-in-law, Malcolm, worked at the builder's yard in the warehouse, so he felt he had a vested interest in knowing what was happening to the business. "Our Malcolm says Jimmy and that brother-in-law of his, Simon, are at sixes and sevens, trying to manage things themselves, now that the boss isn't around. From what he says, a few of his mates have been wondering if they'd get paid at the end of the month, or where their jobs stand. According to Malcolm, quite a few of the suppliers have been in over the last week asking questions too, and no one is telling them anything. Malcolm says some of the deliveries haven't been coming in as usual either, which has been a concern as they can't build without the bricks and cement. If what you're saying is right, then it's good to think that the business won't fold; we need jobs in the town for skilled workers, even if we don't need all those poncy houses they've been building these last few years."

"Hear, hear," chorused the rest of them. Quite a few families' incomes were dependent on the continued success of the Paulson business.

"Well, I'm probably talking out of turn now, but by the sounds of it, getting the business back on its feet is not going to be all plain sailing. Nanny seemed to suggest the solicitor mentioned there were quite a few financial concerns and debts to deal with first. It didn't sound like all was well on that front, especially as it appeared to come as a bit of a surprise to everyone, as I understand it. I'm not sure exactly what she meant, or how bad it is, so I probably shouldn't be saying anything. I suggest you'd better keep that bit to yourselves, we don't want to spread any rumours, particularly if there are problems, do we?"

The Dishonourable Groom

As Wilf picked up his dominoes, to see what his hand looked like, it suddenly dawned on him that by telling someone not to say anything, because it's a secret or is sensitive, was almost the same as saying, "why not just shout it from the rooftops and let everyone know." Ana-Maria would kill him herself if she got wind of what he had been talking about, and would never trust him, let alone let him out of the house unchaperoned, again.

As the game of dominoes continued, the man at the table behind Wilf finished off his pint and returned his glass to the bar before leaving the pub. Having picked up most of the conversation at the neighbouring table he felt he had heard enough for one evening. It was just left for him now to go home and consider what he needed to do about what he had overheard.

Ana-Maria enjoyed her time alone whenever Wilf went to the pub. It was perhaps only a couple of times a week, and maybe then only for a few hours at a time, but it gave her ample opportunity to talk to her lover on the phone, or by video link from the privacy of her bedroom. She lived for the day when they could finally be together, knowing that a few fleeting hours on an afternoon during her one day off a week was never going to be enough for either of them. Since she had met him six months ago, all she could think about was finding a chance to escape with him, and if his response to her was anything to go by, it would not be long before they could be together.

Wilf may have provided her with a passport to England, but she was relying on her lover to provide her with the type of life she wanted to live now that she was here. Mr Paulson's death may well have provided the opportunity she needed, even if the circumstances were not ideal. She just had to bide her time and wait a little longer, and above all be patient until the right opening presented itself.

Chapter 23

It was Tuesday morning, around eleven o'clock, when the phone rang in the hallway at the Old Manor House, the loud shrill echoing throughout the building. At the time, Ana-Maria was dusting in the sitting room and rearranging some of the furniture that had been put into storage due to the wedding, and had now been returned. A team of removal men had carried a selection of sofas, tables and chairs back into the house, carefully removing the protective covers from them as they repositioned them around the property. Ana-Maria had overseen the operation and was now left to make the manor feel homely again. She seriously wondered why she was bothering. Other than Richard and Rosie, who largely spent their time upstairs in their bedrooms or in the kitchen when they were at home, these days there was only Miranda in the house. And from what Ana-Maria saw she too appeared to be hibernating in her room, carefully avoiding having to interact with anyone else. What possible reason was there for her to keep the place cosy for her? Because if what Nanny Tilbury had said was true, she would not be around too much longer to appreciate it anyway. It was ironic to think that only four weeks ago, it was Ana-Maria who thought her cards were marked in terms of living at the manor. How times had changed.

"Hello, Old Manor House, how can I help you?" Ana-Maria answered the phone politely, adopting a tone that did its best to disguise her Romanian accent.

"I need to speak to Mr Paulson, Mr Richard Paulson." The voice was not one she recognised, but the tone of it was undeniably off and it was obvious this was not a friendly call, or anyone who knew the family.

"May I ask who's calling and I'll go and check if he's available."

"Just tell him it's one of his father's associates and I need to speak to him, urgently."

After telling the man to hang on for a moment whilst she went to check, Ana-Maria placed the handset quietly onto the console and walked upstairs towards Richard's room. She had heard him earlier in the day and believed him to still be at home, but whether he wanted to take the call was another question. The man sounded rude and unfriendly, and above all he sounded like trouble. There was something about his accent that Ana-Maria recognised and as she cast her mind back, she recalled the occasion a few months earlier when Frank had invited guests for dinner; guests at the time she believed to be Eastern European. Men who had given her the evil eye; a strange mix of lust and disgust that not only made her feel uncomfortable, but also as if she was in danger. This man sounded as if he could have been one of them, which instantly put Ana-Maria on her guard.

"Hello, Richard Paulson here. Can I help you?"

"Yes. You don't know who I am, but I know who you are and where you live, so listen. Your father owed me money, ten thousand pounds, and I want it back. If you don't pay there will be trouble, do you hear me?"

"Well, I hear you but as I neither know your name, nor what this is in connection with, then how am I supposed to deal with it?"

"I will contact you with details of where and when to drop the cash off, and you will do that, or else there will be trouble. You don't want any more dead bodies, do you?"

"Dead bodies, are you suggesting you know something about my father's death? Perhaps it would be easier if you contacted the police directly. I understand they are dealing with the matter." Richard was unprepared to be fazed by people phoning the house and asking for money. He knew how peoples' psyches worked, and how tempting it was to try to bribe or intimidate people when they were grieving, especially if there was any sniff of money around. Richard was not prepared to be threatened by any man, even if he did have ten thousand pounds to put in an unmarked envelope and leave in a duffle bag somewhere, no questions asked. No, he had seen enough crime thrillers to know how that played out. And anyway, after the contents of his father's will had become clear, it was highly unlikely there would be one thousand pounds swashing around, let alone ten, even if he had wanted to follow the man's instructions.

He was interested to hear that his father apparently owed that amount of money to someone, though, and wondered how long it would take for others to join the bandwagon of issuing similar threats, or sending begging letters believing the beneficiaries were now rolling in money. "How far from the truth can that be?" Richard questioned to himself, almost laughing at the thought.

"No police. We do this on my terms, I will be in touch, in a day or so, so have the money ready." At which point the line went dead.

Ana-Maria had been standing in the wings, attempting to look busy dusting some of the ornaments, whilst trying to overhear the conversation. The caller's voice had spooked her and she was desperate to hear what it had been about. She had only been able to catch half of whatever had been said, however it was clear that it related to Frank's death, which worried her.

"Is everything alright, Mr Richard?"

146

"Oh, Mrs Cuthbert, I didn't see you there. Yes, it was just some crank caller demanding ten thousand pounds, or threatening me with more dead bodies. I told him to speak to the police, which he didn't appear amused by. I think I'll give them a ring, though, just in case, as I'm sure he won't be the last. Anyway, have you any more of that cake you made yesterday? I'm starving." Putting the phone down, he followed her into the kitchen in search of food.

Chapter 24

When DS Jacobs walked into the police station at eight o'clock on Tuesday morning, after a sleepless night, Neil was already standing by her desk, waiting like an eager puppy for her to take her coat off and sit down. Ruth was tired and could do with a strong cup of coffee before having to deal with him. She'd now had two consecutive nights without proper sleep, with a toddler who had refused to settle, regardless of how much Calpol Ruth managed to get down her. She imagined it was nothing more serious than teething, as her daughter was at that age when her back teeth were supposed to be settling, but that did not make it any easier on Ruth, or her husband who needed his sleep too.

She had worked a full shift the previous day, before collecting a fractious child from the childminder and returning home to an empty house. Her husband, Tom, was a teacher at the local high school and had phoned earlier that day saying he had to work late. He mentioned something to do with end of year reports, or parents' evening, but in truth she had not really been listening. It ended up, though, with her having to soothe her daughter alone, before he eventually returned home after ten o'clock, to find them both crashed out on the sofa.

He had called in at the Three Pheasants for a swift pint with his colleagues before closing time. She did not mind him going out for a drink. What she minded was the fact she could not join him and that she had not even had the time to make herself a meal, or even pop out to the garden for a quick cigarette whilst he had been out. She had simply sat on the sofa, nursing her poorly infant as she struggled to settle.

As Ruth sat there watching Tom carefully carrying their daughter upstairs to bed for fear of waking her, she smiled to herself. He was such a kind and gentle man, someone she loved so much, but she could not recall the last time she had told him that. In fact, she could not recall the last time they had shared a date night, or a simple meal out together, without the subject of nappies or feeding times controlling the agenda. Being a full-time police officer, working shifts and weekends was not conducive to motherhood, Ruth concluded, especially having a husband with his own demanding career to consider. Parenting had taken over their lives, forcing them into roles that did not come naturally, especially not to Ruth at least. Roll on the summer holidays, and six weeks of childfree stress, when she could relax a little and let Tom pick up the slack.

"What's happened Dickson, can't it wait until I've at least taken my coat off and had a cup of coffee and a cigarette?"

"No, Sarg. Sorry, Sarg. It's just that the autopsy report came in late last night and I wanted to let you know what it says. I'd chased it yesterday morning, like you'd asked me to, and they sent it through just before I clocked off." He was as excited as a child on Christmas morning.

"So, what does it say? Do we have a murder on our hands, or is it just something innocuous, like you've suspected all along?" Ruth struggled hard to keep the sarcasm out of her voice. She had a million other things she needed to be getting on with today and her head was already hurting.

"Well, it's not conclusive, so I thought I'd ask you to read it and let me know what you think." He handed the document over to his sergeant. In truth he did not really know what he was looking for as it was the first time he had ever received an autopsy report. He had spent the previous evening reading it several times to get a feel for it and to try to understand some of the jargon and medical language that it had used, language he had not really come across before.

Ruth read the document as Neil waited. "Well, it's not conclusive, as you rightly said. What it tells us, over and above what we already know, is that as well as a high level of alcohol in his blood system, there were traces of drugs found. Nothing illegal and consistent with sleeping tablets possibly having been taken. The level was not dangerously high, although it was much higher than it should have been. It could suggest he'd taken something before he went to sleep. Did Miss Swann mention anything?"

Neil took out his notebook and referred back to their earlier discussion with her. "No, Sarg. She didn't mention anything about him taking any sleeping tablets. She said that she'd gone straight to sleep, as she was feeling woozy with the drink, and hadn't noticed when he went downstairs. Do you think he went down to get some tablets and that's when he fell?"

"Well, something doesn't add up. For a fact, we know she was lying about being woozy, as she put it, as she's pregnant so should not have been drinking in the first place. So, if she lied about that, then perhaps she could have lied about the sleeping tablets, too? Although why she would do that is a mystery." Ruth continued reading. "It also says there was a bump on the back of the head, with a slight cut and signs of dried blood, consistent with either a fall or possibly a previous knock. Although, as there was evidence of the deceased's blood on the corner of the worktop, the assumption is that the bump was done prior to death. It goes on to say it may have contributed to the death, if not been the primary cause, and it could have been caused by some form of blunt object, but again isn't conclusive. Well, that's new, isn't it? It also goes on to report there was no sign of any heart failure, or other type of contributing medical incident, whilst noting that the deceased was not in the best state of health. And it says he was overweight, which I suppose we all saw given the way that kimono barely fitted him."

"Yes, Sarg. I noticed that." He was feeling quite pleased with himself that he had picked up most of the main points of the report, if not all.

"So, what are you thinking, Neil? Do we have suspicious circumstances in your opinion; circumstances that would warrant us looking into this as a murder, or at least a manslaughter charge, or is it a case of accidental death? Do you think his wife followed him downstairs and hit him with the frying pan, after an argument because his snoring got out of hand and was keeping her awake? Because if that was the case, I could probably let her off on that one, the way I'm feeling at the moment."

Neil failed to react, the sarcasm going straight over his head. "No, Sarg. If he was sleeping so heavily, why would he need to go downstairs for sleeping tablets, or anything else for that matter? It doesn't add up to me."

"You're right, it doesn't add up to me either, Neil. I think you need to go back through this again, and see if there are more questions that you want to ask the family. They may know whether he was someone who took sleeping tablets regularly. Miss Swann might also be able to shed some light on what the bump on the head was related to, because if you don't buy my theory about the frying pan, then we'll have to find another explanation, won't we? Good work, though, keep it up, Neil. We'll make a detective of you one day."

"Thanks, Sarg."

"Oh, and by the way, Neil, I suggest we might want to contact the family and let them know we're prepared to release the body. They'll want to arrange a funeral, and as much as the morgue is enjoying providing free board and lodgings and a chilled out resting place for the deceased, I guess they'll be looking to move the body on, now that they've done what they need to."

"Yes, Sarg. I'll ring Mr Paulson's son straight away and let them know."

"Oh, and Neil, can you get in touch with the family's solicitors and see if there is any information they can provide us on the contents of Mr Paulson's will. I'm especially interested to know who's set to benefit from it. I understand, from rumours going around the Three Pheasants last night, that it was read to the family last Friday, so it appears to be out in the open. Can you see what you can find out for me, please?"

Tom had mentioned when he'd arrived home that he had overheard people talking about it in the pub, and given that it related to a case he knew she was working, his ears had pricked up. Although, as he was probably hearing it third or fourth hand, that was the best he could offer. From the little he had picked up, though, it did not sound like everyone was happy, he had reported. Ruth had thought it was better than nothing.

As Neil walked back to his desk, his chest all puffed out, he was feeling very pleased with himself. "Good work," she had said. Neil tried to recall whether Morse had ever said that to Lewis, as he contemplated what he would do if he did eventually become a detective. His grandma would be ever so proud of him.

152

Chapter 25

Neil chewed the end of his pencil as he started to jot down the long list of jobs Detective Sergeant Jacobs had asked him to attend to. He needed to call the solicitor and ask for a copy of the will, or at least understand what was in it. That should not be too difficult. He then needed to call the family and let them know they were releasing the body, so that they could start to arrange the funeral. He had James Paulson down as the deceased's next of kin, so a call to him would sort that, again nothing too difficult. He had to arrange to question the fiancée about bumps on the head and what she knew about Frank taking sleeping tablets that night, which would be better managed as a visit, rather than a phone call, so he needed to arrange that too. What he really wanted to concentrate on, though, was pulling together a list of suspects and identify their motives, because with an inconclusive verdict on the autopsy report there was still the chance that the police had a murder on its hands. He quite liked the idea of that. Working on an aggravated murder, with a possible burglary thrown in for good measure, sounded a lot more exciting than being involved in clearing up the paperwork for a simple accidental death.

The first call to Mr Paulson was the easiest to deal with, so he dialled the mobile number he had on file.

"Thank you, Officer." James had appeared content when he told him that he was free to make the funeral arrangements, "I will deal with that now. Thanks again for all your help." The way he said it making it clear James presumed that was the end of the matter, before, almost as an afterthought, he continued, "does that mean you've established the cause of death then?" The way James asked his question left Neil to wonder why he sounded so blasé about it. Surely, he should have been more concerned to learn what had killed his father, he mused.

"The report is inconclusive on the cause, I'm afraid. It did indicate however that your father may have sustained a blow to his head, but this was not understood to be the primary cause of death. It also showed he had drugs in his blood system, consistent with sleeping tablets having been taken, as well as a gash to his head that bled out, which presumably happened when he fell, or collapsed. Although, there was no evidence of any medical condition. Both a heart attack and a stroke have been ruled out as having caused him to collapse in the first place." Neil tried to summarise the findings of the report as compassionately as he could, pleased that he had remembered all the key points. "We do, though, have one or two more questions to follow up on, so for the time being at least we will be leaving the case open."

"Right, okay. Well, thanks for letting me know. I have another call coming through, so if that's all, will you please excuse me?" And with that, the call was ended and the first job ticked off. James' attitude however had done nothing to ease Neil's concerns.

Mr Mears at Laycock, Mears and Campbell was his next call. Neil had never spoken to the solicitor before, so had no idea of the type of man he was dealing with. He'd had limited dealings with solicitors in general, either professionally or personally, although he was aware how difficult and how pedantic they could be if not handled correctly, so he opted for a formal, confident approach.

"Mr Mears, good morning. My name is PC Neil Dickson, and I'm investigating the death of Mr Frank Paulson. We are treating the death as suspicious for the time being, so any help you can offer would be appreciated." As the solicitor remained quiet on the other end of the line Neil continued, warily, some of his earlier confidence lost. "I was wondering if you could spare me a few moments to talk through the key provisions of the deceased's will, particularly who the main beneficiaries are. Also, whether the document contained anything untoward that may be of interest to our investigations."

After a few moments considering the request, Mr Mears replied. "Well, it is highly irregular that I would do that, Officer, without a formal request, that is. Do you mind me asking if there is anything particular you need to know, or that may be worrying you that I possibly could help you with?"

Mr Mears had no obligation to share with the police the contents of a will, although he did have concerns of his own that he would be prepared to discuss, particularly if it helped their investigations. He was not at all surprised the police were treating it as suspicious. He still believed Frank's behaviour had been concerning prior to his death; the need for a pre-nuptial agreement, his detailed list of requirements and the timing of the latest amendments all adding to his belief that Frank had expected his death was imminent, almost planned for it. Mr Mears chose his words carefully as he outlined the little he felt able to share about his client's affairs, at the same time reminding the police that his words were to be treated in confidence.

"So, would I be right in assuming you suspected Mr Paulson was getting his affairs in order, because he feared something was about to happen to him? And, that he may also have had questions around the paternity of Miss Swann's child? Were you aware if there was anyone else he particularly had issues with?"

"Correct, although I would not like to be drawn on names, or be quoted. As I said earlier, these discussions are in confidence. What I do believe is common knowledge, though, is that my client was not a particularly well-liked man, with some of his more recent antics not winning him many friends around these parts. Especially not with some of the local councillors, or some of his workforce. I believe there is already a police report pending on one such complaint."

After Neil had hung up, he sat back in his chair and reflected on how much he had learnt from what should have been two innocuous phone calls. His list of suspects and motives was growing by the day, as was the number of questions for which he required answers.

There were quite a few new leads, especially related to Mr Paulson's dealings with the local council, an angle that had not previously been considered, and possibly people within his business that held a grudge. He would need to look into the database to see what the complaint was to which Mr Mears had alluded. There was also potentially a jealous lover, if the question around the paternity of Miss Swann's unborn baby was genuine, someone he imagined who would have good reason to not want the wedding to go ahead. Any of those leads could easily generate a motive.

In terms of other suspects, Mr Paulson's four adult children could not be ruled out. They inherited the bulk of his estate, which was not surprising, and if they had suspected their father was running their inheritance into the ground, did that give them motive? James, the eldest son, had taken over the business. Did he, or his partner Mr Goodman, need Mr Paulson out of the way for some reason? Were they planning something of which he may not have approved?

It was also clear that none of them liked the idea of their father marrying again, or liked Miss Swann, and from what Mr Mears had said, they had all been blindsided by the existence of the pre-nuptial agreement. They could easily have feared being written out of his will in her favour, which would also have given them a clear motive. Could they have orchestrated it together, perhaps, or arranged for someone to do it for them? Neil had his doubts, as they all appeared to be nice people, but too often it was the nice people who could hide it the best. Clearly something was not right and the way he had witnessed them behaving on the day of the death was odd. They certainly had not acted as he would have imagined children grieving the loss of a beloved parent to act. No, something did not appear right there.

And what about the bride-to-be, Miss Swann? Deliberately cutting her out of his will and requiring her to sign a pre-nuptial agreement was odd, especially for a couple who were so much in love the month before their wedding. Weren't those types of agreements more common with the rich and famous, the Hollywood set, not people living in sleepy backwaters like Chidlington? Although it did support the theory about the child not being Mr Paulson's.

And then there was his child from his previous marriage, a young son he seemed to recall had been mentioned when he'd spoken to Mrs Goodman, Frank's eldest daughter. What was that all about? Why would he cut him out of his will, and did that give the ex-wife a motive? Neil could not see one, but stranger things did happen.

This case was clearly giving his grey cells a bit of a work out, something Poirot would no doubt be very pleased with, Neil thought to himself as he grabbed his tuna and mayonnaise sandwich from his Tupperware box and munched his way through its contents. It might still only be eleven thirty in the morning, but he had earned an early lunch. And with the list of questions he still needed to focus on, he suspected it was not going to be a quiet afternoon either.

"Neil, sorry to interrupt you. Have you got a minute?" WPC Jane Wilson approached his desk as he was just finishing off his lunch. His grandma always added a chocolate biscuit in for his desert, along with an apple or a banana. Whilst he did not like to admit to anyone he still lived at home with his grandma, he did enjoy some of the benefits it provided.

"I have a message here from Mr Paulson, Richard Paulson from the Old Manor House. He phoned the station earlier to alert us to the fact that he'd received a crank call from someone demanding ten thousand pounds, or threatening more dead bodies. Mr Paulson was not overly worried, although he suggested you might be interested. He said the voice was male and had an Eastern European accent, but other than that he didn't recognise it."

"Right, thanks for letting me know, Jane. I'm heading up there later this afternoon, so I'll talk to him about it then." Had that just introduced another strand to an already confused picture, another motive or suspect and something to which, until now, the police had been completely blindsided?

Yes, there was certainly something suspicious about Frank Paulson's death, but Neil was at a complete loss to figure out what that might be. He certainly looked as if he had a busy few days ahead of him trying to figure it all out.

Chapter 26

"Good morning, *SNIPS*, how may I help you?" Katie answered the phone a little out of breath after having run from the other end of the salon. She did not normally answer the phone, however this morning one of her juniors had phoned in sick, so she was having to cover her workload too. It meant she was much busier than usual, backward and forwards to the phone, the desk, the dryers and the styling chair. It was Wednesday, which was normally one of the quieter days at the salon, although today the phone had never stopped ringing.

"Yes, that's fine, Mrs Naylor, when would you like to come in?" Mrs Naylor was one of her elderly regulars, someone Katie often joked had probably been the founder of the Blue Rinse Brigade. Despite her age, she was still active around town, busying herself with a number of charitable causes and an opinion to offer on almost any subject. "No, I'm sorry I can't do Friday as the salon is closed all day. It's Mr Paulson's funeral, so out of respect for him I've decided not to open. How about Saturday, say half past eleven?"

"Oh yes, dear. I'd heard about that. I imagine his death's put the cat among the pigeons, up at the Old Manor House, hasn't it? Especially as everything was set up for that wedding as well. Not the best of times to pop your clogs, I'd say. What a waste, I can't imagine that would have been cheap. A very queer carry on, if you ask me. In fact, I was only talking to that nanny of yours in the chemist last week about it all."

"Shall I book you in for Saturday, then?" Katie was unprepared to be pulled into speculation about how the family was reacting or coping after Frank's death, by Mrs Naylor or anyone else who tried their luck with her.

Katie had run the hairdressers on the high street for several years now, having taken over the lease on the shop a couple of years before her marriage to James. The shop premises were within a commercial property his father's business owned, with her meeting James when he came round one day, toolbox in hand, to sort out a problem with the rendering at the rear of the property.

It was an old building, within a parade of shops that had stood for over a hundred years, and like most of the buildings within the block was at the stage where it required regular repair and maintenance. The lease, though, was affordable, its value reflecting the state of the property, and as it came with a small apartment on the first floor, one that she could move straight into, there was the added bonus of saving rent on her current lodgings. The apartment was basic, the bedroom window leaked and there was damp starting to creep in upstairs, she assumed, resulting from the cracks in the rendering. Problems she promptly expressed to the landlord. Katie was no pushover and wanted them sorting quickly. The winter was setting in and she had no intention of either living in a draft, or having mould growing in her bedroom.

James was sent to sort them out, his calm manner eventually winning her around and a date to go out for a drink secured before he left. Katie, new to the area, had accepted. After all, she did not want to get on the wrong side of her landlord, did she? There was also a twinkle in James' eye when he spoke to her that she found quite attractive, and even in his workmen's overalls, she could see there was a decent body beneath the layers. She was single, so what did she have to lose?

They had been happily married for eight years, with Maia so far their only daughter and Katie had long since moved out of the apartment and into a proper family house in the town. It was a new build and had all the modern conveniences she needed to make her life easy. Housework was not something Katie enjoyed, so anything that saved her time was good in her books.

Nowadays, she rented the apartment above the shop to Hattie, the young stylist who worked for her. Hattie was someone she could trust, and someone who was on the premises should anything ever go wrong. Her rent also helped with paying the lease, because contrary to what James had intimated, Frank had not reduced the charges for his daughter-in-law following their wedding. If anything, over the years it had gone up more than market rate – a point that did not sit well with Katie at all.

James was desperate for more children, a brother or sister for Maia. Coming from a large family he saw the value of siblings and wanted to fill the bedrooms of their home with babies. However, Katie was not so sure. She already had her work cut out dealing with one child, alongside running her busy business and was in no hurry to increase the size of her family. No, she had plenty of time yet. She was healthy and still only in her early thirties, so in her view there was no need to panic. For now, she wanted to concentrate on building up the business, maybe expand or open up another shop. Even look at offering complementary services or beauty treatments to supplement the salon's income.

She had been talking to Frank shortly before his death, enquiring if he was aware of other suitable commercial premises available in the area, but he had not been particularly supportive. In fact, he had been downright rude, arguing she had enough on her plate and should concentrate on that, rather than adding to her workload. Treating her almost like the little woman whose job it was to stay at home and tend the house, not an independent or professional business woman.

The Dishonourable Groom

"What business is it of his?" she had asked James that evening when she got home, seething after her encounter with her father-in-law. "Your dad is unbelievable. I don't know how he survived so long in business, especially with that kind of attitude." At least she no longer had him to worry about.

No, the salon suited her. She enjoyed the opportunity to chat with her customers, always happy to listen to a bit of gossip, whilst at the same time remaining discreet in terms of what she was told. Being a hairdresser was akin to being a priest hearing confession, she often thought. Anything personal that was said in the salon, stayed in the salon, unless of course it was general gossip that was doing the rounds. Then it was fair game.

Her father-in-law's death fell into the latter category. Everyone was talking about it and a surprising number of hair appointments had been generated as a result, so overall it was turning out quite good for business. Ladies just needing a trim, or a blow dry; anything that would give them the opportunity of either sharing or spreading what they had already heard. Or even better, the opportunity to pick up a tasty new morsel. And who better to get the facts from than one of the family, from the horse's mouth, so to speak.

Katie was not stupid, nor blind to what people were doing. She would often stifle a snigger when a customer came in, disappointed to find their appointment had been made with another stylist and not with her. It was a small town and gossip was one of the main currencies in which people traded. Although on this particular subject she had to be careful what she said and importantly how she acted, not only with her customers but around the family as well. She was not sad to see the back of Frank, and whoever had murdered him, as she was convinced was the case, regardless of what the police might be thinking, in her view he'd done the family a huge favour.

In fact, the more she thought about it, and thought about what people were actually saying, the more she realised few people were genuinely sad. Granted, people were shocked, especially at the timing and given the impending wedding, but few expressed real sorrow. The standard platitudes were offered, phrases that people churned out without necessarily thinking about them; words they felt were appropriate for the occasion. None of them felt sincere, though, and although the odd tear had been shed amongst the family and the staff at the Old Manor House, even that had felt a little contrived.

Katie was not a poker player, but if ever she needed to employ her poker face, then now was the time. With the funeral just a couple of days away, perhaps she needed to pick out a hat with a veil that shaded her face. That at least might give her a modicum of protection from prying eyes.

As Katie was locking up the salon for the evening, tired and ready for home, passengers on the 18:12 cross-country service from Oxford to Chidlington were just alighting at platform 1B. Many of them had connected with the earlier train that had come up from Paddington Station that afternoon. It had been a warm day in the capital and most were just relieved to be getting home in time for dinner, after work, or perhaps after spending the day sightseeing or meeting up with friends for a spot of lunch. Even some retail therapy, given the number of bags some were carrying as they made their way off the platform.

As most rushed off, eager to get to their destinations, one passenger held back as long as possible, exiting the standard class carriage at the rear of the train more sedately. The passenger glanced around to ensure their actions were not being noticed, or drawing any attention, before walking purposefully along the platform towards the stairs and the station's exit. It was only a short walk home and the sun was still shining, so there was no need to hurry.

The passenger maintained a deadpan face, but inside could not hide a broad smile. There had been a rather satisfactory outcome to the day. The dealer had been more than happy to provide a valuation, advising he would be able to get a much higher price than had been expected. He had advised that even after his mark-up, and a small amount of touch up that might be required once he got the pieces into his workshop, he was confident the pieces could be resold without any issue. Buyers were always looking for unusual items, regardless of whether they had the full provenance behind them, or not. The markings on the items themselves left no one in any question of their authenticity.

All in all, it had been a very fruitful day and the money, should it ever be required, would certainly come in handy. It was nice to realise how much quality items appreciated in value over the years, especially when so much care had been given to their wellbeing.

Chapter 27

Thursday morning, the day before the funeral, Miranda had taken the 08:27 train into Oxford. She needed a break and to get out of the house. The atmosphere was almost toxic with Richard and Rosie barely giving her the time of day. Judy had also been at the Old Manor House several times over recent days, spending hours at a time holed up in her father's study, the door firmly shut behind her. She was sorting through papers and getting the household bills into some degree of order, as well as preparing Frank's funeral service.

Miranda would have offered to help, had Judy made any attempt to ask for her support, but there had barely been a kind word or a simple greeting exchanged between them whenever they passed in the hallway, or on the way to the kitchen. Miranda knew none of Frank's children had ever liked her, and if she was honest the feeling was mutual, however at a time when they were all supposed to be grieving, she might have expected some polite conversation to have been made.

Miranda had messaged Leo, instructing him when and where to meet her in the city. They had messaged frequently and talked often on the phone, although she had not seen him in person since Frank's death, nor had she gone to any of her usual classes at the leisure centre. She almost missed her Pilates sessions as much as she missed their afternoons in bed; her body ached for the exercise, and the more she got into her pregnancy, with the extra weight she was putting on, the more tired and sluggish she was feeling. The concept of blooming through pregnancy had obviously given her a miss.

The Dishonourable Groom

At one stage, she had considered driving herself into Oxford, or even asking Leo to drive her, but the train was easier. Her little Mazda had become uncomfortable and being seen in his car, driving around town the day before her fiancé's funeral, even for her felt a little too insensitive. So, she arranged to meet him there and then they could find a small, inconspicuous café for lunch and have a serious talk. There were things that needed to be said face-to-face, things for which she needed to see the whites of his eyes when he replied. Miranda was still not convinced he was blameless in Frank's death, regardless of how many times he had professed otherwise.

Her first call, once she had alighted the train at Oxford railway station and walked the short distance into the city centre, was to the jewellers for her ten o'clock appointment. She had phoned ahead to ensure there would be someone there who could carry out a valuation for her engagement ring whilst she waited. They had pointed out it was usual to leave the item and collect it at a later date, as items on occasion needed to be sent away. Miranda had insisted it could not be left, after all, she could not risk turning up to the funeral without wearing it. What would people think? Surely, the sight of the grieving fiancée turning up without wearing her engagement ring would have tongues wagging. No, she needed it with her, eventually reaching a compromise that she could drop it off at ten o'clock and then collect it later that same day. On the basis it was the only item of value she now possessed, she not only needed to know its worth, but equally she did not want to be parted from it, at least not until she knew how much she could get for it.

The ring, a diamond cluster with an emerald set at its centre, had been bought by Frank without any input from her; his proposal remarkably romantic given the circumstances. It had surprised her, not the fact that he was proposing, but the manner in which he did it.

Once she had become pregnant, getting married and getting a ring on her finger was Miranda's priority and Frank was well aware of that. However, the setting had taken her by surprise; soft candle light, a romantic meal at a quiet country restaurant, with discreet but attentive staff hovering in the background. At the time, she had not thought he was anxious to get married. After all, it was her calling the tune; Miranda being very clear that as she was to be the mother of his child, this was what she expected.

Looking now at the ring, she had grown to like it and would miss it once it had gone. In truth it was not a design she would have chosen for herself, although having researched the meaning of emeralds, as well as their value, after he had presented it to her, it had made her appreciate it all the more. It was a very thoughtful and romantic gesture.

"Good morning, Madam. How may I help you?"

"Yes, good morning. I have an appointment for my engagement ring to be valued, for insurance purposes, you understand." It was none of the assistant's business what she needed the valuation for, but Miranda felt better with her little white lie. "I've arranged to collect it later today, so can you please let me know when it might be ready? I have a train to catch, no later than five o'clock this afternoon, so I will need to have collected it before then."

"Certainly, Madam. We close at five o'clock anyway, so provided there are no issues it should be available long before then. Why don't you give me your mobile number and I will phone you as soon as it is ready? It should only take a couple of hours, so probably plan around two o'clock this afternoon."

"Thank you." Miranda gave the assistant her number and took the receipt for her ring, placing it safely in her handbag. As she left the shop and made her way into the main shopping area she had a smile on her face. The idea of being so much richer when she returned in a couple of hours was somehow making her feel very happy, and happiness was a commodity she did not feel particularly blessed with at the moment.

When she arrived at the café forty minutes later, allowing herself a brief mooch around the shops en route, Leo was already waiting for her, looking relaxed in one of the comfy chairs in the window, tapping away at his phone. He was dressed in cream chinos and a white polo shirt, his outfit appearing casual whilst at the same time giving the impression of having made an effort. He smiled as he saw her approach the table and put his phone down.

"Hi, did you drop it off okay? Is everything sorted?"

"It will be when I get it back in a couple of hours. In the meantime, let's order some food, and move to a different table. If anyone walks in, or walks past, they'll see us. I'd prefer to sit somewhere we don't run the risk of being spotted."

"No one's going to see us here, so what are you worried about? We'll be fine. Sit down and I'll go and order us some drinks and a sandwich. Do you want the usual?"

He returned ten minutes later, carrying a tray with two cappuccinos and two paninis, both with healthy fillings. "Take your pick, I'm happy with either, although I asked for them both to be halved in case you fancied sharing." He smiled over and took her hand, unable to hide the desire he felt.

"Be careful, someone might see us." Miranda was becoming paranoid about being spotted with Leo. Why she was worried, though, was difficult to explain. After all, what else did she have to lose, other than her reputation? She had already lost the status she thought she would enjoy as the lady of the manor, along with the man who would have provided for her and the baby. On top of that she would soon be homeless, penniless and without a car.

James had told her only the previous day that he had cancelled the lease and the garage would be collecting it at the beginning of the following week, and all the signs were that the house would be put on the market shortly. Miranda had noticed that a couple of local Estate Agents had already been around to take photos and to carry out a valuation, so she imagined it would be being advertised shortly.

The ring, or more correctly the money she raised once she managed to sell it, was the only thing she had to look forward to.

"So, have you given any more thought to what I suggested the other night, you know moving in with me? I know my apartment's not ideal, but it's okay until we can find somewhere bigger, isn't it? And when I sell it, together with the money from your ring, we should have enough to put down a deposit on something better."

Leo had it all worked out, in his mind at least. He just needed Miranda to agree to go along with his proposal. He had warmed to the idea of the baby and although the timing was not what he had planned, now that Frank was out of the picture, what did it matter?

"I'm not sure. I spoke to Mum and Dad yesterday and they've been surprisingly supportive." The idea of going home with her tail between her legs was something Miranda had no desire to do, however in her mind her options were limited. "They've said my room's still there if I need it, and there's room for a cot, too. Also, Mum's offered to be on hand to help with the baby if I need to go back to work, which I'm sure I'll have to do at some stage. It's an option, at least until things die down, don't you think? If I were to move in with you, everyone will quickly work out it's your baby; there's no secrets in Chidlington. And if I did try to contest the will, or that bloody pre-nup he made me sign, that's not going to help my chances, is it?"

"What about if we leave the area, and find somewhere else to live, an area where no one knows us? That could work and it might even be cheaper. Property prices around here are over inflated. If we moved somewhere where rentals are lower, or house prices more affordable, then we could make it work, couldn't we? I could easily get a job, and if it paid enough you might not need to go out to work at all. You could stay at home and look after our baby. I know you'll make an amazing mum." Leo was desperate to make this work, whereas for Miranda all she could see was the parlous state her life had become. Going from hero to zero, in less than the blink of an eye.

"I'll have a think about it after the funeral. Let's get that over with first, and see what James and the others say to me after that. I might even be able to get them to let me stay in the house, at least until it's sold, which would buy us a bit of time. It could take months, with probate and everything, so I don't want to jump too quickly."

The probability of being allowed to stay in the house was pretty remote, but the probability of agreeing to move in with Leo, at least until she was convinced the police were not looking at him as a suspect, was even lower. A girl needed to keep her options open, though.

Miranda looked over at her phone as it rang. It was two-thirty and she and Leo had been chatting for nearly two hours. "Hello, yes. Miss Swann here. Oh, thank you. I'll be there shortly to collect it."

"Was that the jewellers?"

"Yes, my ring's ready. I'd best get off and collect it, and then make my way to the station. There's a train in forty minutes, which I should be able to catch, if I hurry."

"I'll give you a lift, if you like, and save you the trouble."

"No, it's easier with the train. You never know who's watching."

"Well, at least give me a quick kiss before you rush off. Sitting here, unable to put my hands on you for the last couple of hours, has been excruciating."

"Okay, just be quick." Miranda laughed as she said goodbye to Leo in the doorway of the café, reaching up to kiss him and letting him take her in his arms for a few seconds. "Now, be off with you, before you get me started, too." That feeling, of his body and his lips on hers, was one she had not realise she had missed so much. However, she recognised that as much as she wanted Leo's body, now was not the right time to show it.

Although for Rosie, who was just coming out of the bookshop across the road from the café, it was perfect timing. She was in Oxford collecting some stock for the shop, and had called in to pick up a couple of paperbacks Richard had ordered, before making her way back to her car. So, seeing Miranda, in the arms of another man, whose face she did not recognise, but whose body she would certainly not say no to, was a sight she had not expected.

She struggled to image a plausible reason for their embrace, other than the obvious, given the way he was gazing at her. However, it was certainly something she would be looking into and having words about.

When Miranda got back to the jewellers, she was feeling all buoyed up. Talking with Leo had certainly lifted her spirits. He was so handsome and the fact he was desperate for them to be together she found quite touching. Although, even if he had not murdered her fiancé, and the jury was still out on that, she could not see a life together with him and her baby. She also hated the idea of sinking her money into a house. That was her money and she intended using it wisely. What would happen two years down the line, if things did not work out and she wanted it back? There were no guarantees she would get it, and then where would she be left?

"Good afternoon, Miss Swann. Please take a seat. I'll just let the manager know you're here. I know he wants to have a quiet word with you. I won't be a moment." The assistant indicated a chair for Miranda to sit whilst she waited.

"Miss Swann, would you like to come through?" The jeweller, a middle-aged man in his late fifties, with balding grey hair and dark spectacles, came out of the back of the store and led her to a small side room. "Please take a seat," he said as handed her back her ring.

"Thank you, it's beautiful, isn't it, and quite an unusual setting? I imagine you don't see many like this. Were you able to provide a valuation for me?"

"Yes, I've had a good look at it. With you saying on the phone it was a valuable piece, I have taken my time to appraise it, and have even consulted with a couple of my colleagues on the matter. We're all in agreement that it is a very pretty ring. However, we are also all in agreement that it is not a genuine emerald, as you led us to believe, or that the diamonds are of the quality you imagined. Sadly, I would estimate its value to be in the region of eight to nine hundred pounds, a thousand at the most. Sadly, not the twenty to thirty thousand pounds ball park you led me to expect."

Miranda was speechless. Frank had assured her it was a quality piece, complete with the finest gems and set in twenty-four carat gold. "Eight to nine hundred pounds, you can't be serious? My fiancé assured me it was of value and told me he had insured it for over twenty-five thousand pounds. I can't believe what I am hearing. I need to get a second opinion."

"Of course, that's your prerogative, Madam. However, I have spoken to various colleagues today and, as I mentioned earlier, we are all of the same opinion. I realise this was not what you were expecting and that it has come as a huge shock to you. It is a pretty ring, though, so I suggest you just enjoy wearing it. The value is less important if you have sentimental attachment to it, as I'm sure you do with your fiancé's recent passing. Now, if you would please excuse me, there is somewhere I need to be." And with that he indicated their discussion was over and promptly showed Miranda the door.

Sentimental attachment, after what Frank had done to her she wished she had killed him herself. He had certainly had the last laugh, at her expense by the looks of it, and she was fuming.

Chapter 28

The morning of the funeral arrived with the summer sunshine and the cloudless clear blue sky doing nothing to support the fact it was supposed to be a morose day. It was already warm with the forecasters predicting it would get much hotter as the day progressed. Temperatures were expected to reach the high twenty degrees by mid-afternoon.

The family and some close friends were assembled at the Old Manor House waiting for the hearse to arrive, dressed in their finest funeral clothes and feeling a little hot under the collar. The men particularly were unhappy to be wearing formal suits, with shirts and ties making their outfits even more uncomfortable. At least the women could put a lighter weight summery dress on, provided it was one that was suitable for the occasion. One of Frank's stipulations had been for black to be worn, none of those bright colours that had become so fashionable at funerals over recent years. No, his funeral was to be a formal affair.

The family had arranged to follow the hearse in procession to the small church, for the simple service where other locals and friends had been invited to join them, before continuing onto the crematorium for a private cremation. It was a distance of around ten miles away. Other than the hearse, no funeral cars had been booked. It was an expense they could not justify at this time.

James would drive his car with Katie, Judy and Simon as his passengers. They had opted to leave Maia with Katie's mum, as had Judy and Simon, who were leaving their boys with Simon's mother. Funerals were not a place for children after all. Anyway, they all had school to attend, so why disrupt their routines? Rosie, currently without a plus-one, offered to drive the second car, accompanied by her brother Richard, who could have driven but currently did not own his own vehicle.

The last car he had driven had been written off two months earlier, when an idiot motor cyclist had overtaken him at speed on a blind corner on one of the back country roads, less than a mile from home. After it had sped past, it careered straight into a tractor that was towing a trailer as it emerged through the gate of a nearby field, the trailer full of potatoes recently harvested becoming upturned by the impact. Richard had to brake furiously to avoid the collision and the potatoes, resulting in him swerving and smashing headfirst into a tree. The airbags thankfully took most of the impact. Although Richard was unhurt, the same could not be said for his vehicle, nor for the motorcyclist whose bike had wedged itself between the tractor and its trailer, making it impossible for him to be released until the ambulance arrived.

As it was his father's car, Frank was furious when he found out, taking his fury out not only on Richard for borrowing the car in the first place, but on the young motorcyclist too. He even attempted to have a go at the farmer, accusing him of being a hazard on the road, driving without due care and attention to other motorists. It did not help that the farmer was one of the tenants on the Old Manor House's estate, so although he was in no way responsible, he was made to feel belittled by his landlord. Or, that the young lad was the son of one of the builders who worked for *Paulson's*, who shortly after the incident found his work life become more difficult as his employer made snide remarks to him and his colleagues about it each time he saw them.

Richard had reluctantly called his father from the scene of the incident. He told him about the accident, saying in no way was it his fault before asking for a lift home. The car would need to be towed away, he told his father, once the police had assessed the area. Richard knew he could easily have walked home, but as his legs were feeling a little jittery, presumably due to the shock, he thought better of it. So, by the time the police arrived, Frank was already there and they too felt the onslaught of his temper. He demanded that the young lad be given the maximum custodial sentence possible, or else there would be trouble, adding they would be hearing from his solicitor. Frank was well known for his hot-headedness, as well as his coarse language, neither of which had ever won him friends around the town.

Rosie had even offered to drive Miranda and Nanny Tilbury to the funeral. Her car was more than big enough after all and Miranda's Mazda was hardly suitable.

Miranda did not appreciate the fact that a funeral car had not been booked for her, but accepted that driving herself in a bright red sports car did not appear in keeping with the occasion either, so had accepted Rosie's offer of a lift graciously. Apart from which, with her condition, she had made it known to the family that getting in and out of the low car was quite uncomfortable. Whilst her bump was still not showing, morning sickness was still an issue with which she was struggling, along with an acceptance that the car would not have been the most practical of models she could have driven, once the new baby arrived, even if she had been allowed to keep it. The fact it was going back in a few days was a subject to which she needed to give some serious thought; one more item to add to the growing list of things that was keeping her awake at night.

It had become abundantly clear, following the reading of Frank's will, that her remaining time at the Old Manor House was limited. Frank had left her with basically nothing. Other than the clothes she stood up in and the small trinkets she had managed to amass during their time together, there was nothing in her name. She had no legal rights, not as far as she could see. Even the lease on the car had been in the business' name, and once James had made it perfectly clear that no further payments would be made on it, stating the business could not afford to keep financing it, even if they had wanted to, which they clearly did not, it had to go. Miranda could not afford to keep it herself, so when the end of the month came, her little sports car, with its personalised plates, would be the first of the luxuries of her life to be consigned to the past.

When Miranda had met with Leo over lunch the previous day they had talked over her options, with them both agreeing that until she had actually been given her marching orders she should stay put at the Old Manor House. She may not have legal rights to remain, but that did not mean she should give up so easily, or without a fight, did it? It was her home after all. She had been Frank's fiancée, and as far as the rest of the world knew was carrying his child, so that should entitle her to something.

Leo had also suggested it might be time to engage her own solicitor. She should seek some proper legal advice on what she was eligible to claim, in terms perhaps of broader support, or whether she had sufficient grounds to contest the will. Whilst his idea of claiming benefits was abhorrent to Miranda, and so demeaning, it was still worth considering. Although where she would find the money to pay for legal advice, or how solid the ground was for any claims she might be making, was questionable. She had, after all, signed a pre-nuptial agreement, the fact of which the family was now fully aware.

As she waited with the others, she could not rid her mind of the idea that Leo had done something to Frank, or was involved in some way with his death, and if that proved to be the case where would that leave her? Would she want to tie herself and her baby to him, knowing he had probably murdered her future husband for his own benefit? Because as she stood there now, trying to act the part of the grieving fiancée, she could definitely not see any way that it had benefited her.

As Nanny Tilbury stood with the rest of the family, watching their faces and trying to read into their expressions, she was smiling. She was delighted to accept the offer of a lift from Rosie. Nanny had never owned a car nor learnt to drive, happy to rely on public transport for what little she needed to get herself around. After all, she did not go very far these days, the occasional walk into town or the odd trip out to visit old friends was the furthest she went. And whilst she could have easily walked to and from the church, she had recognised it would have been quite an ordeal to take a taxi, or catch a bus, to and from the crematorium. It was quite a long distance away, so even if the bus had arrived on time, by the time she would have got there the service would have likely been over. And she did not want to miss anything.

Nanny quite liked a good funeral. She always found them a good opportunity to catch up with people and listen to the latest gossip, as well as enjoy a glass or two of something at the wake afterwards, along with a curled-up egg sandwich, if she was lucky. It was amazing what counted as a social activity once you hit a certain age. The wake today would be back at the Old Manor House, provided Ana-Maria and Wilf had got everything sorted whilst the rest of them were at the funeral. Although, when she had looked in on them earlier that morning, to offer any help, it had not instilled her with much confidence.

Mrs Cuthbert had made it clear to the family that she had no desire to attend the church service. She and Wilf would prefer to remain at the house and prepare everything for their return. She assured Judy that drinks and a light snack would be ready for anyone who wanted to return, assuming most would make their way directly from the church and be there before the main mourners returned from the crematorium.

No, Nanny Tilbury had thought, Rosie has plenty of space in her big car, with the added advantage that she could stay close to Richard. She could even hold his hand, if he needed her support. The arrangement suited her perfectly.

It was no secret that Richard and James had always been Nanny's favourites and as Nanny had raised Richard from a newborn, it made their relationship especially close. She became a mother substitute to him, feeding, changing and loving him as if he was her own baby. She lost count of the number of times he had cuddled up next to her on the sofa, desperate for her to read a bedtime story to him. Even as a young boy, he'd had a ferocious appetite for books and would ask for story after story to be read, his concentration on what he was listening to evident.

He soon tired of children's literature and used to turn up with books that were well above his reading age, books that he would take from his grandfather's library, even climbing onto a chair if the book he sought was on a shelf that was not within his reach. The library was a room in the house Frank seldom used, as books were not his thing. Roald Dahl was a favourite of Richard's, which she loved to read to him given he was one of her favourite authors too. It was not long before Richard had mastered reading himself, and that was a mixed blessing to Nanny, as she sought to find alternative ways of remaining close to him, now that their special reading time was over.

Frank had been grieving at the time, which was understandable having just lost his wife, Susan. He also had three other children to care for, children he had already developed relationships with, something he had never managed to achieve with the new baby. Without Nanny's love,

Richard would have been almost forgotten, abandoned to the nursery. The fact she had stepped in, and stepped-up on all levels with all four children, meant that over time she developed a strong bond with each of them and a very protective streak towards them all. She would not hear a single word said against any of them, by anyone. They were her family.

Nanny was also very close to James and remembered how much his father had on occasion bullied him, or ignored him as an adolescent. James was growing up without his mother's love and as an inquisitive teenager she had on more than one occasion been forced to step in to console him after an argument had broken out between him and his father. She would spend hours patiently answering his questions, even watching as he brought his first girlfriend home, determined to make sure she was made to feel welcome in the house. She was delighted when he eventually met and married Katie. She was such a pretty little thing, and such a hard worker, Nanny often thought on the occasions she called into her salon to have her hair done.

Judy had always been Frank's favourite child. That was no secret either. She was the one who looked and acted most like Susan, which perhaps explained why he felt most aligned to his eldest daughter. Nanny recalled the moment Judy first introduced Simon as her boyfriend at the age of eighteen, and how aghast Frank was at the thought of his little girl becoming a woman. Simon in his mind was James' friend, not Judy's boyfriend, so how had that happened? It took him a long time to get his mind around the fact she had grown into a beautiful young lady, no longer Daddy's little girl. Eventually, what his little girl wanted, his little girl got with Simon accepted into the family.

After Simon graduated from university and started to discuss his options and job opportunities across the country,

Frank had been quick to react. He instantly created a role for him within the business, one that aligned to the type of career he had been seeking elsewhere. The idea of Simon taking Judy far away from home was something of which Frank could not conceive, so anything that was in his power to prevent that happening, was what he needed to do.

Rosie, being effectively the middle child, had always been fiercely independent and like Richard was as bright as a button. She was happy to meander her way through whatever family politics and relationships developed, diplomatically never taking sides or making alliances, unless it suited her purpose to do so. She was always focussed and intent on her own course, her own agenda remaining clear in her mind at all times. She had never wanted to rely on family handouts, or trade on the family connections, with the thought of being indebted to anyone anathema to her. She just wanted to provide for herself and show that as a woman she could make her own way in the world, as easily as any man could.

Her independence at times had got in the way, especially in terms of her own relationships and love life, as she was never prepared to compromise on what she wanted out of life. Men had come and gone, none ever becoming too serious or dependent on her. She would not give her heart easily to anyone.

Granted, she still lived at home, but that suited her purposes for the time being, whilst she focused all her attentions on getting the business established. She was not ready to fly the nest yet. Although, the threat of Miranda's position, had she become lady of the manor, would have upset her plans. It was something she had not been at all happy about.

No, Nanny wanted to be there to offer whatever comfort she could to all of them as they were all special to her, in their own way.

Judy had been left to make the funeral arrangements, assuming the role when no one else stepped forward to take charge. After all, she only had two children to look after, so they argued had plenty of time on her hands. James and Simon were keeping the business going, Katie had the hairdressers to run, Rosie the dress agency and Richard, well he had 'serious thinking' to do. He was loveable, but not the most practical of people, with the thought of Richard arranging the service something none of them wanted to contend with.

Judy had eventually approached Miranda and asked for her comments, including inviting any input she might want to make in terms of what they were already considering. She was forced to recognise that Miranda had spent several years with her father and would have her memories, some of which she may be prepared to share.

Judy diplomatically made it clear however, that as Miranda was not his next of kin, nor technically his family, they would be taking the lead. No one wanted her taking charge, or assuming a key role in the proceedings, the fact of which Miranda was secretly relieved. She would attend, obviously looking glamorous in her black designer dress, just not as the grieving widow, simply as his fiancée.

As Miranda now stood with the others waiting for the hearse to arrive, she pondered where life had brought her. Had circumstances been different, she would still be on her honeymoon, not standing outside a house that she no longer felt comfortable to call home, waiting for a coffin carrying her dead fiancé to arrive. With the prospect of then spending an hour in a cold dark church, when all she really wanted to do was to be outside, in the sunshine, working on her tan.

The small parish church of St Bartholomew's, out of respect for the Paulson family presumably rather than Frank himself, was packed to the rafters for the brief funeral service. People from the town, tenants of the farms and employees of the businesses had turned up to witness the event, all crammed into the ancient and extremely uncomfortable wooden pews.

Judy had followed her father's instructions for the funeral service almost to the letter, having been given a detailed list of his wishes, passed down from Mr Mears, Frank's solicitor. The list had been very specific in terms of the readings, the hymns and the people who would be invited to provide the eulogy for him. It was almost as if her father had not only anticipated his death, but had prepared well for it.

Judy noticed from some of the arrangements, the instructions appeared to have only been made recently, as the names of the people invited to speak were not necessarily long-standing or family friends, but more recent acquaintances. In fact, the list was woefully light on long-standing friends, leaving Judy to wonder where her father's friends had gone, or if he still had any.

Surprisingly, the only thing her father had not done was pay for his funeral ahead of time. So, whilst he had made certain more extravagant requests, in terms of the funeral procession and some of the finer things about the day itself, that was where Judy had drawn the line. She could not justify spending more money than was strictly necessary, certainly not on horse-drawn carriages, or wreaths of white roses, to name but a few of his more quirky requests.

As the six pallbearers carried the coffin into church, the family members arranged themselves behind it ready to process down the aisle. Miranda stood behind the four siblings and their partners; mindful of the similarities to the aisle she should have paraded down in her wedding gown only three weeks ago. In fact, as they made their way slowly towards the altar and took their seats, she noticed that several people were staring back at her, smiling compassionately. They were people who should have been there for that occasion too, and obviously sensed her distress.

Finally, Nanny Tilbury brought up the rear, a solitary old lady acknowledging people as she walked past them, giving a gentle wave, almost as if she was visiting royalty. None of the mourners were surprised to see her there, simply happy that Frank's children had included her and were treating her as family, and not the hired help, or the trusty family retainer that she was. Had it not been Frank in the coffin, they were assured that would not have been the case. He would not have thought to include her in such a pivotal role.

Sitting at the back of the church, at the end of the aisle furthest away from the main entrance, were DS Ruth Jacobs and PC Neil Dickson, quietly watching on as the family entered and took their reserved seats at the front of the church.

The police had arrived early, in plenty of time to see who else was attending and to soak up the atmosphere outside the church. It was a glorious day after all, so why not enjoy an extra few minutes in the sunshine? They had mingled around as people arrived, listening in as the conversations began. Speculation was still rife about what had happened to Frank, with new theories emerging daily. News of the contents of his will had started to trickle out, which only added to people's desires to theorise. Who would benefit the most from seeing him dead, assuming of course it was not an accidental death?

Most people had instantly jumped to the conclusion that it had to be murder. After all, that was a lot more exciting than believing Frank had simply slipped and banged his head after one too many whiskeys the night before. Where was the gossip factor or sensationalism in that? No, people were happy to think the worst and had already started to ask who had a motive, who had a grudge against Frank and who would inherit most from his estate? The questions of motive, means and opportunity all being bandied around as if it was a given.

Some believed the family should be under suspicion, as far as the talk in the graveyard and around the town was concerned. After all, they were in the house when it happened, so certainly had the opportunity. Although there seemed to be no consensus on which of them had done it, or whether they had worked together or alone in orchestrating it.

Others believed Miranda was the obvious suspect, but then again why would she kill the hand that fed her, and did she have the means to do it? She was a fit woman, but was she strong enough to overpower Frank? Many of the locals still knew her as the barmaid at the Three Pheasants and believed that since she had taken up with Frank she had become too pretentious for her own good, swanning around town in her fancy sports car and expecting everyone to fawn all over her, as if she was someone special. Whereas, she was just a kid from town, someone from a working-class background, who had gone to the local comprehensive and not really amounted to much. Working as a barmaid was not rocket science, was it? Then again, what would her motive be? Her parents were nice people and were reportedly horrified at what had happened to Frank, but could their daughter have done it?

Some of the more astute ladies around town had already made the connection between her and Leo, their regular chats after Pilates classes not going unnoticed. They always appeared friendly, perhaps too friendly some would say, especially given she was engaged to be married to another man. So, what about Leo? The tall dark handsome stranger who had recently come back to the town. If he was some thwarted ex-boyfriend, who did not like the idea of his rekindled love being ruined by his lover tying herself to a man old enough to be her father, was that motive enough to get Frank out of the picture? He certainly could have overpowered

Frank, and he had a motive, but did he have the opportunity? Some of the older townsfolk recalled that Miranda and Leo had been friends as teenagers, so had Leo returned to claim his prize and killed Frank out for some sort of revenge?

Others looked beyond the family and towards Frank's business interests. *Paulson's* as a family firm had once been a respectable business, a name whose reputation could be trusted and relied upon. When Lady Susan was still alive she had always pushed for her husband's company to build homes for local people at affordable prices. She knew she had come from a privileged background, being brought up as the daughter of a wealthy landowner, and wanted to ensure her family put something back into her local community. She saw the value of community and having homes that the younger people could afford. Homes that would enable them to stay close to their own families and not need to move elsewhere because property in Chidlington had grown beyond their budgets.

Following Susan's untimely death, any altruistic acts by the company were scaled back, and over time Frank began operating on a profit first basis. For years now, making money had been his principal driver, and who he used or trod on in the process of making his next million was not his concern. He threw his weight around in more ways than one, bullying suppliers into giving him favourable terms for his materials, pushing hard to get the maximum prices for the houses he developed. And, if rumours were to be believed, he thought nothing of bribing his way through the planning processes, or making promises that he would invariably renege on. His business scruples were not to be trusted, and the Paulson name had lost a lot of its glisten.

As people scanned the congregation, looking to see who they recognised and wondering what their reason for being there was, there were various faces that jumped out.

Faces of people that had sufficient motive for wanting to see the back of Frank Paulson. In fact, it was not difficult to imagine a pretty long queue of suspects forming.

"So, Sarg, what do you think?" asked Neil quietly as the service got underway. "Do you think we've got our murderer in the church, or not?" Having seen many a detective programme, Neil knew it was generally considered that the murderer returned to the scene of the crime, as well as turning up to the funeral, even if he was hovering behind a gravestone so as to avoid being spotted. It was one of the main reasons DS Jacobs had suggested they both attend the funeral, keeping their ears and eyes open at all times. They would even call into the wake afterwards, if they had the chance, believing the prospect of a glass or two of wine might help loosen tongues even further.

"I wouldn't be at all surprised, if it was murder, that is, Neil. We've still not ruled it out, equally we've no evidence to support it either. Let's see what more intel we can pick up after the service as that might give us a better idea."

Sergeant Jacobs was still in two minds on the subject of it being a murder, a manslaughter or an unfortunate accident. Her heart was telling her one thing, whilst her head was suggesting another. Police work was all about dealing in facts, not suppositions or guesswork, and for now there were no facts that pointed them in any one direction.

"All I can say with any real confidence, Neil, is that Kleenex won't be making its fortune out of this funeral. I don't think I've seen a solitary person reach for a tissue yet, have you? And in terms of mourning, the family look like they've dressed for a society wedding, not a funeral. Some of the dresses those ladies are wearing are straight out of Vogue, and how they've stayed upright, tottering down the aisle in four-inch heels I can't imagine."

"You're right, Sarg.   Something definitely doesn't feel right, does it?" Neil was certainly learning a lot from his sergeant about detective work, and he was lapping it up.

Chapter 29

By the time the family returned from the crematorium, after having watched Frank's body disappear through the velvet curtains to the strains of Frank Sinatra and My Way playing over the music system, the house was full of well-wishers. Most had walked the short distance from the church to the Old Manor House, knowing that at least that way they could partake of a few free drinks, without the worry of having to drive home, or the expense of calling for a taxi.

The cremation had been short and sweet, with James offering a few words into the brief service the celebrant conducted. It sounded sincere, and although he recognised that Frank had perhaps not been the best father in the world, he said he spoke for all of them when he said Frank would be missed. There was no clichéd eulogy or maudlin words spoken, just factual sentiments that noted his passing. If anything, his words were more heartfelt than the gushing eulogy that had been offered at the church by Councillor Dent, who had delivered what had sounded both incredible and insincere, making Frank out to be a model citizen, an honourable gentleman, a pillar of their local community, a friend to all.

It did not go unnoticed among the congregation how people moved a little uncomfortably in their seats as his words were spoken. Honourable was not a word normally associated with Frank.

"Well at least that's over," James announced as soon as they pulled into the driveway. "Just the wake to get through now, and then perhaps we can start getting our lives back to normal."

Katie gave him a sideways glance as he got out of the car, one that suggested he needed to be careful what he said. People expected the family to be in mourning and throwaway comments like that would not give the best of impressions. The remaining family members had a reputation around town, and for the sake of all their businesses, they needed to ensure that reputation was not tarnished further by their own insensitive words or behaviours.

"I know what you mean," Judy replied, equally glad it was all over. The last few weeks had been quite an anguished time for her, having to prepare the funeral and deal with an unending list of requests. Some of which were frankly bizarre and had left her wondering what had been going on in her father's mind. She had felt torn on more than one occasion in terms of doing what Frank wanted, or doing what was best for the family and its future financial position. The news of the state of his estate, following the reading of the will, had left Judy speechless, with her still struggling to absorb the enormity of what they had all heard.

However, of the four children, she sensed, all things considered, she felt his loss more than the rest put together. James, Rosie and Richard she knew had grown distant from their father a long time ago. They had tired of trying to maintain or force a relationship that had not come naturally. They were adults, and as such could choose how they spent their time, or with whom they socialised. And for a long time now that had not been their father.

Her relationship with him had perhaps been the strongest, although saying that, they too in recent years had drifted apart. Come to think of it, she could not recall the last time her father had come over to their house for a simple meal, or to play with his grandchildren. Rosie and Richard lived in the same house as him, and by all accounts barely interacted on any level, managing to keep their distance if they happened to be at home at the same time. Even working on a daily basis with Frank, as Simon and James had, did not necessarily result in them having a good relationship. If anything, they saw a side to Frank that she had not personally witnessed and the more that had come out over recent days, as she learnt of things he had said or done, the more she had not liked it. That man she was learning about was not the same man she had grown up with. The daddy she had run to as a little girl, desperate for his attention.

Thinking back, she realised she had perhaps started distancing herself from him when she learnt about his behaviour towards Alison and Mason, behaviour that had not endeared father to daughter in the slightest. And subsequently, taking up with Miranda, a girl her own age, had only added fuel to the fire. Judy was frequently embarrassed by things he had said or done during his affair, and had often felt the need to defend his actions, mostly against her better judgment.

So now, having prepared the funeral, she had a good idea of what people thought about him and what they were saying about the way he had lived his life, with little, if any of it being complimentary. No, as much as she hated to admit it, life would be a whole lot easier for the family with her father no longer around.

"Right, let's go in and face the wolves."

Once inside the house the family dispersed and went to speak to people who had attended with a view to expressing their condolences. James approached a group of councillors, at the centre of which was Gregory Dent. James made a show of shaking his hand.

"Gregory, I want to thank you for the kind words you said about my father at the church. It was very much appreciated by the family."

"That's no problem, James. Happy that I could oblige, although why your father requested me to do it is a mystery, I'm afraid. I know our paths have crossed on numerous occasions, but I wouldn't have considered we were particularly close, so I do admit to being a little surprised when your sister approached me to do that."

"Yes, I can understand that, and that's why it's appreciated. It appears Dad had a way of getting what he wanted, even from the grave." A nervous laugh accompanied his comment. "Well, I'm sure I speak on behalf of the whole council when I say, planning meetings won't be nearly as colourful now that your father isn't around to contribute to them as he has done over recent years. He's been very vocal, that's for sure."

"Hear, hear." The other councillors nodded their agreement.

"And do you mind me asking, James, what's your intention in terms of the business? Do you plan to continue running it, like your father did?"

"Well, that's an interesting question. I certainly intend to continue running it, but perhaps not in the same way as my father did. Si and I have other ideas, and once we get everything back fully operational we would like to talk to the council a little more about them. I'd like to think they're plans you and your colleagues may find much more palatable. Now, if you wouldn't mind excusing me, I need to circulate."

As James left the discussion, he could almost feel the intrigue being sparked between the others and the appreciative nods his comments had received.

Stepping back, as he and Simon had done over recent weeks, and discovering the true state of the business had been a real eye opener, with them embarrassed to realise it had come to this without them ever being aware. Frank had been a devious operator, his practices sharp and self-serving, his behaviour rarely honourable. He and Simon discussed wanting to run the type of business that contributed to the local economy, not one that leached off it, as they feared had become the case under his father's management. If nothing else, listening to the professionals and employees alike over recent days had really resonated with them. They had learnt a lot about how not to run a business, and even more about how not to irritate people. The message was clear, Frank had not only destroyed a lot of the good faith the family had built up, but he had also destroyed any bridges to the local community and the town council, bridges that in his mother's day had been so strong. He and Simon saw the reconstruction of these as their first priority.

As James was talking to the members of the council, Simon was working the other end of the room, where a few representatives from some of their employees and sales teams had gathered. Everyone had been given the opportunity to attend the funeral, should they wish, with around twenty people making the effort to do so.

As Simon approached, the chatter went silent, and the atmosphere changed. Mrs Ellington, Frank's long-term secretary, was currently enjoying a glass of wine along with another of the ladies who had come along, someone Simon recognised from the admin team.

"It was a well-attended service, wasn't it, Mr Goodman?" Mrs Ellington said to Simon as he approached her. She was old school and liked to maintain a formal air at all times. Managers, in her book, deserved respect to their face, whether they had earned it or not. What was said in private however was a different matter.

"Yes, Mrs Ellington, it was. It was clear Frank had a lot of contacts in the area, if not all friends, I might add." Simon was astute enough to realise that even if people had offered condolences on the family's loss, one could not automatically assume there were feelings of sadness attached to them.

"Yes, I know what you mean. As loyal as I have tried to be to him over the years, there have been occasions when even I have not seen eye to eye with him. He was a difficult man to work for, and could try the patience of a saint."

"Well, I hope you won't be saying the same about Jimmy when he takes the reins, or of myself for that matter. We're both hoping for your support, especially helping us to navigate some of those areas Frank kept to himself over the years. The number of files or papers we're discovering that we've never seen before is worrying. Once we've got to grips with everything, we're looking to change the direction of the business."

"I'm not too sure about that, Mr Goodman. I'm perhaps a bit long in the tooth for change, and I'm not sure about starting again with someone new. And, as I was saying to Mr Ellington the other evening, I've been thinking about retirement for some time now, so this may be just the opportunity I need to call it a day."

"Well, whatever you decide, Mrs Ellington, both Jimmy and I will support your decision. However, please don't be too hasty as you're an asset to the business, and for the time being we couldn't afford to lose you; we've got a job on our hands." He patted her arm as he moved on. It was clear there was some real uncertainty and discord within the workforce, leaving Simon to conclude that he and James had their work cut out if they were to steady the ship.

As the family moved among their guests, acknowledging their presence and thanking them for their support, Miranda had basically stood in the corner of the room, alone, nursing a glass of mineral water. It was surprising to note how few people actually took the time to engage with her, or offer her their condolences. The occasional person would approach, and after a few moments move away, their duty done. She had no discussion or real engagement with anyone. Even some of the people who had been invited to the wedding, who she thought of as her friends, kept their distance. She felt out of place and extremely uncomfortable, desperate to leave the room as soon as she could and get back to the relative safety of her bedroom.

Surprisingly, the one woman who did engage with her was Alison, Frank's ex-wife. She had turned up after the service to offer her condolences to Frank's children. Like most people, she felt their loss, without showing any degree of sadness. Frank was history to her, and had been so for some time, effectively cutting both her and Mason from his life. Yet his behaviour did not mean she could not show kindness to his children. They were not the ones who had hurt her. If anything, they had sided with her against their father, a fact for which she would always be grateful. Especially given their support had helped her in terms of the divorce settlement she was able to negotiate.

"So where does this leave you now, Miranda?" Alison enquired as the afternoon was drawing to a close, her tone as solicitous as she could manage. "I imagine with a baby on the way and no husband to support you, your position in the house will be quite precarious. Have you decided what you're going to do next?" News of the pregnancy had become difficult to contain.

"Thank you for your concern, I'm sure it's well meant." The sarcasm was evident in the tone of her voice as she replied. "If you'll excuse me, I think I need to go and have a lie down." At which point she headed towards the door and quietly made her way upstairs.

Throughout the afternoon, Mrs Cuthbert and Nanny had handed out vol-au-vents and sandwiches to people as they mingled, inconspicuously trying to listen into their conversations as they politely offered the food around. Wilf had stepped in to help with the drinks, carrying trays of wine or sherry, or offering cups of tea to anyone who was driving. There was no free bar today, much to the chagrin of some of the mourners.

Nanny thrived on gossip and was happy to join in where she felt she could add anything, or better still learn a juicy detail of which she had previously been unaware. Whereas Mrs Cuthbert was on her guard, choosing to keep her eyes lowered and remain silent for fear of anyone either trying to engage her in conversation, or worse still recognising her. She scurried back to the kitchen whenever she had the opportunity and stayed there for as long as she could, before Nanny would return and suggest they take the next tray of food out. Her sense of danger was heightened with so many new faces; faces she neither recognised, nor felt comfortable being around.

For some months now, Ana-Maria had felt like she was living on a knife's edge, never comfortable nor relaxed, either at home or when outside the house. When shopping, faces would spook her, people she thought she recognised from her homeland coming out of the shadows; Romanians to whom she had no desire to become reintroduced. There had also been occasions when she had felt as if she was being followed or watched. None of which made her feel any easier about leaving the house. Even the occasions when mysterious phone calls had been made, the caller hanging up whenever she answered the phone. Wilf had tried to ask what the issue was, why she had suddenly become so edgy, but she could not tell him. How could she put into words that she thought Frank's murder was mistaken identity, with the intended victim actually being herself? Her fear that the bad people had finally caught up with her.

Eventually the room began to thin out as people made their excuses to leave. They had said what they needed to say, and that was that. There had been a distinct lack of bonhomie around the room, or funny anecdotes exchanged. It was all very sombre, with a distinct lack of warmth or atmosphere on display.

The two police officers had generally kept their distance throughout the day, happy to simply observe people's behaviour and make note of who had bothered to show up, along with any titbits of information they had managed to overhear. Today was not the day for questioning, but the events had given them plenty of food for thought, as well as a few interesting leads to follow up on, once they got back to the station.

Chapter 30

Nanny Tilbury had noticed Mrs Cuthbert's behaviour throughout the afternoon, the way she had studiously avoided people and done whatever she could to stay out of the limelight. It was so out of character for her, as she was usually someone who would seek to take charge in the house and make her presence known, not shy away from a situation as she had. She was usually outspoken and whilst not the most sociable of characters, was not someone you could easily ignore.

Having arrived at the Old Manor House to take up the position of housekeeper five years ago, she and Wilf had proven themselves to be hard workers, both settling into a lifestyle that was completely alien to them. Wilf had worked as a train driver before taking early retirement, so was used to working shifts and long hours. It had been a manual job, so hard work had never fazed him, although now having turned sixty he was careful what heavy lifting he took on.

Ana-Maria had been unused to running a home of any description prior to applying for the position of housekeeper. However, she had blagged her way through the interview, confidently convincing Alison, then Mrs Paulson, of her ability to do whatever was needed. She even promised some Romanian cuisine, grateful she at least knew her way around a kitchen and had learnt to be a competent cook, thanks to the time she had spent with her grandmother. As Alison had Mason, who was only a young baby at the time, she was simply relieved to be getting help. And, with Wilf offering his services too, that was a bonus. After all, the position had been vacant for some time, so having willing applicants was a godsend.

What it did mean, though, was that Alison perhaps did not research into the couple's references as closely as she might, and as her husband was busy at the builder's yard, it had been left to her to make the final decision. If truth be told, over the years it was not a decision that any of the family had found cause to regret, as yet. Wilf and Mrs Cuthbert had simply settled into their positions and generally speaking it had worked out well for all concerned.

Nanny had a sense, though, that things were about to change. There was something about the situation that left her with a worry bead. Something she could not quite fathom, and above all else Nanny hated not knowing what was going on.

Eventually, around six o'clock, the final guests had departed and the process of starting to tidy up and get the house back in order began. As the front door closed on the last mourner, there was a sense that what needed to be done would not only involve collecting the dirty pots, or stacking the dishwasher, or any of the usual tasks that were required once a party or social event was over. No, the atmosphere felt as if it would take a lot more than rearranging the furniture to get this household back into shape.

The events of the previous three weeks had certainly taken their toll, emotionally and physically. The family was unsettled, tempers on occasion were short and the overall dynamic between the siblings was not as it should be. The formalities of the funeral were over, but there remained questions still to be answered. Things that needed to be said, and importantly decisions that could not be put off much longer.   There was a sense that they needed to regroup and pull together, more than they had ever done before.

The Dishonourable Groom

As the rest of the family took their drinks and moved into the sitting room, no doubt to relax and mull over the events of the day, Nanny considered her options. She could go straight back to her annex over the garage, to have a rest and make her dinner. After all, it had been a long day for her too, and she was not getting any younger. She had also not eaten very much since breakfast and was starting to feel a little hungry. At her age, her appetite had shrunk, but she still enjoyed her food and liked to cook on occasion. She had her own facilities in the annex, a small kitchen, where she made her meals and a cosy sitting room, where she could relax, with a television and a radio to keep her company on an evening. Over the years she had made it feel very homely, adding the odd ornament, or picture, or photo she had found around the place. All in all, it was very comfortable and she had no complaints.

Alternatively, she could stay behind and offer to help Mrs Cuthbert and Wilf with the cleanup. She was technically no longer in the employ of the family, so there was no expectation on her to do any activities within the house, or to spend her time in the kitchen helping out, but on occasions like this, or when the family was together, she liked to make herself useful. After all, she knew how much work had gone into catering for all those extra people in the house.

Wilf, assisted by James, Simon and Richard, had already cleared the main room, replacing the furniture where it needed to be, whilst Rosie, Judy and Katie had sorted out any food that was left over, boxing up what could be saved for later, before disposing of the rest. So, effectively it only left the kitchen to sort out, the dirty glasses and crockery to stack in the dishwasher.

If she stayed, Nanny thought it would also give her an opportunity for a quiet talk with Ana-Maria, in private. Nanny had befriended her and Ana-Maria had begun to trust her, so if anything was worrying the housekeeper, as Nanny suspected to be the case, then she might be able to get her to open up. On balance, she felt obliged to stay and help.

"Why don't you take your paper through to your lounge and have a quiet read, Wilf? I know you've not had a minute's rest all day. I'll stay and help Mrs Cuthbert with the dishes. It shouldn't take us too long, I would imagine," Nanny volunteered. "Would you like me to make you a nice cup of tea and bring it through to you?" She did not offer him any alternative, other than to agree to her suggestion.

"If you're both sure, then that would be great." He was feeling a little weary and welcomed the offer. "I might just be able to catch the news headlines, if I'm lucky." Unlike his wife, who was uninterested in British politics, or what was happening around her, Wilf liked to keep himself abreast of the latest news. He liked to form an opinion on most things, opinions he tended to share with his cronies at the Three Pheasants on the odd occasion he strolled down there for a quiet pint, or his game of dominoes.

Left alone the two women continued with their work in companionable silence for around another ten minutes. The radio was gently playing in the background and although Nanny was anxious to find out what was going on in Ana-Maria's mind, she knew she needed to bide her time. She sensed if she pushed too hard, Ana-Maria would simply clam up and the opportunity would be lost. That would leave Nanny none the wiser in terms of what was worrying her, or whether there was anything she could do to help.

All the time, as Ana-Maria was loading the dishwasher, the housekeeper's mind was racing. She was glad Wilf was out of the way and no longer fussing around her. She cared for him, and appreciated the way he was so considerate towards her, but there was no way she could ever let him know what she was thinking, or what she had gone through prior to them meeting all those years ago. It had been a difficult day for everyone, but on a personal level Ana-Maria was just glad she had got through it unscathed. Now all she needed to do was decide on her next course of action, because the only thing she knew for certain was she could no longer stay at the Old Manor House, or anywhere near Chidlington for that matter. Her sense of concern had been heightened after the events of the afternoon and she had to do something about it.

There had been a man there whom she had recognised, a Romanian she remembered from her home country. He was not someone she had seen at the Old Manor House before and was not one of the men who she remembered coming for dinner some weeks previously. He knew them, though, and had stood with them, all talking in Romanian, she had noted, on the occasion she passed by with her tray of drinks. She could not quite overhear what they were discussing and as her head was bowed he appeared not to recognise her.

It was six years since Ana-Maria had fled her home country, and although the years had been kind to her, she had aged a little. She was no longer a thirty-one-year-old woman, who could have passed for someone much younger. She was now in her late thirties and although those extra six years would not have been sufficient to make a huge difference, when coupled with the fact that her hair had changed, both in style and colour, and she now wore glasses and carried a little more weight, the similarities were not so obvious. Also, seeing her out of context added to her protection, her occupation now so far removed from the life she had once led in Romania, the life he would recall without a second thought if anything prompted him. No, someone would need to look very closely to recognise her, and even then would be careful what they said if they did make the connection.

Nevertheless, that had not allowed her to rest on her laurels, or ever led her to drop her guard. Until recently, Chidlington had felt like a safe haven, with Ana-Maria confidently able to walk around town without fear of recognition, relaxed in the surroundings she was beginning to call home.

That confidence had even seen her become a little more sociable, prepared to go out more by herself and even venture further afield on her days off. On one such outing into Oxford six months ago, to mooch around the shops and look to buy some new clothes, she had met a man in a café whilst she waited to catch the bus home. She had missed the earlier bus so had forty minutes to wait for the next one. They chatted over coffees and soon discovered they were both living in Chidlington, and both destined to catch the same bus.

He mentioned that his car had recently been scraped so had gone into the garage to have its paintwork treated, along with a couple of minor repairs. The garage had offered him a courtesy car, which he had declined, deciding to take a bus trip instead. It had been years since he had taken a bus and the thought of driving through the countryside appealed to him. He would get the bus back into Oxford the following week when the car needed collecting.

While they sat and chatted the first bus came and went, as did the second. By the time they caught the third bus it was as if they were old friends. Ana-Maria found herself responding to him in a way that she had not experienced in a long time. He was interesting, roughly the same age as she was and extremely good looking, with a very nice manner about him and no wedding ring on his finger. She recognised she was attracted to him, and from the way he responded to her the feeling appeared mutual. He, however, had noticed the wedding ring on her finger.

As they spoke, she discovered he had travelled widely with his work and had a wealth of stories to tell, and a way of telling them that left her wanting more. Sitting next to him on the way home, their bodies close, their arms touching, sent a bolt of electricity through her that she could not explain. By the end of their journey, there was no doubting there was a spark between them, an intangible feeling that she had never experienced before. Love or lust was a feeling that was new to Ana-Maria. When they parted on Chidlington high street later that evening, having exchanged names but not telephone numbers, something told Ana-Maria that destiny would bring them back together again, one way or another. She was sure of it.

Two weeks later, she was walking down the high street carrying two heavy shopping bags. It had started to rain and she was desperate to get home before the heavens opened. Showers had been predicted, although not the downpour that looked imminent. Hearing a car horn beeping beside her, she looked around.

"Do you want a lift? I can see you're struggling with those, and if you're not careful, you're going to get drenched." Ana-Maria looked over to see Carl smiling back at her, at the wheel of an expensive looking car. She did not recognise British models, but it was impressive. "Jump in, you don't live far, do you?"

As she got into the car, it was almost as if her destiny had been sealed. She had predicted they would meet again and this time she was not prepared to let him off so lightly. She was prepared to do whatever she needed to make this man part of her life.

Since then, she and Carl had met up on several occasions on her days off, generally at his home about a mile out of town. They also messaged each other frequently, whenever she had time alone, or Wilf was down at The Three Pheasants. Each encounter drew them closer, and the frisson she enjoyed whenever they were together outweighed the risk of being found out. It was exciting and made her feel attractive, and above all young again. In the scheme of things, the prospect of Wilf finding out about her affair was something she was prepared to deal with. If the Romanians however had found her, that was something she could not leave to chance.

"Ana-Maria, why don't you sit down and I'll make us both a cup of tea. Then you can tell me what's worrying you, because I can see something's troubling you. As your friend I'd love to be able to help, if you'd let me."

Ana-Maria considered the suggestion Nanny had made and smiled at her. She liked Nanny Tilbury, and over the years had grown to trust her, even to consider her to be a friend. She could see how loving she was, particularly to his lordship's children, how much she cared for them, even though they were adults and no longer needed her nurturing. She had also heard the wise words she imparted to them whenever they had a problem. It was usually Nanny they turned to, and, as far as Ana-Maria could tell, she had never let them down. Should she talk to her, and put her trust in her? After all, she needed someone to talk to, because she was in danger of driving herself mad if she continued to keep everything bottled up. And with Wilf not someone she could turn to, on either of her two concerns, who else did she have? Although, she was aware how fond Nanny was of Wilf, so perhaps talking about her feelings towards Carl may not be appropriate.

He had been at the house earlier, attending the wake along with some of the other local councillors. Ana-Maria had not realised he and Frank were friends, but as they lived in the same town and Frank was so high profile, she did not think too much about it. There were a lot of people there she had not known. Carl had watched her as she walked around the room, occasionally smiling if she caught his eye. His presence was comforting, although she did notice he was one of the first to leave.

"Come on, dear." Nanny placed a cup of tea in front of her and took the seat opposite at the kitchen table. The doors to both the main house and Ana-Maria's rooms were closed, meaning they would neither be overheard nor disturbed by the family, or Wilf. He would be well into his news programme by now, or more likely would have dozed off in the chair, and the family rarely ventured into the kitchen at this time of night.

"A problem shared is a problem halved, is one of my mother's old sayings. Do you want to let me know what your problem is? Because I can tell from the look on your face that you have a real dilemma going on inside that pretty head of yours."

"Oh, Nanny, I wouldn't know where to start, and if I did I can't imagine what you would think of me once I've told you, or how I could ever tell Wilf. He's been so kind to me, and I care for him so much."

"Well, my advice would be to start at the beginning. It's usually the best. And I'm sure you've done nothing that will make either Wilf or I think badly of you, my dear." Her kind open face made her so easy to talk to.

"Oh, where to start...."

For the next few minutes Ana-Maria outlined her life in Romania, describing how she had grown up as an orphan and been raised by her grandmother, after both her parents had died in an accident when she was only nine years of age. Her grandmother was not well off, and life had been tough for them, especially after all the troubles the country had gone through, and continues to face as a result of the wars and revolutions that had taken place. Born whilst the country was still ruled by communist dictators, Ana-Maria explained how she had lived through many political and economic changes, as politicians fought to establish a free market and a different country.

Ana-Maria was a bright girl, but not at all academic, and when she left school at sixteen she had few options for employment. Her qualifications did not entitle her to apply for further education and even if they had, she could not have afforded to continue studying. They lived on the outskirts of a city that was still struggling to rebuild itself and she needed to start earning money to help her grandmother, who by this stage was in her late-sixties and not in the best of health.

As Nanny listened, she sensed she was being told a version of the story that was not only true, but was very painful in the retelling. Some of the things she heard tallied with what Wilf had said over the years about his wife's background, others did not. Also, the way Ana-Maria told her story was almost detached, dispassionate even. It was as if she was talking about someone else's life, not her own. There was however no question over the tears in her eyes as she spoke, those were genuine. It was a story she had never expressed to anyone, least of all her husband, and as she spoke it felt good to be sharing it.

Sensing she had come to a difficult part, Nanny prompted. "So, what did you do once you left school?"

Ana-Maria took a long drink of her tea as she decided how to go on. "I'm ashamed to admit it, but I turned to prostitution. There's always a demand for that, isn't there?" Ana-Maria gave a nervous laugh as she said it, conscious that she had probably embarrassed the old lady. After all, sex was not a subject you just launched into in polite conversation.

"Oh, my dear, I am so sorry to hear that, or that you felt that was your only option."

"Well, it paid the bills, and although I didn't enjoy it, I was very good at it. It's illegal in Romania to sell sex, but I eventually managed to operate under the protection of a high-class agency, with the politicians and authorities largely turning a blind eye. After all, a lot of them were clients, so were protecting their own interests." Noticing Nanny was neither shocked nor judgemental gave Ana-Maria the confidence to continue. "Anyway, by the time I was in my twenties I had begun to earn serious money. I was what you would call a high-class hooker and could afford the finer things in life, including designer clothes and a stylish apartment in the city. I was a bit like a Romanian version of Julia Roberts in Pretty Woman, with some influential clients who liked to tip well if they got good service. By this time, I had moved out of my grandmother's home as she didn't like what I was doing, although it never stopped her from accepting the money I continued to send her each month to pay for her bills. She died just before I came to England."

"I'm sorry to hear that, my dear." Nanny patted her hand to show her continued support. "It sounds like you had quite a life over there, and a complete contrast to what you have here. What made you come over to England, if I might ask, because I'm sure Wilf said something about meeting you online?"

"Well, life was good up until a point, and then things changed. I had a new client that soon became a regular, who was rich and demanding and well connected. After a time, I tried to get out of seeing him, using various excuses that I was busy, or unavailable. Nevertheless, he always insisted it was me who he wanted and wouldn't take no for an answer. If I refused to see him, he started making my life difficult, started to demand that I was exclusively his. I even sensed I was being stalked when I was out, seeing faces in a crowd I knew worked for him. It made me feel uncomfortable, the thought of being watched, and if I am honest I felt unsafe. I needed to get away, so I started looking for a way to leave Romania. That's when I started to look online, and met Wilf. I really liked him and thought that we could build a new life together in England. Somewhere where I could be safe as well as happy."

"So, Wilf provided you with both a reason for moving and a chance for love, did he?"

Ana-Maria sensed Nanny did not believe the last part of her question. "If I am being completely honest, it was more the opportunity to leave the country that I most needed, and I needed it fast. Finding love was never my priority, whereas getting out of the country was."

"So why did you have to leave so fast? If you had money, a career and a nice home, what was so pressing, especially if Wilf was not the love of your life? Why did you commit to come to England and marry him, as you did, in such a hurry?"

Something was not adding up for Nanny. There was no doubting Ana-Maria was a very attractive young woman and the concept of her working as a prostitute was not something Nanny had struggled with at all. What she could not work out was why such a beautiful, young and independent woman, with financial security, who enjoyed the expensive and materialistic trappings life had offered her, would saddle herself to a widower. Why marry someone who was twenty plus years her senior, and then choose to hide away in a quite country idyll, acting as a housekeeper? No, there was at least one piece of the jigsaw that was still missing.

"Am I right in assuming you've never told Wilf your story, or the real reason you agreed to marry him, because from what you're telling me, love was clearly not your driver, was it? And, why tonight of all nights has this resurfaced, to the extent that you're visibly shaking as you're telling me your story? If this is all ancient history, what's happened that has suddenly brought this all into focus?" Nanny could tell by the look on Ana-Maria's face that she was starting to get to the crux of the real problem.

Taking a deep breath, Ana-Maria decided she had to continue. "Today one of my old clients was here, in this house, and I'm scared that he may have recognised me. He was with two other men, men who had been here for dinner as guests of Mr Paulson before his death. I think they had business with him. I remembered them from then, but I remembered the third man from back home."

"Surely, seeing an old client shouldn't have worried you that much, should it? And, if it was so long ago and out of context, I imagine he will have forgotten you anyway. I can't remember who I saw last week, never mind six years ago."

"He will remember me, I am sure. He will remember the look in my eyes as I saw him kill another man, with his bare hands, simply because that man would not do what he wanted. I witnessed a cold-blooded murder, and I don't want to wait around to see if he will come back again, to find me and finish me off, too."

"What do you mean, again? I thought you said this man had not been in the house before." Nanny was starting to get a little confused, with what Ana-Maria was saying starting to sound far-fetched.

"I'm not sure, but I don't think Mr Paulson was the intended victim that evening. I think the other two men told him I was here and he came looking for me; looking to shut me up so that I could not speak about what I had witnessed. I am not safe here and I know I have to leave."

As Nanny watched Ana-Maria's face as her story reached its conclusion, another piece of the jigsaw fell into place. Nanny was still not convinced she had heard everything that was worrying her friend, but at least she now had some understanding of the concerns Ana-Maria was facing.

Chapter 31

At half past five on Saturday morning, as the milkman was doing his usual rounds, delivering fresh milk and orange juice to the houses in Wilton Drive, he was surprised to see a young woman standing on the corner of the lane. She had a large bag in her hand and was wearing a dark jacket with her hood up. It was unusual to see people out and about this early, and as it was still slightly raining it was not even ideal weather to be going on an early morning dog walk, or a jog. Clearly, though, she neither had a dog with her, nor was dressed to go running, so that did not explain why she was out so early, or alone and standing on a corner with her bags packed. The early morning sunrise meant the light was clear enough through the drizzle for him to get a good look at her, and she was not someone he recognised from his early morning rounds. In his job he was used to bumping into the same people, or chatting to them when he collected his money at the end of the week. Having worked as the local milkman for over thirty years, he was proud to say there were few people that he did not recognise in Chidlington.

As he watched her, he could see she was looking around, and appeared to be quite anxious. In his view, he guessed she must be waiting for something or somebody. He resolved to say good morning as he passed her, and check she was okay, after he had walked down the driveway and delivered the two bottles of milk he was carrying to number 75. He did not want to go shouting in the street, certainly not at this time of the morning.

By the time he had delivered his milk, though, she had gone. He could just about see a car pulling away in the distance, driving in the direction of the dual carriageway. So, happily whistling away to himself as he walked on to his next delivery, he simply presumed her lift had arrived to collect her.

He thought nothing more of it until later that week, when he overheard a conversation between two of his customers about the housekeeper at the Old Manor House, and how she had absconded with the family silver in the middle of the night, after murdering his lordship!

As Ana-Maria got into the car and threw her bag onto the back seat, she leaned over to the man next to her and kissed him passionately. "Thank you for agreeing to pick me up, Carl. You don't know how much I appreciate it, or how much I needed that." She sighed, as she relaxed back into the seat.

"It's not a problem, but what on earth's the matter? I presume something's seriously wrong, otherwise you wouldn't be calling me in the middle of the night, would you? You nearly gave me a heart attack. I'd only arrived home a couple of hours earlier, so had just got off to sleep, when you messaged. I'm shattered, it was a long day yesterday, what with the funeral and then having to drive down to London to attend that meeting." A client had phoned at short notice and Carl could not get out of seeing him, or staying for dinner. At least at that time of the night the roads were quiet for his drive home.

"I'm sorry about that. I'll explain later, but just drive, please. I need to get away." Ana-Maria did not have time to listen to his woes today.

"Okay, but where to?" he asked, putting the car into gear.

Carl was just glad the garage had managed to repair the problems with his car. He had phoned them first thing on the

Monday morning, three weeks ago now, letting them know he'd had to abandon it at the Old Manor House on Saturday evening, after the party, as it would not start. He'd asked that as he had a business trip planned, could they recover it and do whatever was necessary whilst he was away. Until yesterday, he had been forced to rely on the train or taxis to get him around as the garage had struggled to get the part it needed to do the repair. At least he now had it back, with whatever the problem had been sorted.

"Do you want to come back to my place, and we can have some breakfast and you can tell me what's happened? Have you left Wilf, is that what this is all about?"

"No, I need to leave the area, possibly the country, so I can't go back to your house. Someone may see me there, or put two and two together about us, and then come looking for me. That's too dangerous." Ana-Maria knew Mrs Dent was one of Carl's neighbours and she was perfectly capable of joining the dots, once she learned Ana-Maria had left the Old Manor House, the news of which would probably spread around town at an alarming rate.

"Ana-Maria, you're scaring me now, what's happened? Has he hit you, or something?" Carl could hear the panic in her voice, leading him to believe it was something more serious than simply an argument with her husband, although as soon as he said that he knew it was not the case. Whilst he had never spoken to Wilf directly, he had seen him around town, and occasionally in the pub, and he did not look like the kind of man who would lay a hand on his wife. It was obvious from the way he behaved, whenever Carl had seen them out together, that he adored her, which did give Carl more than a twinge of guilt acting the way they were behind his back. He had been on the receiving end of a deception himself, so knew it was not pleasant and how painful it was for all concerned when things eventually came out into the open, as they invariably did. Carl consoled himself with the thought that he had never actively pursued Ana-Maria, or gone about to break up a happy relationship. They had simply met, been drawn together by fate and fallen in love, with the romantic in him believing they were destined to be together.

"No, it's nothing like that." Ana-Maria smiled over at him, trying to give him the reassurance he needed.

After she had finished talking to Nanny the previous evening she had gone back through to her lounge and found Wilf still sitting in his armchair, his newspaper open on his lap. He appeared to have nodded off in front of the television. The cup of tea Nanny had made him remained untouched on the coffee table beside him. So, she left him there and walked quietly into their bedroom, afraid to disturb him and face the need to explain herself. He would see that her eyes were red and blotchy through all the crying and would expect an explanation. Talking to Nanny had been quite emotional, bringing back a mix of happy and sad memories, and she did not have the energy to go through that again. She instinctively knew, though, that she had to get away and fast, although where she would go, or how she could achieve it, was still a mystery.

As she sat on her bed, pondering her future, her bag hastily packed at her feet, a text message came in from her lover, Carl. He was letting her know he'd been called down to London at short notice, so would be in touch in a couple of days, adding that he missed her and could not wait to see her again.

Carl had been overseas or away on business a lot in recent weeks and she had missed him too. Seeing him at the wake unexpectedly had made her realise just how much she had missed him, as well as their afternoon lovemaking sessions when she would sneak around to his house on her day off, on the pretext of going shopping or visiting a friend for coffee. A couple of hours of escapism, great sex and the simple feeling of being desired again had managed to keep her grounded these last few months. She knew Wilf loved her. Desire, though, was not a feeling he had ever expressed or acted upon, and he certainly did not have that effect on her. Meeting Carl and falling for his charms had shown her what her life was sorely missing.

Carl was sexy, his body providing her with what she craved. It was not just the sex, though, she enjoyed his company, his humour and the fact he had a wealth of experience of life. He had travelled extensively, with his work and for pleasure, and as far as she could tell had nothing, or importantly no one holding him back. He had never married, nor had children – just a cat, who was independent enough to sort itself out whenever he was not around. In her eyes he was perfect.

Over the last few months, as they had sneaked around enjoying a clandestine affair, she had grown to know him; his likes and dislikes, his interests and what his passions were, not only in the bedroom, but in life in general. He was open and did not appear to have a devious or malicious bone in him. Above all, he made her feel safe, as if she could really trust him.

Trust was a feeling she rarely felt, although as she had never told him her real story, the question of whether she could trust him with the unabridged version remained unanswered. She had preferred to stick to the same highlights she had told everyone over the years. It was less complicated that way. But, if they had any future, something she had started to hope would be the case, what option did she have, other than to be more open about herself?

Seeing a signpost to London on the dual carriage way, Ana-Maria suddenly had an idea. London was a city where she could easily lose herself, and it was also a city with major airports and connections should she need to get anywhere fast. She had her passport and her savings, so if she had to make a quick exit she was prepared. She had nothing to come back for, or anything tying her to Chidlington.

"Can we perhaps drive to a hotel and book in for the night? Preferably somewhere quiet, where they won't ask too many questions. After we've had a couple of hours sleep, I'll tell you what's going on, then hopefully you can help me decide what I need to do next."

Carl agreed to her plan and ten miles down the road pulled into a Travelodge. It was one of those places weary travellers stopped to break their journeys. It was also somewhere he could easily book a room, without the fear of unnecessary questions being asked. He was just thankful he'd had the foresight to pick up his wallet as he had left the house in such a hurry.

Carl realised he needed the sleep almost as much as he wanted an explanation. Having flown through the night from Dubai only three days earlier, and then having to hit the ground running so soon thereafter with another trip to London, he was exhausted and was struggling to keep his eyes open. He had only been away for three days, so it had not been a particularly gruelling trip, but that was the nature of the consultancy work he did. Regular travel, long-haul or short-haul, but most with hardly any notice.

Recently the increased frequency of his travelling and his need to be in London was playing havoc with his life, to say nothing of his duties as a local councillor. In terms of the council work, he was finding that it was all becoming too demanding, nowhere near as rewarding as he'd hoped. He wanted his life back, so had decided to step down from the council at the earliest opportunity. He had even mentioned it to a few people the night before Frank Paulson's death, at the drinks party. It had not gone down too well with some of the more established councillors, nor Frank himself for that matter who had made his feelings known on the matter.

When Wilf woke up later that morning, at seven o'clock to the sound of his alarm beeping, he found that his wife's side of the bed was already empty. He had eventually made his way to bed around midnight, having woken uncomfortably in his armchair, feeling a chill blowing in from the open window. Ana-Maria was already fast asleep, so they had not spoken. He had simply got in next to her, kissed her forehead and gone straight back to sleep.

Presuming she was already awake and in the kitchen preparing breakfast, he had no cause to worry. He simply got up, got dressed in his gardening clothes and made his way through to the kitchen. She was not there either. Again he was not unduly concerned as she could be anywhere in the house and it was not unusual for her to get up long before he did. Recently he had worried that she had not been sleeping at all well, but each time he asked he was told not to worry, she was fine.

As the housekeeper she had the full run of the property and after all the activity of the previous few days Wilf presumed there would be a million little jobs she needed to attend to around the place. She would be busy somewhere.

Wilf boiled the kettle to make himself a cup of tea and a flask for later, before popping two slices of bread into the toaster and taking the jam out of the fridge. He was not someone who enjoyed a huge breakfast. A pot of tea and some toast would suit him nicely, although a fry-up at the weekend was something he would never say no to.

Half an hour later he pulled on his wellies and put on his sun hat, and with his flask and newspaper tucked under his arm he made his way to the shed at the bottom of the garden.

It was his own little haven, where the lawnmower and other gardening tools were safely stored away.

It was a beautiful Saturday morning. The ground still looked damp from a bit of overnight rain, but the sun was shining and the prospect of a quiet day gardening appealed to him. Being indoors over the last two days, helping out with the preparations for the funeral and the wake, had been frustrating. He much preferred to be in the fresh air where he could happily lose himself among the hollyhocks and the rose beds, both of which were in full bloom at this time of year. And with his early start he would possibly have time to cut the lawn too, before Ana-Maria called him in for his lunch. It was usually a sandwich or some homemade soup, but whatever it was, after all his exertions it would be more than welcome.

Gardening and working outdoors was one of those pleasures Wilf had only experienced in later life, and the more he did it and learnt along the way, picking up tips and cuttings from whoever or wherever he could, the more he grew to love it. The Old Manor House had a beautifully established garden that needed maintenance rather than anything drastic, which suited Wilf perfectly. The peace and quiet, even the solitude, listening to the birds chirping away as he worked, or sat with his flask and newspaper on one of the old deckchairs he kept in his shed, was more than enough for him. And the bonus was that the exercise helped justify the couple of pints of beer he would be having later that evening. After all, gardening could be thirsty work.

By the time noon arrived, Wilf had started to feel weary. He had finished his flask of tea before ten-thirty, sitting for around thirty minutes to catch up on yesterday's newspaper, before resuming his work, weeding and pruning the roses. He had been too busy to read it the previous day, and when he had eventually sat down around teatime to catch up on the news, he had promptly fallen asleep. He needed to keep abreast of what had been happening in the world if he was planning on meeting his cronies at the pub later that evening, because no doubt their conversation would veer onto sport, or politics, or something else that had been newsworthy that week. He needed to have his opinions ready. And Saturday night was also dominoes night, so not one to be missed.

As he walked up the garden towards the house, his back was aching and his stomach was telling him it was time for lunch. He was surprised Ana-Maria had not called him in by now. Normally she would be popping in and out of the garden throughout the day, but he'd not had sight nor sound of her all morning. He had seen Nanny cross the courtyard from her annex to the kitchen earlier, and had heard Rosie drive away from the house an hour or so ago, with Richard in the passenger seat, laughing and joking about something. Other than that, it had been a very quiet morning. Just him, the birds and the gentle sound of his old transistor radio playing in the background.

"Ana-Maria, is lunch ready?" he asked as he stood in the doorway of the utility room, pulling off his muddy wellingtons. He would not dare to enter the main house until he had taken off his boots and washed his hands, removing any signs of his hard labours as the mud rinsed away down the plughole. Receiving no reply, he walked into the kitchen and asked again. "Ana-Maria, are you there?" His wife's chirpy response was nowhere to be heard.

Nanny had heard him coming back towards the house, the sound of his gait and his whistling an immediate give away. She pulled on her cardigan and made her way down her stairs and crossed the courtyard, towards the kitchen. She could see him wandering aimlessly around, clearly confused.

"Ah Nanny, have you seen Ana-Maria by any chance? I can't seem to find her anywhere, and I can't remember if she said she was going out today. It's Saturday, isn't it, not one of her usual days for shopping? I've looked all over and through the back, but she doesn't appear to be there. Her handbag's nowhere to be seen either, so she's probably out shopping after all. Unless she's gone for her hair done and I've forgotten. I'm just surprised she didn't say anything to me before she left. Do you have any idea where she might be, or what she could be doing?" Wilf's voice, although not panicked, was clearly concerned.

Having witnessed Ana-Maria leaving the house earlier that morning, carrying what appeared to be a large holdall stuffed with what she presumed to be her clothes and other possessions, Nanny could have said with certainty that her friend had not popped to the shops, or gone into town to have her hair done. And whilst she almost certainly suspected his wife had done a moonlight flit, she had no direct proof of that either. And even if she had, it was not her place to suggest it to Wilf, was it?

After their discussion the previous evening, Nanny had suspected Ana-Maria was planning to go on the run at some stage. When people got cornered or became worried, their bodies instinctively prepared for fight or flight, and the look in her eyes was a clear sign she was preparing for flight. Staying and fighting someone she perceived as a danger, for Ana-Maria that was clearly not an option. All the evidence, from what Nanny had seen this morning, supported that view. It had just happened sooner than she had thought.

"Why don't you message her, or perhaps give her a call and see what she says?" Nanny suggested in an attempt to be helpful. "There may be a simple explanation, something she told you that you have perhaps forgotten."

Nanny cared for Wilf and hated the thought of deceiving or misleading him. At the same time, it was not her story to tell. And as it was clear that Wilf was none the wiser to either his wife's background or her whereabouts, at least if Ana-Maria answered the call she could assure him she was safe. She may still not feel able to let him know why, or where she was running – or with whom, because she had clearly had an accomplice to help her with her runaway. That was the final piece of the jigsaw Nanny now had to turn her mind to solving; with whom had she run away?

Although, if the casual glances she'd witnessed at the wake, being exchanged between her friend and the man she now recognised as Carl Gilbert, were any indication, then she may not have to look too far to find her answer.

Chapter 32

On Monday lunchtime, a couple of days after Ana-Maria's disappearance, a phone call was received at the police station, alerting them to the fact that Mrs Cuthbert, Mr Paulson's housekeeper, had gone missing. The young female desk officer, PC Jane Wilson, answered the call and after attempting to take some basic details, tried to reassure the caller that as the missing woman was an adult and not someone who was considered vulnerable in any way, or to their knowledge had committed any crime, then as far as they were concerned it was not a police matter. She would come back, or not, in her own time, Jane had said, adding that if she had left by her own accord, which by the sound of it she had, there was nothing that the police could do anyway.

The caller, a woman who the officer later described as well-spoken and sounded to be in her mid to late thirties, would not provide her name. She was agitated by the response she received, so went on to say that she believed the woman had possibly fled the country, potentially taking with her some valuables from the Old Manor House. Items she had allegedly stolen. And, most importantly, she could be a key witness in the death of Mr Frank Paulson. At which point, the desk officer asked the caller to hold whilst she called her sergeant. She knew DS Jacobs was working on the case of Mr Paulson's death, along with her colleague, PC Dickson, so presumed they may be interested in what the mystery lady had to say.

"Ma'am, I have a lady on the phone who won't provide her name, but says she has some information relating to the death of Mr Paulson. I'm not sure exactly what she is calling to tell us, as she originally called in to report a missing woman, before suggesting the two incidents were connected in some way. Would you like to talk to her, or should I pass the call onto PC Dickson? He's in today and is sitting at his desk."

"I'm a bit busy at the moment Jane, so yes perhaps if you can see if Neil's free to talk to her, that would be good."

Ruth had a hundred and one other things to do, and going back over Frank Paulson's death again was not one of them. Whilst the coroner had ruled the death as unexplained, to Ruth it still felt suspicious. However, no matter which angle she and her colleagues worked, there was no evidence whatsoever to support a murder, or even a manslaughter having been committed. And there was certainly no evidence of a murder weapon. Ruth had almost got to the point where she was ready to close the case, knowing every avenue they had followed until then had led them to a dead end, and with no new leads she was fast running out of ideas.

As PC Jane Wilson was walking out of Ruth's office, the DS looked up and turned to her. "Before you go, Jane, did she sound like a crank to you, or someone who was credible? The more I think about it, for someone not to want to provide their name sounds suspiciously like they're trying to cause trouble. If it was a serious missing person report, you'd think they'd be keen to provide whatever information we needed, wouldn't you?"

"Yes, Ma'am. She didn't sound like a crank, though. She sounded quite well spoken, mid-thirties I'd say and local if her accent is anything to go by. Although I don't think she has any relationship with the missing woman as she struggled to provide any real detail about her. When I asked about her age, height, weight, what she might have been wearing, you know all the standard stuff, she drew a blank."

"Yes, Jane. I know what you mean and that does sound strange. Perhaps I will have a talk to her after all. Why don't you patch the call through and ask Neil to join me, if he's not too busy? It'll do him good to listen in."

Half an hour later, Ruth and Neil were still sitting around Ruth's desk, reflecting on what they had just heard. They were both staring into space, drinking their afternoon cups of coffee and trying to make sense of it all over a packet of chocolate digestives. What Miranda had alleged all sounded a little weird and farfetched, but it was not beyond the realms of possibility if they were honest. Something sounded distinctly odd.

"I still can't work out why it was Miss Swann who reported the housekeeper missing, and not her husband, or one of the family? That sounds strange, doesn't it? And why was she so reluctant to tell us who she was? She must have known that it wouldn't take a rocket scientist to work it out, once we'd heard her voice. She must think we're stupid." Ruth laughed at the absurdity of Miranda putting on a posh voice in an attempt to disguise her identity, as she brushed biscuit crumbs away. "What was she trying to achieve?"

"Yes, it was quite bizarre, Sarg. When we spoke to her after the incident, she didn't appear to me to be a woman who'd play games, especially not if they were connected with her fiancé's death." Neil had taken notes throughout the call, trying to make sense of what Miss Swann was saying. "I got the feeling, though, without having anything concrete on which to base her assertions, she probably did not want to identify herself as the one making the accusations. She couldn't even list what items were supposedly missing, or how she believed Mrs Cuthbert was connected with the death of her fiancé, which added no credence to her story whatsoever."

"But again, why didn't Mr Cuthbert report her missing, if he was concerned about her whereabouts? He would surely have got in touch with us himself if he was worried, wouldn't he? If there were questions about her disappearance, why was it not him asking them? That's the bit that's baffling me." Ruth continued staring out of the window, chewing the end of her pencil, a habit she had got into in lieu of being able to have a cigarette in the office.

"Perhaps. Although, if Mr Cuthbert suspects what Miss Swann is alleging might be true, he might not want to drop his wife in it. Or, he might know where she is and be in on it with her. He might be off next to join her, wherever it is she's gone. They did appear to be a very odd couple to me, if you don't mind me saying, Sarg."

Neil remembered how he had found the Romanian housekeeper extremely attractive. There had been something about her eyes that he had been enchanted by, which he had to admit had left him quite distracted when he took her statement. As he had listened to her unusual accent, and watched her pretty lips moving, all he could think was why she was married to such an older man. For the life of him he could not work it out. Her husband appeared nice enough, but rather plain and far too old for her. What a waste, in Neil's view.

Had Neil perhaps missed something when he'd spoken to her, overlooked a clue as he'd allowed himself to be beguiled by her? Looking back at his note book now, he searched through it for a record of her interview, desperate to confirm the facts he had recorded, also wanting to confirm there was nothing that he had neglected to take into consideration.

"Well, I suggest you get yourself over to the Old Manor House tomorrow and ask around a bit more. See if her husband can shed any light on where she's gone, or give you any more details that might help in finding her, assuming he wants her back, that is. It might also be worth checking whether she has left the country, as Miss Swann suggests. Try to find out if she took her passport with her, or what else might be missing, assuming she may have stolen some trinkets on her way out. I'm sure there's plenty of takings in that place."

"Yes, Sarg."

Ruth continued to mull it all over, trying to justify the actions she was asking Neil to take. His overtime levels were already higher than she liked, so asking him to spend even more time on this would do nothing to ease the pressure on her budget. However, Miranda's words had left a niggle, an itch that needed to be scratched.

"I suppose there's no harm in doing some digging to see whether she's a missing person, or not, is there? Or whether there's any truth in her hightailing it with the silver? The family can help with that. I just can't see any link to Frank Paulson's death, though, can you? Or if there is, why it's taken her over three weeks to scarper? If she was guilty, wouldn't she have run sooner? And if she had in any way been involved, what on earth would her motive be? She didn't stand to gain in any way by his death, did she?"

"No, Sarg, not as I recall." Neil had managed to eat six biscuits already and was contemplating whether to call it a day or sneak in another before he left. He was taking his grandma out for a birthday tea later than afternoon so needed to watch his appetite. "I'll drive over there first thing in the morning, unless you need me to go now? It's just my shift finished ten minutes ago, and I've made plans that I can't get out of."

"No, tomorrow morning's soon enough, just report back if you find out anything interesting." Ruth was sure it was not serious enough to warrant his plans being changed. "Thanks Neil, go and enjoy the rest of your day off."

Looking at her watch, Ruth thought what she would do with an afternoon off. Probably just crawl back into bed and get some sleep. "The demands of being the full-time working mum of a cranky toddler are certainly taking their toll," she thought to herself, as she reached for her now cold cup of coffee and the almost empty packet of biscuits.

Chapter 33

As PC Dickson pulled his car into the gravel driveway of the Old Manor House, around ten o'clock the following morning, he parked directly outside the front door. The house looked quiet and there were no other cars around, or lights on inside the building. Given it was a mid-week morning, it was perhaps not surprising there appeared to be no one at home.

"Maybe I should have rung first to let them know I was calling," he thought to himself after he had rung the bell several times without getting any response. He knew both Mr Paulson's youngest son, Richard, and Rosie the youngest daughter stilled lived at home. As presumably did Miss Swann, given she had made the call to the station alerting them of the housekeeper's disappearance. In terms of anyone else, he was unsure. He hoped Mr Cuthbert was still around, but whether the old lady who had greeted them the first time they arrived, and said she was the nanny, was still living there, he was not certain.

Neil decided to walk around to the back of the property to explore, and as he rounded the side of the house he could see the old lady descending the stairs from the annex above the garage, carrying her handbag and a lightweight jacket over her arm. He considered turning around before she saw him. The thought of being propositioned by her again, without his colleague next to him for protection, was a little scary. He could not quite remember her name, all he could think of was Miss Marple, the name with which Ruth had christened her when she had described her as an interfering old busy body, or words to that effect. Rightly or wrongly they had not gone out of their way to engage her in conversation since; Ruth arguing life was too short. Perhaps, though, she might have seen something, Neil wondered to himself as he steeled himself to ask her.

"Good morning." He spoke in a relatively loud voice so as not to startle her. He also recalled she had poor hearing, so felt it appropriate to speak up.

"Oh, good morning, Officer. How nice to see you again and what a beautiful morning it is. I was only thinking when I looked out of my window earlier that it was going to be a lovely day, and now to have a visitor on top of that, how exciting. I was just planning on having a walk into town for something to do and a little company. There's always someone to chat to when you're walking around the shops or stopping for a cup of coffee, I find. A time to catch up on the gossip and see what's been happening around the place. It can get quite lonely up here at the Old Manor House sometimes, you know, living all by myself. Especially now that all the children have grown up. They don't need me like they used to. They still come to visit and bring their little ones, but it's not the same." She gave a wistful glance towards the house, and Neil could see small tears forming in her eyes as she spoke.

"It was completely different when they were all youngsters, running around the house or playing in the garden. All their noise and fun kept me feeling young and gave me a purpose in life. I don't have that anymore, and I really miss those old days. Lady Susan and I would be run off our feet with four little ones to care for, but I wouldn't change a thing. I used to love our times together and am just glad Richard and Rosie are still here to keep me company."

Neil began to wonder whether she would ever take a breath, or come up for air. He began to understand what Ruth had meant.

"Now, young man, can I perhaps invite you to come inside and I'll make you a nice cup of tea? I'll see if there's any cake left, or at least try to find a biscuit I can offer you. I'm not sure what's left in the cupboards as the housekeeper has had to go away suddenly and I don't think she's done an awful lot of shopping recently. I have suggested to Wilf that we should consider doing one of those online shops, you know where they deliver your groceries to your door, as neither of us has a car and it's a lot to carry back from the supermarket, especially the big or heavy items. He agrees it's a good idea, but he doesn't know how to go about it either, so we'll have to think of another way around it, won't we? Although, thinking about it, I'm sure Richard or Rosie will know what to do, if I ask them nicely. They were such lovely children and have grown into such beautiful young people. I have to say, I'm proud of all of my children and have a special place in my heart for them. It was such a shame when they lost their mother at such a young age, so awful. To think, all she did was go out for a meal and never came back. It was a tragic accident. For them to grow up as they have, she would have been so proud. Now, what do you say to that nice cup of tea?" The expectant smile on her face seemed to leave Neil with little option, other than to accept.

"Thank you. I would also like to talk to Mr Cuthbert, if he's at home, and Miss Swann too, if she's around."

"I'm not sure about her, but I think I saw Wilf earlier going down to his potting shed." The way she said *her* made it clear to Neil what she thought about Miss Swann. "It's where he spends most of his time in the spring and summer months, or whenever the weather's fine, to be honest. He loves to garden and keeps everywhere looking lovely, so well maintained. I find the flowers are pretty at this time of year too, and they attract all manner of bees and butterflies into the garden, which is a bonus as we do have to help the environment, don't we? Although I have to admit to keeping my windows closed most days to stop them getting into the annex. I wouldn't want a wasp buzzing around in there and stinging me, would I? No, for someone who's not had any formal training to be a gardener, I think Wilf does a marvellous job, don't you?" she asked rhetorically, not waiting for an answer.

"Between you and me, I think he also loves to sit and listen to his radio, or read his newspaper and enjoy a bit of peace and quiet by himself. Not that it's particularly noisy around the house anymore, but I think he still prefers his solitude, like most men, I imagine. Richard is the same. He tends to sit in his bedroom most of the day, if he's not out at work, that is. He has himself wired up to his computer with his earphones in, listing to music, or whatever else it is he does on that computer. I can't say I understand them at all, technology is not my thing. He's a very bright boy, though, very intelligent. I imagine he inherited that from his mother, as she was always very sharp. Such a sad loss.

"Anyway, I get the sense he's not too bothered about getting a job. He's enjoying his life too much, without the worry of having to work for a living, although once the house is sold, presuming they decide to sell it, that is, then that will be another thing. He might need a job then to pay his rent or to get a mortgage, might he? Because as we all know, the shambles his father left his estate in is not going to keep the children in the lifestyle they're used to. No, the children have got a right job on their hands to sort it all out and I really don't envy them that, do you? Mr Mears, the solicitor, is going to help them, although what he can do I don't rightly know. He's always struck me as a bit of a cold fish, quite standoffish.

"Anyway, Jimmy, that's Frank's eldest, and his friend Simon, you remember him, the one who's married to Judy? Well, the two of them are trying to sort the business out. I can't imagine what state that's in, as there are rumours that there are debts left, right and centre, and they will all need paying once the house is sold, won't they? I do feel for all those people who have bought houses from the business and might not now get them finished on time. As I said, Richard is bright and I'm sure he and the others are applying some thought to that too, because they won't want to let people down, will they? People are already talking about the family and they don't want to do anything to make that worse. Although having Miss Swann still living here isn't making that any easier, is it?" Neil managed to shake his head, in an attempt to show he was following.

"She's a proper madam, that one. I don't imagine any of the children are disappointed that she didn't succeed in marrying their father. I think they'll all be pleased to see the back of her, once they can decide how to get her out of the house, that is. I suppose being pregnant isn't helping, though, is it? They'll presumably not want to throw her out if she's carrying their father's child, will they? Although, there's a question hanging over that too, isn't there? I wouldn't want to be accused of being someone who spreads gossip, but there is talk around town that she's been carrying on with another man, which surely raises the question of whose child it is, doesn't it? She's probably upstairs now, locked away in her bedroom, where she appears to be spending most of her time these days. I'm not sure if she's moping or scheming up there, but I'd bet she's not mourning her fiancé's loss, as much perhaps as the loss of his money. I bet she'd had her sights well and truly set on living it up at the Old Manor House for a good few more years, before inheriting the whole lot when Frank eventually died. Although thinking about it, that pre-nuptial agreement she apparently signed probably put paid to that. It's funny how things turn out, isn't it? One minute, she's lording it over the family, the next she's hiding away from them, fearful of when her number's up and they show her the door."

Before Neil could interrupt, she continued. "She wasn't at all happy yesterday by all accounts, when that fancy sports car of hers had to be handed back. According to Richard, Jimmy cancelled the lease and asked the garage to collect the car. She was fuming, he said, her language not at all ladylike as she was forced to hand over the keys. In fact, I think she threw them at the poor man from the garage who'd been sent to collect it. It did give Wilf and I something to smile about after the earlier events of the day, because if you're not aware yet, his wife has left him and he's not feeling himself, which is understandable under the circumstances, don't you think? No one wants to be left by themselves, do they?"

Sensing she had finally run out of steam, Neil seized his opportunity and aimed to get a word in quickly before she started up again.

"Actually, that's why I'm here, and why I would like to speak to both Mr Cuthbert and Miss Swann, if they're around. I did try ringing the front door bell earlier, but nobody answered."

"Oh, you should have said sooner, dear. No, I imagine neither Richard nor Miss Swann would have heard you if they're both upstairs. I can't hear the bell myself either, unless I'm in the main house and I haven't got the radio switched on. And Wilf, when he's at the other end of the garden stands no chance at all, does he?"

"No, I imagine not," was the best Neil could offer after the barrage of questions he had just had hurled at him.

"Why don't you come on in and I'll put that kettle on, like I said earlier, and then I'll go and see if I can find either of them for you. Now, is it milk and sugar or just milk? I can't remember what you said the last time you were here. It was such a confused sort of day, wasn't it? If I'm honest, I'm not sure everything's settled back down yet, but it will do, I'm sure. Why don't you sit yourself down and have a little rest and I'll be back in a minute or two to finish off your tea. I'll hopefully have Wilf in tow, especially if I promise him a biscuit, or a slice of cake to go with his drink. Although I should probably check what there is in the pantry before I go. I know how partial Wilf is to his lemon drizzle cake, and he'll be disappointed if I suggest that and then there's none left. Does that sound like a plan?"

"Thank you. That would be lovely, you're most kind."

"Oh, what lovely manners you have. I noticed that the first time I met you, and such a handsome face too. I bet you can charm the ladies, can't you?" Neil blushed as she walked off into the pantry, acknowledging at the same time he was not going anywhere for quite some time. He felt like prey, trapped in the spider's web she had spun to entice him, or an insect caught by a Venus fly trap, powerless to fight its way out.

And for someone who said she did not engage in gossip, she had certainly given an epic one-woman monologue that put paid to that argument. Neil only wished he'd had his notebook open to record some of the things she had said, admitting to feeling impressed by how she had managed to cover so much ground, without hardly taking breath. She was certainly living up to the Miss Marple characterisation Ruth had given her, her nose clearly in everyone's business. He only hoped that some of the gems she had thrown his way would help him to solve the conundrums the police were grappling with. For not only did they still not know what had happened to Mr Paulson, they also now knew Mrs Cuthbert was confirmed to be on the missing list, and with a query still hanging over her disappearance and whether there was any connection between that and the death, any further questions he may have for both his star witnesses, could prove to be vital.

Two hours later, Neil walked back into the police station feeling exhausted and looking completely drained. He was a young fit man, but the morning's activities had certainly taken their toll on him. He flopped down into his chair, desperate for a strong coffee and a chance to review his notebook.

Earlier he had spoken to Wilf, who simply confirmed he had woken up on Saturday morning, as usual, and gone straight out to the garden to get on with his work. He admitted it was not until later that afternoon that he suspected his wife was not around, when he returned for his lunch and his soup was not ready. While he spoke, Nanny had remained sitting next to him at the kitchen table, gently patting his hand to provide him with the reassurance he needed.

"I suggested he should phone Ana-Maria and ask her where she was, which he did. The call went to voicemail, didn't it, Wilf?" she chipped in, presumably feeling a little left out that no one was asking her any questions.

"Yes, that's right, Nanny. I left her a message, but I'm not good at those types of things, so I just asked her to phone me, and I'm still waiting to hear from her."

Neil had tried to conduct the interview without Nanny in the room, assuming she would head straight off into town as she had earlier planned, once she had tracked down the people to whom he needed to speak. He had failed miserably, though, with Wilf arguing it would be good for her to sit in, especially as she had been there to help him at the time he discovered Ana-Maria was missing. As the man already looked distraught, Neil did not have the heart to say no.

"And may I ask, why didn't you contact the police yourself? Especially if you thought there was something suspicious by her leaving as she did. I presume she was not in the habit of going off by herself, especially not at that time of the morning?"

"I can help with that, Officer," Nanny chipped in again. "It dawned on me later that I'd seen a car pull up outside the gates, at the end of the lane, earlier that morning. I can just about see it from my kitchen window. I wasn't sure if it was a taxi, or a car, as it wasn't a car I recognised. Anyway, when I told Wilf, he said that if Ana-Maria had chosen to leave him, then she was entitled to do that, didn't you, Wilf? You said she was free to go."

"Yes, I'm surprised she's stayed as long as she has, if I'm honest. I was punching well above my weight, as you youngsters like to say." He smiled across at Neil as he said it, his smile forced. "And as she's been muttering about leaving for the last couple of months or so, I simply presumed she'd decided to go, especially when I saw her handbag and some of her clothes had gone too. She'd been talking about finding somewhere else to live and possibly getting a new job, even saying she didn't feel safe here any longer. But I like it here and have no desire to move. After Mr Paulson's death, I suppose she got more edgy, so in truth I wasn't surprised. That's why I didn't bother reporting it, Officer, I didn't find it particularly suspicious."

"You just said, she didn't feel safe. What did you mean by that, Mr Cuthbert?"

"Not sure, it was her words, not mine. And no matter how many times I asked her to explain, she couldn't or wouldn't, so I don't know." At this stage, as the police officer had directed his question directly at Wilf, Nanny Tilbury decided to keep quiet. After all, it was not her story to tell, and whilst her input might have helped clarify the situation, she did not want Wilf to be any more upset than was necessary.

Later Neil spoke to Miss Swann, who appeared equally distraught, although not necessarily about Mrs Cuthbert's departure. She had been more concerned about sorting through her wardrobe, wondering what she could possibly sell if she was forced to raise some money quickly. There were a couple of designer dresses and an expensive leather jacket she had earmarked, even two pairs of Christian Louboutin stilettoes, shoes she could not begin to imagine she would wear again, especially not pushing a pram around town.

When Neil started questioning her and scratched beneath the surface, he found her accusations were completely unfounded. She had no evidence to support anything going missing or being stolen, or had any real connection with the disappearance being related to her fiancé's death. All she could say was that the housekeeper's bedroom was nearest to the kitchen, so there was no way she did not know what had happened.

"The police need to find her and make her answer some questions." It all sounded pretty lame, reminding Neil of Ruth's initial concern that she was probably some sort of crank, wasting police time.

Finally he spoke to Richard, who had been in his room, dusting off his CV, at the time Nanny knocked on his door. She asked if he could spare a few moments to talk to the nice policeman who was waiting downstairs. Neil almost cringed at the foot of the stairs, as he heard her say this.

Richard, of them all, appeared the least concerned by the whole state of affairs and could not understand what the fuss was all about. He had no idea what had happened, or if anything was missing, and he certainly did not suspect the housekeeper of stealing, or being a thief. He quite liked her and admitted to the fact he would miss her around the place, especially her cooking. Other than that, he wished her well, wherever she may have gone, or with whomever. He was convinced she had finally run off with some younger chap, and although he did not voice that opinion aloud, Neil sensed exactly where he was coming from.

Richard then put his earphones in and went back upstairs to his room to finish off updating his CV. He had decided the time was right to start looking for something useful to do with his life and just needed the space to focus on it.

He asked Nanny to see the officer out.

"Of course, my dear," she had replied, smiling over at him mischievously. "In fact, do you think that if I ask him nicely, he'll give me a lift into town, on his way back to the station? After all, it is his questions that have delayed me this morning."

"So, Sarg, I don't see what any of this has got to do with Mr Paulson's death, do you?" Neil had finally summoned up the energy to go in and debrief his DS before the end of his shift. "I don't think it's a missing person situation and I don't think there's any evidence to suggest a theft has taken place either."

"What's your take on the point about her safety, that she'd told her husband that she didn't feel safe. That sounds strange, doesn't it?"

"It does, but I've nothing else to base it on. The husband wasn't giving anything away and for once Miss Marple appeared to have nothing to add." He rolled his eyes as he said this. Feeling pressured to give her a lift into town, and being forced to listen to even more of her stories of the children growing up, had been the final straw.

"Yes, you're probably right, Neil. It doesn't sound like I could justify launching a full-scale man hunt, even if I had the budget, or issue a missing from home report on the back of a hunch. Especially when the hunch doesn't even constitute a formal complaint. If the husband was worried about her going missing, surely he'd have said something, or asked us to look into it? But as he hasn't put in any type of complaint or report, I don't see what we can do."

"No, Sarg, me neither. In my view, for what it's worth, I think she's probably done a runner with another fella. They were the oddest of couples after all. I even think the husband believes she's run off with another man, and doesn't blame her. He didn't appear at all fazed when the old woman mentioned she'd seen a car picking her up at the end of the lane, around six o'clock that morning. I also suspect the son, Richard, does too. Although, as it stands no one has any idea who the mystery man might be, assuming he exists."

"Well, it wouldn't be the first time, would it?" Ruth added philosophically. The whole day had proven to be a bit of a damp squib by the sounds of PC Dickson's debrief. One moment they thought they had a plausible lead, even a potential suspect. The next they had nothing. That was police work for you, frustrating.

"Let's ask around and see what, if anything, turns up. Run her details through the system, but otherwise don't waste too much time on it. I'm sure there's plenty more for you to be getting on with."

"Yes, Sarg."

Neil hated the thought that he had not got to the bottom of the case. He'd harboured thoughts of getting all the suspects in a room and doing the big reveal as to 'who'd done it', like they did at the end of every episode of Death in Paradise. How they worked out some of the most obscure crimes always baffled him, but the devil was always in the detail. Yet here they neither had credible suspects nor details to follow. Every lead led to a dead end, and every suspect had a great alibi. What were they missing?

Chapter 34

It was Wednesday evening and the family was once again gathered at the Old Manor House, their agenda principally to decide what to do about Miranda, now that the funeral was behind them. They had various wheels in motion in terms of sorting out their father's financial affairs and had got into the habit of meeting up frequently to plan their next moves. Although none of them was outwardly grieving, they did find their times together quite cathartic. Time to reflect and discuss what they wanted for their lives and the legacy their father had left them. They had decided on the key tasks that needed attending to and for the time being they were slowly working their way through the list.

The house was of principal concern. Even if they had wanted to keep it, they could not afford to, nor could they justify the running costs when it was just Rosie and Richard living there. No one wanted to see them without their home, but what alternative did they have? Miranda would have to be asked to move out. Where she went was of little concern, but they had agreed that as soon as the funeral was over they would address it. Wilf would also have to be given his notice, although technically it was not him that was in their employ. Mrs Cuthbert had been the housekeeper, Wilf largely pottered around and lived rent free at the manor.

What really tore at their heartstrings, though, was Nanny Tilbury. If the house was sold, they could hardly offer her up as a sitting tenant. But where would she go? To their knowledge she had no other family or close friends. They were her family. Offering her the vacant cottage on the farmland was an option, although whether that could be made to work was debateable. It would need a considerable amount of money spending on it to make it habitable, and money was something they did not have.

Judy had contacted a couple of local estate agents, with a view to getting the Old Manor House valued and on the market as soon as possible. At the same time James and Simon were beavering away at the building site, trying to get to grips with a business they had worked in for years, but were finding they barely knew the workings of. With Frank out of the way they were faced with a new set of challenges, challenges that saw them walking a fine line between keeping the business operational or closing the doors for good. Some of their suppliers were proving supportive and were happy to give the men more time to sort themselves out, others were being less so. It was taking all James' and Simon's efforts to either win them round, or find alternatives that would enable the business to keep going.

Mr Mears had put them in touch with a good business and financial advisor, someone who would understand the numbers and work with them to assess the contracts they had, as well as advising where they stood as a result of them. The process was already showing where the challenges existed, and at the same time it was identifying opportunities that could be taken, if they were of a mind to take a risk.

Frank, whilst believing himself to be an astute business man, had never been particularly progressive in his methods, and modernisation of his office or business systems had never been critical to his operations. The analyst was quick to identify techniques and processes that could easily be improved and with some proper structuring, and the bank's support, he believed the finances could be made to work. In fact, some of the so-called debts had disappeared with Frank, along with some of the more dubious accounting practices he had employed. The situation, thankfully, was nowhere near as bad as they had previously feared.

Richard was playing his part too, working with Mr Mears on the matter of probate. After all, nothing could really be finalised until that had been sorted. He had begun the process of cataloguing assets and arranging valuations for some of the items in the house. Judy reminded him their grandparents had collected several antiques and other items of value over the years, so Richard was given the task of determining what these were, and getting them valued accordingly. So far he was struggling.

Rosie was the last to join them, having called and collected pizzas for everyone on the way home. After the events of the last few days no one felt like going out to eat, or could be bothered to cook, arguing they could just as easily talk over a pizza and a bottle of wine in the privacy of their home than go to the pub and risk being overheard. Gossip was already rife about their family and they did not want to fuel that any further.

Miranda had thankfully gone out, a taxi arriving a few minutes earlier, with the front door slammed behind her a clear indication she had left the building. Where she had gone, or with whom, no one knew, or cared. It was clear she was still furious with James for cancelling the car lease, and having to give it up the day before had almost been the last straw. Her language, as she flung the keys back to the man from the garage, was not at all ladylike or becoming for a woman in her position.

Nevertheless, she was out, which meant they had the house to themselves, apart from Nanny Tilbury and Wilf, who were no doubt watching television together or tucked away in the private sitting room in the housekeeper's apartment. Since Mrs Cuthbert's departure it had been noted that the two of them had gravitated towards each other for companionship, and there was certainly no harm or gossip in that.

"So, what have I missed and what's left on the agenda?" Rosie handed round the pizzas whilst Richard topped up the ladies' wine glasses and got himself another beer from the fridge. Simon and James were both driving, so had passed on the offer of a top up.

"Well, we still need to decide about Miranda and how we approach the topic of her moving out." Richard managed to say, between mouthfuls of pizza. "I don't know if we're drawing straws, in terms of who's going to be the lucky one to tell her, but after yesterday's fiasco with the car then I'm not stepping forward, not without full body armour!"

"I'm not scared of her. In fact, I'd love to be the one to tell her. I'd also love to hear her explanation of who it was she was seeing in Oxford last week, because it sure looked pretty cosy to me."

"What do you mean, Rosie?" Judy knew they all had their suspicions about Miranda, but so far there had been no actual proof of anything going on. "What did you see?"

"I saw her kissing a guy and they didn't look like they were strangers. He was fit, about her age, I'd say, and was quite tall and good looking. Not anyone I know, although come to think of it, it could have been one of those guys she invited to the pre-wedding party. Some of them were quite good looking, weren't they? Anyway, they were outside the café, the one opposite the bookshop. I saw them when I was collecting Richard's books. It looked like they'd just been in there, as they kissed in the doorway, then each went their separate ways. I'd have followed her if I hadn't had to collect Richard's books."

"That's interesting. I wonder what else she was up to in Oxford?" Richard was intrigued. He had seen her leaving the house early one morning last week. She had not taken the car, which had got him wondering where she was going. She rarely walked anywhere.

"I don't know. I do know, though, that the way he touched her stomach left me in no doubt that he knew she was pregnant. And I wouldn't be at all surprised if he's not the child's father. I think I'm going to ask her to get a DNA test, what do you think?"

"Wow, hold on there, Rosie. That's a bit extreme, don't you think?"

"Actually, Jimmy, it's not. I tend to agree with Rosie, and if the gossips around the hairdressers are to be believed, I'd say it's pretty common knowledge that she's been messing around with her Pilates instructor for some time now. I've heard rumours circulating for a while, and even saw her myself driving through town with him a long time ago, before your dad died. I think his name might be Leo, the way some of them go on about him being the fit, good-looking one." Katie rarely liked to engage in, or repeat, gossip. Where the family was concerned she generally made an exception.

"Leo, is it? God, she's a lucky bugger, I wouldn't mind being under that star sign," Rosie muttered under her breath, unsure whether her comment had been overheard or not. The thought of a private Pilates session of her own suddenly had quite an appeal. Although the thought of second-hand goods, after Miranda's hands had been all over him, soon brought her back to her senses.

"Knock, knock, do you mind if I come in for a minute?" The door opened slightly and Nanny Tilbury could be seen peeping around it. She had been hovering outside the room long enough to overhear the name Leo used in connection with Miranda, and cast her mind back to a late-night phone call she had overheard some weeks earlier. At the time she could not piece together who he was, so to hear them now mentioning he was the Pilates teacher it suddenly made sense. It also went some way to explaining Miranda's ideas of converting her annex into an exercise studio, for private tuition. Something else she had overheard Frank and Miranda arguing about. Well, at least that had been avoided. Nanny was just glad the little mystery had now been solved as she hated loose ends. And by the sounds of Rosie's suggestion, to ask Miranda to do a DNA test, so had the others.

"I don't want to disturb you, dears. I would like to talk to you all, though, while you're together."

"Come on in, Nanny. Do you want a slice of pizza?" Richard offered her the box with the last remaining piece. He'd had his eye on it for a while now.

"Thank you, dear, but Wilf and I have already eaten. We had a lovely piece of steak for our dinner, with some fresh vegetables from the market and a fresh fruit tart for dessert."

"Oh, I miss your cooking, Nanny. I used to love Sunday lunches best. Your huge roast dinners, with all the trimmings." Richard could almost feel his mouth salivating at the thought of her Yorkshire puddings and rich juicy gravy.

"Me, too. I especially loved your jam roly-poly and custard for pudding," Rosie said.

"That's very kind of you all. It was a pleasure cooking for you. You always had such healthy appetites, and there was hardly anything ever wasted. Especially not on your plate, Richard. How about I cook us all a farewell lunch, for old times' sake, this Sunday if you're all free? You can bring the children over. It will be lovely to say good-bye to them too."

"Farewell, what do you mean, Nanny?" Judy was confused. This was the first time she had heard that Nanny was planning to leave, and by the others' reaction it was news to them too.

"That's what I wanted to talk to you all about, love. I've decided it's time for me to move on. You don't need me anymore, and with the house up for sale it's only a matter of time before I would need to leave anyway. In fact, Wilf and I have decided we're going to leave together. We've been talking about it these last few days and we've found a nice little cottage to rent. Somewhere quiet. Now that Mrs Cuthbert has left, he's at a loose end too, and we find we enjoy each other's company. It's nice to have the companionship on an evening." She smiled over at them as they digested the information. "Anyway, I don't have a lot to take, so I'll arrange to rent a small transit van on Monday to take our things. Wilf says he's happy to drive it to the cottage if needs be, so we'll be no trouble."

"Oh, Nanny, what will we do without you? It will be the end of an era." Judy was almost in tears.

"You'll all be fine. You have dealt with your father's death admirably, and if nothing else it's brought you all a lot closer. I'm very proud of you, and it's clear you don't need me around to protect you anymore. So, Sunday lunch it is. A full roast dinner with jam roly-poly and custard for pudding."

And with that, she left the room, leaving then to wonder what had just hit them.

Chapter 35

The following morning as Rosie was standing at the top of the stairs, just about to go down to get her things before heading out to work, she heard the front door open and a car driving off, its wheels crunching on the gravel driveway. She waited and watched as Miranda almost crept across the hallway towards the bottom of the stairs, careful not to make any sound or draw attention to herself.

It was just before ten o'clock, and unless Rosie was mistaken it looked decidedly like Miranda had been out all evening. She was dressed in the same clothes Rosie had seen her leave in the previous evening, and her hair was not styled the way it had been. Miranda was particular about her hair, and in all the time Rosie had known her she could not recall a single occasion it had not looked immaculate.

As they had passed on the driveway the previous evening they had barely acknowledged each other. The briefest nod and hello was the most they achieved. Rosie had still noticed how well she was dressed and how much attention she had made with her appearance. She had wondered at the time where she was going and having seen her the previous week in Oxford, she had her suspicions she was meeting her lover. Nevertheless, Rosie, with her arms full of pizza boxes, had simply made her way inside, whilst Miranda, after getting into the taxi that had pulled up alongside Rosie's car, had sped off.

As Miranda reached the second stair, Rosie decided to begin her descent, determined she would say something as they passed each other.

"Late night was it Miranda, or should I say early morning?"

On realising she had been caught red-handed, Miranda did not know what to say, or where to look. "Oh Rosie, I didn't see you there. Are you off to work?"

"Yes, I am, although I'm in no rush. I'd be happy to chat, if you wanted to tell me where you've been all night."

"Oh, nowhere special. I just stayed over with a friend. We'd watched a movie and it was too late when it had finished to get a taxi home. She said I could sleepover on the couch."

As Miranda concocted her lie on the hoof, Rosie continued to stare at her as she gradually made her way down the stairs.

"On the couch? That probably wasn't too comfortable, especially not for someone in your condition, I'd imagine? Does your friend not know you're pregnant? I'm sure if he, sorry she, had known then they would have let you sleep in their bed."

Miranda tried desperately hard to sidestep Rosie's questions as she continued to climb the stairs and make her way up to her own bedroom. She was tired and needed her sleep and she was never at her best at this time of the day. Her morning sickness may have settled, but the tiredness was getting worse. A fact not helped given neither of them had slept much the previous evening.

Once she had got to Leo's apartment it had not taken any time for them to strip off and get between the sheets, and after several weeks of not being close she realised she had missed him almost as much as he had missed her. When the time came to head home, he had begged her to stay. Now, she realised she should have insisted he drive her home, although given he'd had a couple of bottles of beer that would not have been such a good idea.

Deciding to stay until after Leo had left for work, allowing the traffic to have died down, Miranda had not expected either Rosie or Richard to be around when she came home. By ten o'clock, Rosie would normally have left and Richard would still not have surfaced. He, like her, was not a morning person. So, her story had not been at all rehearsed and as she stood mid-staircase she was struggling to defend her position.

"No, I've not told many people about the pregnancy yet. I wanted to wait another few weeks, at least until I started to feel well enough. Having just lost Frank, everything is still very raw." The sympathy vote clearly was worth a try, Miranda imagined, although sensing from the expression on Rosie's face, as she moved alongside her on the stairs, it had not worked.

"What about the friend I saw you out with in Oxford last week? You both looked to be very close. In fact, I'd say very cosy outside the café when you appeared to be saying goodbye to him. Have you not even told him?"

Miranda was stunned. How on earth had Rosie seen her and Leo together, and having been seen how could she now deny it?

"Oh, that's just an old school friend I bumped into when I was out shopping. I'd popped into Oxford to get a couple of things for the baby. We started chatting, so decided to catch up over a coffee. I haven't seen him in ages."

"Well, it certainly didn't look like that to me. In fact, I'd go as far as to say you acted as if you were particularly close, with the way he touched your stomach as you left very intimate; almost proprietorial I'd say. He surely knows you're pregnant, doesn't he?"

"Err, yes, I think it may have come up in conversation, now that you mention it." However, any confidence Miranda felt that she could wheedle her way out of her embarrassment was lost when Rosie threw her killer blow.

"When we were chatting yesterday evening, and I mentioned to the others I'd seen you in Oxford, I learned that it's not the first time you've been seen around town with this friend, is it?" The way Rosie said 'friend' made it clear exactly where her thought process was going. "So, we were wondering, have you considered perhaps having a DNA test, you know, just to confirm it's Dad's baby?"

As Rosie stared her out all Miranda could do was stare back. Her guard was completely down and with not a single cohesive thought in her head, in terms of how best she could defend herself, or Leo's baby, she was at a complete loss. They were onto her and there was nothing she could say, or do, that would ever change that.

Five minutes later Rosie had left the house, leaving Miranda alone in her bedroom hastily packing her bags. She could see no value in keeping up the pretence any longer. All she could see was that she needed to get out of the house as quickly as she could. She needed to move on and staying at the Old Manor House would not allow her to do that, not with the atmosphere as toxic as it had become.

"Dad, can you please come and collect me from the house, as soon as possible? I'm coming home, to stay." Going to live back with her parents was not what she wanted, or needed, but for the time being it was her only viable option.

As she looked around the bedroom checking she had packed everything that belonged to her or had been given as gifts, she toyed with the idea of leaving her trinket engagement ring behind on the dressing table. She needed no reminder of Frank, or his family, and for what it was worth she questioned was it worth the hassle.

Then again, a thousand pounds was a thousand pounds, so it was worth having. Throwing it into the bottom of her handbag, she thought the sooner she could get it sold, the better.

Chapter 36

The Eve of the Wedding........

By seven o'clock the pre-wedding party was in full swing at the Old Manor House. The guests had arrived and the champagne had started to flow, with the bride and groom-to-be walking around hand in hand, talking to their guests and accepting their best wishes and congratulations for the forthcoming nuptials.

There were around fifty people milling around, both inside the house and in the gardens, where the pop-up bar had been set up. It was a balmy evening and the weather promised to hold for the following day when the actual wedding would take place. A small staff of waiters was wandering around offering canapés and glasses of champagne, or taking orders for other drinks. It was a free bar, so most people were taking the opportunity of exploiting their hosts' generosity.

When Miranda had mentioned wanting a formal Rehearsal Dinner, as she had read and heard about as being all the rage in America, her fiancé had initially objected. Frank could see no value in hosting an additional event, believing the main wedding breakfast was more than sufficient. Why did he have to pay for two events, had been his position? Especially given it would largely be the same people attending each. It was one of the many things they had argued about leading up to the big day, and as with all the rest, in the end Miranda got her way. Although the format was toned down with a formal sit-down meal giving way to a more informal drinks party, with nibbles the extent of the catering Frank was prepared to sanction.

The Dishonourable Groom

Nevertheless, the caterers had gone to town with a seemingly endless series of plates of tasty food emerging from the kitchen. Eduardo, the party planner Miranda had employed for the whole event, had supported her in arguing that as the marquee was erected anyway and the garden was already set for the wedding, there was no point in wasting all that hard work, or cost, on just one day. He said the caterers may have to work extra hard and come in early the following morning to get everything shipshape again for the wedding itself, but that was for him to worry about, not Mr Paulson. Eventually, as with everything, Frank had given in, seeing some sense at least in their arguments.

Now that the night was here Frank was determined they would have a great time, simply mingling with their guests in a relaxed setting. He would put people at their ease, make them feel welcome in his home. It was all part of rebuilding his image. For the town, the wedding would be a big event, something the locals would talk about for years to come, especially if they got it right. Frank was convinced friends and family, along with his business acquaintances and other local dignitaries, would all be anxious to get involved. Invites to either the wedding or the pre-wedding drinks party had become hot tickets around town. A veritable who's who of Chidlington and the surrounding areas of Oxfordshire.

Miranda had managed the guest list and it was fair to say there were still a lot of people who would be attending to whom she had still not been formally introduced. People Frank did business with that he wanted to impress, or more importantly looked on her to impress for him. After all, she was his trophy bride; the young and beautiful woman who would look stunning on the arm of any man in his sixties, let alone his. And with a baby on the way, he was clearly someone who was still virile and very much active in that department. Frank had his image to consider, and with Miranda by his side he believed that was very much enhanced. He intended showing her off and getting maximum benefit from the weekend. For what it was costing him, he expected to see some return on his investment.

Councillor and Mrs Dent were there. Frank did not care very much for Mrs Dent, who he found to be quite a busybody. Someone who always wanted to know what other people were up to, her finger in everyone's business. It also did not help that she was friendly with his old housekeeper, Nanny Tilbury, who he was convinced knew too much about what went on around the house already.

Frank was careful what he mentioned when she was around, for fear of it leaking out and making its way to the wrong ears. He knew how much women could gossip if fuelled with the right information. Some of the things he was considering, and had been talking about recently, were certainly not points he wanted Councillor Dent to become aware of too soon, or via the wrong channels. Not until the time was right. And if the old nanny found out, it would surely get to his ears, one way or another, before Frank was ready. Councillor Dent was one of those councillors who stuck to process, and remained above reproach, a rare breed in politics today. If he got wind of any underhand dealings, it would certainly not bode well for what he was planning for their future relationship.

Frank had been in discussions for some time with some influential Romanian developers, who had their eyes firmly set on investing in the UK. They were looking at opportunities to develop some high-class apartments, with even higher price tags. Frank saw a chance to make some serious money out of them, especially as most of their funding had not been obtained through entirely legitimate processes, or through transactions that were strictly above board. The money was coming from sources Frank did not want to question too deeply, although it was clear they were looking to launder dirty money through an authentic enterprise; a project that had the right paperwork and clearances behind it.

Frank had already been advanced around ten thousand pounds to help oil the wheels of the local planning council and to start the process of getting some of them on his side, but he knew it would take a lot more than what they had already invested to make the deal work. It was not a fast process and buying council officials was proving more difficult than it had ever been. Their *fees* over the years seemingly linked to an inflation rate that was almost criminal.

No, Coronation Terrace, a site he had long since set his heart on, was proving a lot more difficult to get control of than he had ever imagined. Every step he believed he was taking to move it forward, fell by the wayside as each planning application failed. His tactic of arguing it was for affordable, rather than luxury, apartments did not appear to be getting the traction he had assumed with the council. If it went on much longer, he would seriously have to reconsider his strategy, because his current approach was clearly not working.

The amount of money Frank had been forced to part with, to secure the approvals for his previous two developments, had cost him sorely. It had left him and his business exposed. All Coronation Terrace was doing, the longer that delay went on, was to add to his woes. He had been forced to take out loans against his assets, his house and his land. The councillors in question had not only accepted his money, but they had become greedy. They had even started to threaten him on the two occasions he'd missed the payment plans they had imposed. Ongoing monthly instalments was their price for keeping quiet. How they had the audacity to bribe him, with their own reputations on the line, was difficult to understand. They were as guilty as he was, but somehow they had managed it and now Frank did not have a leg to stand on. He was in too deep.

What had started out relatively innocently, if bribing a government official could ever be termed as that, had soon turned nasty, with the stakes for Frank's business, and his family's reputation, now too high to contemplate. He had to keep them sweet, whilst at the same time watch his back, as nothing was beyond them.

Now, as he wandered around the room, with Miranda on his arm, he did his best to steer his path away from them. He had considered not inviting them tonight, however the consequences of that would not have been worth considering. The thought of being slighted was not something that would have gone down well for them, and could have raised even more questions among the other council members as to why they had not been included on the guest list. Frank was not prepared to deal with unnecessary questions, and certainly none for which he did not have the answer.

He had also avoided his eldest son and son-in-law for most of the evening, partly due to the guilt from what he was about to put Simon through. In fact, he could barely look any of them in the eye, and he was finding it extremely uncomfortable. He'd had a discussion earlier that day with an associate, someone who was known to operate on the more shady side of things. Between them they had concocted a way out of one of the financial holes into which Frank had recently got himself, but it involved implicating his son-in-law in a fraud. Provided Frank got away with it, the business' insurance policy would pay out and everything would be okay.

Granted, it would not be good for the family, especially his daughter, Judy. But desperate times called for desperate measures, and one thing was for sure, Frank was desperate. In time, he would work hard to win his family back and regain their trust. Well, that was his plan. Although he knew it was a high-risk strategy, as he was not starting from a position of strength with his children, especially not as far as their love, or their respect, was concerned. They were content to continue taking his money, and benefitting from his connections, just not pleased with the way he lived his life, or the choices he made.

It was clear that none of his children was happy about being there tonight, or that any of them supported him getting married again, but it was his life, not theirs, so his choice to make. Frank would not kowtow to his children or their desires ever again. He had done that once before when he divorced Alison, by agreeing to give her a greater settlement than he felt comfortable with, or that his lawyers advised was necessary. All because his children put pressure on him to be decent, if not to Alison, then at least to their son, Mason. They argued Mason was an innocent party in his parents' divorce, and he should not be penalised as a result of his father's affair, with a woman half his age.

Frank supposed, looking back that was the point at which his relationship with his children soured. He guessed Mason would be around five or six years old by now, but if he was honest he did not really have too much to do with him, or Alison for that matter. The terms of their divorce settlement had put paid to that, and for that at least he was grateful.

That was a chapter of his life that was best forgotten. Miranda was his future, and he needed to concentrate on her, although where the baby had come from was anyone's guess. He for sure was not the father, having had a vasectomy on the quiet after his last mistake. He'd decided he'd no intention of getting caught out in that way again.

What Miranda's motivation was for forcing him into marrying her was also unclear. He was happy enough to go along with her idea, though, on the basis that at his age having her on his arm was better than not. Being a sad, lonely old man did not play well into the image he wanted to create, and once they were married he would soon find out who she was involved with and put a stop to any of her shenanigans. She had no idea he suspected anything, believing her secret to be safe, and that he was happy at the thought of another baby. The pre-nuptial agreement had at least protected him from being taken to the cleaners again, or for an illegitimate child to have a claim on him or his estate. So, either way, he could not see how he could possibly lose from the arrangement.

As he looked around the room there were a couple of candidates that potentially met the criteria Miranda would probably look for in a lover. Young, fit and good looking was the type he imagined she would go for, and presumably someone who was good in bed. When they had first started their affair, she had been anxious to please him in that department, whereas now she was less so, and if he was honest he had lost the urge, too. There was a lot to say for getting old, especially for men, particularly in that respect.

She was obviously getting it somewhere, though, the small bump, which was just about disguised by the designer dress she had chosen to wear this evening, a testament to that. He wondered who in the room either knew or suspected she was pregnant, other than the family. Her condition was something she had been at pains to hide, at least until after the wedding. In fact, he was unsure if she had even told her parents.

Thankfully, his future in-laws were not here this evening. He would have to endure them tomorrow, though, as there had been no getting out of inviting them to the wedding. He could just about manage one day, especially if he had a few drinks inside him. He found them a frightful couple, but imagined at least they would be happy at the thought of becoming grandparents. The idea of them becoming regular visitors at the Old Manor House, though, once the child had been born, was one that certainly gave him the shivers.

Presumably, if the daddy was in the room, he would know. He could not imagine Miranda keeping that to herself, unless of course that was part of her plan. Maybe she wanted to continue the pretence indefinitely. What went on in that tiny little mind of hers, he sometimes wondered.

Was it perhaps Carl Gilbert, the man he'd recently had dealings with on the local council? Carl was a relatively new councillor, who was struggling with the whole business of council meetings and all the politicking it involved. He was finding it too demanding and time consuming, and had even confided in Frank that he was considering stepping down.

By trade Carl was a quantity surveyor, working for a multinational development company based in London. He commuted to and from the capital whenever he could not work from home, staying in a small apartment that apparently was owned by his parents, Frank seemed to recall him once saying. He was also a jetsetter, regularly flying around the world wherever his company needed him to deal with an overseas project, or meet with a potential client. He had been telling him only earlier that he was due to fly out to Dubai later that week for a few days to advise on a new project they were involved in there.

Their conversation had got a little heated as they debated the merits of British builders against their foreign counterparts, and the relative costs of each. Frank had attempted to defend the local industry, whereas Carl clearly saw a lot of merit in what the country could learn from overseas. They had agreed to differ, but was Carl perhaps the daddy? He was certainly good looking and looked to have a reasonable body, and with such an interesting lifestyle with all his travelling, Frank could imagine he would be good company.

In fact, he quite liked the chap and would be sad to see him step down from the council.

Or was it one of the men Miranda had invited from the leisure centre? Frank had not thought people from her exercise class were suitable guests, but as she had not asked to invite anyone else, he struggled to argue against it. It was not as if she was asking for them to be invited to the full wedding, just for drinks the evening before. She spent a lot of time at the leisure centre, so it was understandable she would have made friends there. She certainly had not made friends anywhere else, at least not since they had begun their affair. He sensed some of the local woman now blanked her, even taking Alison's side after the divorce. The wronged wife rather than the scarlet woman, the homewrecker.

Frank certainly did not want to get involved in that, and provided Miranda was friendly with the people he needed her to be friendly with, and kept up her end of the marriage, what more did he need?

Looking over now, there were a few young men within the sporty group that could fit the bill. Men with athletic bodies that made Frank feel the need to breathe in as he stared at them, his paunch suddenly feeling more noticeable than he would have liked. He noticed some had partners, and even imagined from the way another behaved that he might be gay, so he ruled those out immediately. In terms of the others, though, could any of them be the daddy?

Or was it one of the councillors? They were not all old and staid like Hargreaves and Dent. A couple of them were still in their forties, married, granted, and although they were not quite as athletic as the sporty set, there was no reason why Miranda would not have been attracted to them. After all, she had set her sights on him, and he was married at the time, and also far from the type he had classified.

No, it was certainly a mystery and something he would park until the time was right. He was sure there would come a point when he would need something from her, or to work out a trade, and that would be the time to show his hand. For now, he needed to keep his powder dry.

"Hi, darling." Miranda sashayed over, conscious most eyes were focussed on her, the last dregs of a mock-cocktail in her hand. He smiled. She certainly knew how to work a room.

It was getting close to midnight and the party had started to die down, with only a couple of stragglers left. Frank had drunk more than was good for him and he knew that if he had any more he would be suffering in the morning.

"I'm starting to get tired, Frank. Why don't you suggest it's time they all left?" She stared over at the remaining group, who looked like they had no intention of going home. As they were not attending the wedding itself, they had obviously banked on making the most of the night. "I need my beauty sleep and we've got a long day ahead of us, as well as a very early start. Apart from which, I don't think I can stand a moment longer in these heels."

How she had lasted so long remained a mystery to him, or how she had maintained her glamourous look throughout the evening, whilst pregnant. Frank had heard her throwing up most mornings, so knew she was suffering badly with morning sickness, and had even seen her refuse food, hardly eating enough to keep a bird alive. So to keep up the pretence was something for which she had to be applauded. She was one hell of an actress, he had to give her that.

"Yes, I'll sort it. Why don't you head up to bed. I'll follow, as soon as I can get locked up. I think the caterers stopped serving food a couple of hours ago and appear to have already cleared away most of the mess. Although looking at what's left to do, they're still going to have their work cut out tomorrow morning."

"Thanks." She smiled over at him, barely able to hide her tiredness. She was paying a wedding planner to manage the details, so how they sorted it tomorrow was not her concern. They just needed to ensure it was done on time, as she did not want anything to ruin her big day.

"Just remember to leave the alarm off, please. I don't want it waking me up any earlier than necessary, when the caterers arrive, do I?"

Frank had been the last one to head upstairs, having locked up after everyone had eventually left. The house felt eerily quiet as he climbed the stairs, the loudest noise being the thumping sound in his head. He really should not have drunk so much and he definitely should not have mixed his drinks. Champagne was bad enough, but then to hit the whiskey had perhaps not been his finest hour. He needed his bed, hoping that a good night's sleep would be sufficient to rid him of his headache. Getting through the day tomorrow would be bad enough, without the thought of having to attend to a hangover as well. Why on earth had he agreed to go along with this charade, he kept asking himself?

Miranda was already sound asleep as he slipped into bed next to her, having stripped off in the bathroom to avoid waking her. She was generally a sound sleeper, but he knew she was struggling at the moment, so trod carefully. Having her grumpy through lack of sleep, on top of everything else, was not something he wanted to contend with, tomorrow of all days.

He must have fallen asleep, although around an hour later his mobile phone went off, the vibration and flashing on his bedside table sufficient to wake him up. He leaned over and saw the caller's name, and knowing the way their call had gone earlier that day decided there must be a good reason for him to be calling at this hour. He picked it up to answer it.

"Just give me a minute, I'll go downstairs," he whispered. "I can't talk here."

Frank grabbed his robe from behind the door and padded his way silently downstairs, careful to avoid the steps that were known to creak. As he reached the kitchen, he closed the door quietly behind him.

"What is it? What's so urgent that you need to call me at this hour? Can't it wait until after the wedding? I need time to think." Frank's head was spinning. His body was tired, whereas his mind would not rest. The conversation he'd had earlier that day had continued to vex him and he could not think straight. All evening he had tried to switch off and relax, tried to enjoy the event that he was hosting, but he had failed miserably and just drank more and more to numb the pain.

People had approached him all evening, offering their congratulations and best wishes, and all he could do was smile and pretend that it meant something to him. Being married was neither here nor there, what he was worried about was keeping himself out of trouble, alive. Unless he could get his hands on some money, and fast, he feared there would be serious consequences. He owed money left, right and centre, and although some of it was through legitimate sources, the majority was not. Those were the lenders he feared. Having his assets repossessed was the worst the banks could do. The others would not be anywhere near as forgiving.

Framing Simon for fraud was part of the picture, and even that was not failsafe, but if it worked and the insurance paid out it would relieve some of the pressure. If it failed, Frank seriously feared for his life.

"As I said earlier, I've sorted it. I've found a way of implicating Simon, and I believe I can make it look like fraud."

"I know what you said earlier, Frank, and I've been thinking about it all day too. And the more I've thought about it, you're not going to get away with it. What's more, I don't want any part of it. Simon's not stupid and he's not going to go down lightly, is he? And what about that wife of his, your daughter, Judy? She's never going to believe her husband is capable of doing what you're suggesting. It's a hairbrained scheme, Frank, and the insurance will see straight through it. So I'm just letting you know you can no longer count on my support."

"You're not walking out on me now." Frank's voice was getting louder and louder the angrier he became. "You've got to follow through with what we discussed. I'm convinced I can get the insurance to buy it, and in terms of what Judy thinks, or what it does to her marriage, or the rest of the family for that matter, I don't care. This is about protecting my own skin, because if I don't, they will get me and it won't just be the money I lose."

"Well, sorry Frank, but you're on your own. I've got my own family to think about and I can't go down for this. Enjoy the rest of your weekend, mate. Just don't call me when you get back from wherever it is she's booked you for your honeymoon."

As the caller hung up, Frank was furious. His plans were unravelling, knowing that without the support of his friend he would not be able to pull the scheme off. It was too risky to try to do it by himself. So far it had been the only option he had, one that would buy him time, if not realise all the money he needed. But was it his only option?

Frank was racking his brains trying to think, his headache getting worse. He realised he needed some painkillers, before going back to bed to get some sleep. Deprived of that he would have no chance of getting through the rest of the weekend without seriously losing his rag. He felt his life was on a knife's edge, and the slightest provocation would be enough to destabilise him.

As he ran the tap to get cold water, from nowhere, a potential solution came to him. There was an original painting, an old master his father-in-law had once told him was valuable. It was hanging at the top of the stairs. He rarely gave it a second glance, as it was not something he either liked or appreciated. Although, if it was of value, he could possibly sell it and the proceeds could help tide him over, at least until he could think of something better. He would need to get someone in to value it before he committed, but it was feasible and offered a glimmer of hope.

After taking the tablets, he turned around, towards the door. He could see something, or someone lurking in the shadows, and could hear the gentle sound of their breathing. The full moon had created a soft light in the kitchen, but there were still corners of the room that were not illuminated, and without the noise of the phone call, or the running of the tap, it was eerily quiet. Apart from the sound of the breathing.

Frank felt afraid. "Who's there? Show yourself," he shouted out. Every instinct told him there was someone there, even though he knew he had locked up himself and had ensured everyone had left the party. Had someone snuck back in, or laid in wait, ready to burgle the house as soon as the occupants had gone to bed?

As Frank looked round he could see no sign of forced entry, or broken glass, or any disturbance. There was clearly someone there, though. A shadow moved.

"Come out, show yourself," he repeated, his voice almost quivering as he spoke. He had suspected people were after him, but had always assumed he would be safe in his own house, his own fortress. Why had Miranda insisted he leave the alarm off, tonight of all nights, allowing someone to get in?

"What the hell are you doing here?" Frank staggered forward, the glass in his hand, the only weapon available to face off to the intruder. The verbal abuse and the tone of his voice, as he approached and saw who it was, was akin to the type of language normally associated with a group of dockyard workers, not the lord of the manor.

Frank's mind, once he realised his earlier conversation had been overheard, began to work overtime. The impact of what he had said getting back to his family was indescribable. Was there anything he could say, or do, that would mitigate the impact of what had been overheard earlier? From the look in their eyes, he imagined not, and as he got within a foot of the intruder, in a fit of rage, he saw out of the corner of his eye something large swinging towards him. In an attempt to avoid it, and protect himself, he tried to move backwards. In his panic, he lost his footing and stumbled forward.

As the heavy blunt object made contact with the back of his head, he crumbled to the floor. His fall was broken by a further knock to the front of his head as it came into contact with the granite worktop, before finally smashing against the cold, hard stone floor.

As Frank lost consciousness, the intruder looked around to check no one had witnessed what had happened, before quietly making their way out of the kitchen.

Chapter 37

Present day……….

"Nanny, that smells amazing. Are you sure there's nothing I can help you with?" Richard had come down just before noon on Sunday morning to the aromas of meat roasting in the oven and the sweet smell of baking. He eyed the lemon drizzle cake that was sitting on the counter top waiting to be iced.

"No, dear. I think everything is in order. I found a lovely leg of lamb in the freezer that was more than big enough to feed us all, so I thought I would cook that. Roast lamb was always one of your favourites, wasn't it? And I couldn't imagine either you or Rosie cooking it once I'd left, could you?" She smiled across at him. Richard loved his food, although the thought of him cooking for himself was completely alien to her.

Nanny recalled how concerned she had become those three years Richard had been away at university, having to fend for himself without any homecooked meals to rely on. How she had counted the weeks down before he returned for his holidays, and how many times in between she had considered catching the train to his digs, just to check he was eating something. Anything, other than ready meals or snacking on take-aways.

"Sounds good. I hope we've got roast potatoes and Yorkshire puddings and gravy, with mint sauce to go with it?"

"Don't worry, I have. There's also jam roly-poly as Rosie requested. You won't go hungry, my boy. I've made plenty." She smiled as he bent down to give her a small kiss on her cheek.

After having told them all earlier in the week that she and Wilf were leaving on Monday, moving to a small cottage by the sea, Nanny had been busy. As well as all the arrangements to get her clothes and valuables packed away ready for the move, which had involved calling on an old friend with a van, she had invited Mrs Dent and Mrs Hargreaves to meet her for coffee. They were the only people with whom she intended staying in touch, so wanted to tell them a little of her plans. She did not want to do a moonlight flit, as Ana-Maria had done, then find the whole town gossiping about her, as they now were about the housekeeper. Especially given Wilf was coming with her. That at least needed some positioning. After all, what would people think of her if she did not put the record straight? No, it was important she told them of her plans, well, some of them at least.

"Why don't you go and set the table for me, Richard? I've counted and there will be eleven of us sitting down for lunch, as I've asked Wilf to join us. You don't have a problem with that, do you, dear?"

Richard, appreciating it was a rhetorical question, simply smiled. He was not sure what Nanny's interest was in Wilf, but that was not his concern. The concept of Wilf trading Mrs Cuthbert in for Nanny, though, did give him something to smile at. He still wondered where she had gone and who the lucky man was with whom she'd scarpered.

"No problem. I'll go and do it now. Give me a shout if you need anything else. What time's lunch, by the way, as I'm already starving?"

"You and your stomach. It won't be for another couple of hours, so why don't you grab yourself a snack to tide you over. There's some cold meat in the fridge, if you want to make yourself a sandwich. Or there are some biscuits in the barrel, if you'd prefer something sweeter. But keep your fingers off that cake."

Richard considered his options. "I'll probably have both as two hours is a long time to go without food, and you wouldn't want me to pass out while I'm waiting, would you?"

"Away with you, you cheeky monkey." Nanny laughed, as she flicked her tea towel at him to shoo him away. She would certainly miss the manor and the years of happy memories she had with the children. They were her family, so moving on had been a tough decision, but it was definitely the right one. It was time, and if nothing else she had earned her retirement.

"Now, let me get on, or else it may be three hours before everything is ready, and you wouldn't want that, would you?"

The rest of the family started to arrive around one o'clock and had gathered in the sitting room for a couple of drinks and a chat. James and Katie, with their daughter Maia, were the first to arrive, followed shortly by Judy and Simon, with their two boys. The children all started to run around, the sound of their laughter as they chased each other brought the house back to life.

Hide and seek was one of their favourite games, with the Old Manor House a great place to play, its endless rooms and hiding spaces offering countless opportunities in which to get lost. As Nanny listened to the children's noise she knew the house needed a family again, and if that was not to be one of Frank's children with their children, then it was right that it should be sold. A new family could enjoy the house and gardens as they had growing up over the years, and fill the house with new memories. With Rosie and Richard rattling around the place, if felt as if the heart of the old property had been ripped out.

At two o'clock Wilf popped his head around the sitting room door. "Nanny has asked me to let you know lunch is just about ready. She says if you want to come through, or help carry the plates into the dining room, she would appreciate it."

Wilf felt a little uncomfortable socialising with the family, having said he would prefer to eat his meal in his own rooms, if that was alright with Nanny.

"Nonsense, you're eating with the family, as am I. This is our farewell meal and I plan to leave in style. Now, why don't you pour me a small sherry while I finish off." As Wilf did as he was told, he wondered what it was that attracted him to strong women. Nanny took charge, as had Ana-Maria before her, leaving him to simply follow happily in their wake.

When Nanny first discussed her plans to leave the manor, Wilf had felt desolate. First Ana-Maria leaving him, and then Nanny. He was going to be left all alone. What would he do, and importantly, where would he go once the house was sold? He had never had a formal role, so even if new owners moved in, there would be no place for him, an aging odd-job man. Now in his mid-sixties, neither the idea of starting again nor being alone appealed to him, and the more Nanny spoke about her plans for a quiet retirement by the sea, the more he thought that would suit him, too.

"Did you say it was a two-bedroomed property?" That was all it took to convey his interest, with Nanny eager to invite him to join her. Going anywhere by herself was not what she really wanted either, certainly not after being surrounded by family and friends all her life. The idea of Wilf being by her side suited her nicely. They got along well and his companionship was something she would enjoy.

As James carved the leg of lamb and passed the plates around, Nanny smiled to herself, and as the plates were cleared she felt she had achieved her task admirably. Before the desserts were brought out, the doorbell rang. They all looked around with questioning stares.

"Are you expecting anyone, Richard, Rosie?" James asked.

"No, but I'll go and see who it is." Richard rose from the table and went to open the door. "Oh, it's Officer Dickson, isn't it? How may I help you?"

"Sorry to bother you, sir, especially on a Sunday. I wanted to speak to Mr Cuthbert, if he's around?"

"Yes, please come through. We're in the dining room, just finishing lunch."

If PC Dickson was surprised to hear Mr Cuthbert was eating his lunch with the family, he was professional enough not to show it.

"It's PC Dickson, to speak to Mr Cuthbert. Would you like us to leave you to it?"

"No, lad. I'll be alright. What can I help you with, Officer?" Wilf was of the opinion he had nothing to hide, and if the family listened in then at least he would not have the bother of having to tell them separately.

As PC Dickson took out his notebook, there was a look on his face that clearly showed he was unsure whether he should speak in front of an audience, or not. There were children around the table, laughing and joking, and it was a little off-putting. Nanny also noticed him looking at the food, and even from where she was sitting could hear his stomach rumble.

"Why don't you come through to the kitchen and talk to Mr Cuthbert there. It will be much quieter and I could make you a nice sandwich, if you'd like? I imagine you haven't had your lunch yet and you'll be hungry? Wilf, will you please carry the plate of lamb in and we can come back later for the rest?"

Wilf dutifully picked up the meat and followed Nanny and PC Dickson into the kitchen.

Nanny placed a sandwich and a cup of tea in front of PC Dickson as he sat at the table.

"I really shouldn't," he said, as he eyed the food. He was starving, with the aromas in the house not making it any easier to resist.

"Don't worry, lad. We'll not tell anyone. Anyway, what was it you wanted to tell me?"

"Oh, yes. There has been some activity on your wife's bank account that we thought you might want to know about. She was caught on camera at one of the cash machines, withdrawing a sum of money. The amount was not high value and the circumstances were not suspicious, so we did not feel there was anything to get too concerned about. What it did tell us, though, is that she's alive and well, and she appears to be living in London. Here is the image the camera took. Can you confirm that it's her?"

Wilf and Nanny both looked at the image. It was very good quality and clearly showed Ana-Maria, her face smiling. In the background of the photo Nanny could also make out the face of the person standing directly behind her. He was also smiling, as if the image had captured them both in the middle of a joke or a funny story. It was Carl Gilbert, the nice young man who had called at the house on occasion to see Mr Paulson, the man Mrs Dent's neighbour occasionally cat sat for whenever he was out of the country, on holiday or on business. He seemed to have a good job, she recalled, but she had no idea of his connection with Frank.

As Nanny looked at the picture, she tried to work out the meaning of it all. She recalled seeing him from her bedroom window the night of the party, leaving his car behind as he headed off to walk down the driveway. At the time, she had also seen Ana-Maria standing in the kitchen doorway. Nanny had just presumed she had popped out for some fresh air, but had Ana-Maria been watching him as he left, or had they just had a tryst in the driveway? Nanny had noticed the following day that the car looked to have a flat tyre, but she was not mechanical so anything could have been wrong with it. A few days later she had also noticed a mechanic come round to look at it before towing the car away, which explained why it had not been collected earlier.

Nanny had not seen Mr Gilbert again. She had, though, heard Mrs Dent's version of events, where clearly he was involved in Frank's murder in some way. Added to the fact he had fled the country, shortly after the so-called murder, was sufficient evidence for Mrs Dent to convict him.

Now, piecing the jigsaw together, Nanny suspected his motives may have been entirely different. With the fact he had not returned to Chidlington more to do with the realisation he was holed up in London with Ana-Maria. Nanny decided to keep her observations to herself, after all it was none of her business what Ana-Maria or Mr Gilbert got up to, was it?

"Yes, Officer. That's Ana-Maria," Wilf said, smiling at the image. "I'm glad she's well."

"And have you still not had any contact with her? She's still not been in touch in any way?"

"No. I've not heard anything. Neither of us has, have we Nanny?" Nanny shook her head.

"Well, if we find anything more out, we'll let you know. In the meantime, at least you know she's safe. And if she does get in touch, please let us know."

"Thank you, Officer, we will. Now drink your tea before it goes cold. Would you like another sandwich before you go, or one to take with you for later, perhaps?"

"No, thank you, and if my Sarg knew I'd had that, she'd have my guts for garters."

"Well, it's our little secret then. Shall I show you out?" Nanny smiled at him as she led him to the front door. "Good luck with the rest of your enquiries. Goodbye."

As Neil got back into the car he thought what a nice lady she was. Not at all interfering, as Ruth continued to imply. He found her very helpful and the lamb was very tasty.

As Nanny watched him drive away, she thought to herself what a lovely young man he was. Perhaps not the brightest, but still lovely and with impeccable manners. He was obviously intent on getting to the bottom of the crime and would no doubt continue searching until he found the answers he needed.

The following morning at eight o'clock, a small white van arrived at the Old Manor House. The burly driver, around thirty years old, with arms full of tattoos and enough piercings to make Wilf look twice, got out of the driver's side of the vehicle and walked towards the annex. As Nanny opened the door, he took her in his arms and hugged her. Wilf was surprised to note they were clearly not strangers.

"Good morning, Darren. Lovely to see you again and thanks for driving over, come on in. There's a few boxes upstairs that I need help carrying down, and a couple of pieces of furniture I'd like to take too, if there's room in the van? Nothing much really. And Wilf here, he's got his things, mainly clothes. If you let him know where you want them, he can start loading the van while you're bringing my things down."

"Don't worry, Auntie Maggie, I'll sort it. Nice to meet you, Wilf." He extended his hand to shake Wilf's.

Nanny had not told Wilf much about her life, and until then he had never even learned what her first name was. Over recent weeks he had however pieced together enough to realise that the image she presented to the outside world was not perhaps totally authentic. She had a past and one that he imagined was perhaps a little more colourful than his own, and the more he got to know her, the more she surprised him with the way she got things done. Effortlessly and without a second thought. A simple phone call to people he had never heard her speak of before was all it normally took to get things arranged. The cottage, the move, in fact everything appeared to have been organised without any effort at all. Wilf had just gone along with it all, amazed at how easily everything fell into place when Nanny was in charge.

Half an hour later, the van was loaded and Nanny and Wilf were seated in the cabin ready to be driven away.

"Are you sure you don't want to say goodbye to Richard and Rosie? We've plenty of time and they'll probably be upset if you just leave without letting them know." He had no qualms about leaving, as after all it had only been his home for a relatively short period of time, whereas Nanny had thirty years of memories of the place and the people who lived there.

"No, Wilf, I said my goodbyes to everyone yesterday. I'll be in touch when we're settled, in a few weeks, or so. They need to get on with their own lives now, and so do we." She patted his arm as she spoke. "Come on then, Darren, we're ready when you are, so let's get a move on before the traffic gets bad. I know what Monday mornings can be like, especially at rush hour."

And with that, the van reversed out of the driveway and Darren drove Nanny and Wilf to their little cottage.

"By the way, if you want you can call me Maggie. After all, I can't call myself Nanny any longer, can I?"

Wilf pondered that for a moment. "No, I don't suppose you can, Maggie. I quite like that name, thank you."

Chapter 38

Epilogue – Three months later........

It was around eleven o'clock in the morning and Richard was just preparing to leave the house when the doorbell rang. He had a train to catch and needed to leave to get to the station within the next forty minutes. He had a taxi booked to collect him for eleven thirty. Any later and he would run the risk of missing his train into London, and potentially his interview. It was for a job he had applied for two months earlier, finally deciding he needed to do something to get his life back on track. Still in his late twenties, it was too early to give up and settle for casual jobs. With his skills, the types of jobs he had been doing had paid well. They were just not something he found particularly rewarding. Apart from which, he needed to get back out into the real world again and start meeting people, and importantly get back into the dating game.

The role he had applied for was as a business analyst in the city, working for an investment bank. It involved dealing with statistical information and analysing trends in the market, looking at qualitative and quantitative data to determine patterns in people's behaviour and spending patterns. It had his name written all over it, just the sort of role that would get his grey cells back in order, and he was determined he would get it. He had been brushing up on his interview skills and was mentally prepared. He had even had his hair cut and bought a new suit to make himself look more respectable. First impressions counted, and being a slob at home, lounging around in his tracksuit all day, was not quite the image he was aiming for.

The Dishonourable Groom

It was too early for his taxi and he was not expecting anyone to call. Rosie had left for her dress agency around eight o'clock, arguing she had lots of new stock to sort through, so needed an early start. She and Vanessa had more work than they could cope with and were working long hours to keep ahead of the game. With just the two of them in the house now, and with Rosie out most days from dawn until dusk, it had started to get lonely. Secretly Richard longed for the house to sell and for them all to move on. The house did hold some happy memories, just not enough to justify him getting maudlin about it.

Summer had turned to late autumn and his father had been dead for over four months. James and Simon were doing a good job of getting the business back on track, with building work having begun on a new development of affordable housing. Rosie's business was doing well, as was Katie's. Everyone always needed a hairdresser. Even Judy had looked to find herself a role, both boys now happily settled at school, with her eye on opening her own small business. Everyone was moving on, and once the house was sold and the debts were settled he would be forced to, too. Probate had been cleared, and the situation, thankfully, was not as dire as they had all imagined. There would be enough to keep them comfortable, if not in luxury. Richard could live with that.

Mr Mears had worked with the family to partition off the farmlands from the house and grounds, and working with their accountant they had determined that if the property sold for a fair price, the farmlands could be retained, thereby protecting the tenant farmers and giving the family a regular income. Judy had even come up with the suggestion of opening a farm shop on a piece of land that ran adjacent to the house, and operating a business from there. The land had an old cottage on it that had not been lived in for some years, and with a little redevelopment it could be modernised and converted into business premises. Richard recalled at one stage how they had considered that cottage as a suitable home for Nanny.

Judy envisaged her farm shop selling local produce, fruit and vegetables, along with plants and flowers, with a small tearoom to which people could drive out to enjoy freshly baked cakes. It would also act as a great place for the locals to get their fresh produce without having to traipse out to the big supermarkets. She was excited at the prospect of going into business, and had plans to move forward as soon as the house sold and the paperwork could be done. Councillor Dent and the council's planning committee had already approved the plans.

The doorbell continued to ring and Richard considered ignoring it. He was already pushed for time and did not need a distraction, especially if it was someone who had driven past, seen the For Sale sign and decided to call in on spec, hoping to get a nosy around the Old Manor House without an appointment. He was not in a mood for those types of people today. People who had no interest in buying, just in having a gawp around.

Deciding he could not ignore it any longer, he shouted down. "Hang on, I'm coming."

"Sorry to bother you, sir. It's just I need a signature. It's recorded delivery, so I couldn't just leave it." The postman handed Richard an A5 sized padded envelope. Richard noted it was addressed to him. "Good day, then. It looks like it's going to stay fine, doesn't it?" the postman said cheerily as he walked back to his van.

"Yes, thank you," Richard replied, already distracted by the package. He recognised the handwriting instantly, with his curiosity immediately becoming piqued. Although knowing he did not need the distraction, today of all days, he put the envelope to one side. He had a train to catch.

Richard arrived home later that evening, around seven thirty, after a very successful day. The interview had gone well and he had completed the tests they had put before him with ease. Two hours after the interview had completed, as he had been wandering around London sightseeing, he had been surprised to receive an offer of the job, subject to his references checking out. The text asked him to confirm back if he was still interested, providing details of a contact within their HR department if he wanted to take up the position. Overall, a very productive day indeed.

Now, back at home, he could turn his attention to the contents of the envelope that had arrived that morning, which he had succeeded in putting to the back of his mind all afternoon. He knew that if he'd allowed his mind to think about what it contained, he would not have been able to concentrate on getting through the interview. Part of him had been surprised to receive it, whereas the larger part of him had been expecting it. Although its contents were not at all what he had expected.

The letter was handwritten, and as he took it from the envelope a key fob fell to the floor, with two keys hanging from it. The fob had no markings to identify where it belonged.

Richard settled back to read the letter, a wry smile on his face as he slowly digested its contents, and importantly the implications of what was being said.

"My dearest Richard,

"I wanted to write to let you know that I am well and settled, and above all happy. Wilf and I have rented a pretty two-bedroom cottage, overlooking the sea, with a small garden where Wilf is happy to potter around. It's not the same as the Old Manor House, although it is starting to feel like home and

we're both quite contented together. I've even put some pictures up of you and the others, who I will always consider my family. Above all it's nice to have some companionship in the evenings, especially now the nights are drawing in.

"I know you of all people understood when I decided it was time to move on, and I've suspected for some time that you probably knew the real reason why I had to go. You were always the brightest of boys and very little ever fazed you, or created problems that you were unable to solve. I used to love our evening chats over hot chocolate and ice cream, a combination that only you and I ever understood, and used to love to read to you. Bedtimes became my favourite time, when you snuggled up to have stories read to you, or in later life read stories to me. Roald Dahl was always one of our favourites, wasn't he?

"Anyway, enough of the reminiscing. I don't want to get too maudlin, do I? And I'm sure by now you're wondering what the real reason is for me to be writing to you after all this time. It's just that I wanted to tell you about some of the events leading up to your father's death, and perhaps answer some of the questions you may still have lingering around.

"What you decide to do with what I tell you is your decision, even down to whether you share it with the others. I have always trusted your judgement, and whatever you decide I'm sure will be for the best. Just remember that what I did that evening was for the good of the family and with no other motivation than to protect you all. I have always loved you and that will never stop, regardless of what your next move is."

Nanny's handwriting was very neat and precise and as Richard moved onto the second page, there were small tears forming in his eyes. He had a love and a fondness for this lady that he knew he would take to his grave, regardless of what he was to learn as he read on.

"So, here goes. The day before the wedding, Saturday morning, I was in my kitchen tidying up the breakfast pots. It was a beautiful day and the window was open. It was too early in the day for wasps, so I felt safe. You remember how I always hated wasps, don't you? Anyway, below my window, in the courtyard, I could hear your father talking on his phone. From where he was standing, I believe he thought he was somewhere he could not be overheard or seen by anyone. You will remember that day, I'm sure? The house was overrun with the caterers and all the deliveries for the wedding, so there was a lot of people and noise.

"Your father's voice was louder than normal and the tone of it, along with the odd word I picked up, indicated he was clearly agitated about something to do with money. He kept mentioning half a million pounds, in a way that suggested he needed to get hold of that amount of money fast. I couldn't help but overhear, especially when he mentioned Simon's name. He suggested he was prepared to fix the books and lay the blame on him, adding that if Simon went down for it, then so be it.

"I couldn't imagine what he was talking about, but it worried me at the time, as it implied it was something dangerous or illegal, or both. Since the details of the will, a few things have become clearer to me. I believe your father had taken money out of the business and the house via various mortgages, to pay people off, maybe as bribes. Whatever his latest plan had been, something had obviously backfired.

"By this stage, he was not only agitated, but he was getting angry. He ended the call five minutes later by saying he would sort it, one way or another.

"I didn't see your father for the rest of the day, and as you know I wasn't invited to the pre-wedding drinks party, so I can't say what happened there. I kept myself to myself for the *remainder of the day. I even managed to have a long nap in the afternoon, which meant by bedtime, I struggled to get back to sleep.*

"I'd heard people coming and going from the party all evening, until around midnight when it started to quieten down. Around one in the morning, I decided I wanted some ice-cream. You know what I'm like for my night-time cravings, don't you? It was one of the things you and I shared, that love of ice cream and hot chocolate before bedtime. Those were such happy days."

Richard turned to the next page, his memories swirling around in his head. There were good memories, chatting with Nanny late at night, laughing over their shared tastes, tastes that everyone else in the household thought were bizarre. Mixed with bad memories, of his father and the type of man he had been, the way he had treated him. He was regularly angry and agitated over something, with rarely a kind word to say to him, or anyone else for that matter. The man Nanny described was one with whom he had no difficulty identifying.

Richard continued reading.

"I went to my small freezer, only to discover that I had run out of ice-cream. So, I had the idea to come over to the house and take some from the freezer there. No one would mind, after all there was only you and I that ever ate it, wasn't there? I came downstairs and unlocked the kitchen door and made my way into the pantry. It was a full moon, so the kitchen was light enough and I didn't need to switch on any lights, or risk waking anyone. I took a bowl and a scoop and headed towards the freezer. I was just about to put the ice-cream back, when I heard your father come into the kitchen and close the door behind him.

"He began talking on the phone and, by the nature of what he was saying, it appeared to be the same person I'd heard him speaking to earlier. He'd obviously had a few drinks as he was slurring his words, but I could just about make out the fact that he said, "I've sorted it," adding that Simon would get what was coming to him.

"He'd come up with a way of implicating Simon in what would look like a fraud, as if he'd stolen the money from the business. Your father said he didn't care what it did to his family, or Simon and Judy's marriage for that matter. He was just worried about protecting his own skin, as it was clear someone was out to get him.

"After he ended the call, I saw him reaching for a glass of water and some of my sleeping tablets, which I'd accidently left in the kitchen next to the painkillers. I guess he was after the painkillers and took my tablets by mistake. They're quite strong, and you only need one. I presume he took two. After he'd taken the tablets he turned around and saw me lurking in the shadows, my hand on the freezer door, which was still opened. I hadn't wanted to shut it, as it always made such a racket and regularly jammed, and I didn't want to make any noise.

"Anyway, he stood and looked at me and started talking to me in a most unacceptable way, using language that I found quite distasteful. I imagined it was the drink that was talking, and his fear of being overheard. He accused me of being an interfering old woman, adding that the sooner I left the Old Manor House the better.

"As he approached me I felt scared. I don't know what came over me, and it was certainly not premeditated, but I reached out and grasped the frozen leg of lamb from the freezer. I don't know what I thought I would do with it, but as he got closer, by this time shouting and swearing, vowing to kill me if I ever repeated what I'd overheard, I swung it at his head, *hitting him directly over his left temple. I've always had a powerful right arm, even if I say so myself.*

"He obviously wasn't expecting it, as it caught him off guard. He stumbled and fell over, banging his head heavily on the corner of the kitchen worktop as he fell. It created a nasty gash and blood started to pour instantly from the wound as he lay on the cold stone floor. The tablets he had taken were fast working, and having taken double the dose I didn't think he was dead, but I knew there was no chance of him waking up soon.

"I was a little in shock, and I didn't know what to do, so I simply replaced the lamb in the freezer, along with the tub of ice-cream and left the bowl of ice-cream I'd scooped out on the worktop. I no longer had a craving for it. I went back to my room, although in my haste I forgot to relock the kitchen door behind me. I stayed in my rooms until I heard the caterer's scream several hours later, at which time I came across to the house to see what had happened."

Richard had read Nanny's words so far, and having put some of the pieces together himself a long time ago, he was interested to now learn the full story. He could clearly remember going into the kitchen with Simon and seeing his father's body sprawled out, lying in a pool of his own blood. He remembered feeling quite removed from the scene; shock being his key emotion, before he noticed the bowl of melted ice-cream that was clearly out of place. As he took in the wider scene, he saw Nanny, standing at the sink, desperately trying to tidy away the dirty pots, before the police insisted she leave the room and preserve the evidence.

There was something about the look in her eyes when the police said 'evidence' that had shaken him. No one in the house ate ice-cream other than him and Nanny, and his dad certainly did not. It was a clear give-away that she was involved in some way. It was the context he had struggled to piece together.

He gave a small smile that he had been on the right track, but an even bigger smile when he realised that not only had he and the family eaten the murder weapon, but so had the policeman. Nanny was a canny old bird. He smiled as he continued reading.

"By the time I saw your father it was obvious he had died at some stage during the night. I had certainly not set out to kill him and probably should have called for an ambulance when he fell. Although, over the coming days and weeks, after understanding some of the implications of his death, I would be lying to say I was not glad he had gone. He would have sacrificed you, his family, for his own ends and I could not let that happen. I had sworn, on your mother's life, that I would protect you until my dying breath.

"Now that you know the truth, I will leave it up to you to decide what to do with the information, and If you do choose to go to the police, then so be it. I'm sure my letter will help answer a few of their outstanding questions. If nothing else it will stop them from looking for Mrs Cuthbert, who by the way is fine and living her own life, somewhere where she feels safe.

"If the police do ever catch up with me, I suppose my defence would be that it was a crime of passion; my love akin to a mother's love, prepared to protect her young, regardless of the personal costs.

"And, if you decide not to go to the police, which is obviously my preferred option, I hope you can all forgive me for what I have done and get on with your lives, free from the dangers your father was creating for you. I'll admit that I have been keeping a watchful eye on you all these last few months, and I am so proud to see you all doing well. I believe your father's death has been the making of you.

"With my love always, Nanny Tilbury.

"P.S. As you have probably worked out by now, Nanny Tilbury is not my real name, so if you do want to involve the police, you may want to let them know that. After all, I'd hate to waste their time any further."

Richard saw that although Nanny had signed off her letter, there was still another piece of paper left to go, so he turned straight to that to see what she could possibly have to add. Hadn't her revelations already been enough?

"Richard, I forgot to mention the keys."

Richard picked up the keys that had fallen from the envelope that had been placed on the small table next to him. There were two keys, one large and one small.

"The larger key is to a lock-up at the back of Coronation Terrace, Number 46. I think it would be a good idea to go over there as soon as you can and have a look around. I have been using it over the years to store items from the house. Items that were of value to your mother, and your grandparents before her. They were mainly things in which neither your father, nor Alison or Miranda for that matter, had any interest, and importantly did not see the value of.

"My upbringing, which I won't bore you with as it was such a long time ago, taught me a lot about the art world. It also introduced me to some interesting characters, some of whom I am still in touch with and have helped me over the years. I knew what was fake and what was forgery, it was just the way I was brought up. Being with your mother in those early years, I soon learnt what was of value in the house, and

some of the stories that went with the various pieces. Not everything is of value monetarily, but some items were of sentimental value, especially to your mother.

"You will find paintings, pieces of artwork, even the odd object d'art that was around the house. In fact, there's some rather nice Fabergé jewellery that your grandfather gave to your grandmother on their wedding day, which your mother occasionally wore when she was dressing up. For some reason, she never kept it in the vault at the bank, preferring to keep it close to her. You'll find the jewellery, along with a few priceless items and a couple of original oil paintings. I'm not sure they are all masterpieces, but they are of significant value nonetheless.

"When you see them, you'll notice that similar ones already hang in the house. The ones in the lock-up are the originals, and the ones that hang at home are clever replicas. I had my sources do the copying for me, and all the transportation, as well as arranging valuations, whenever I needed them. Everything is insured and properly stored, and the policy is in your name. All the paperwork is in the filing cabinet, which you can access by using the second key.

"I always feared your father would sell them off if he knew their true value, or he would lose them in one of his many divorces. So, I've been keeping them safe for you, along with the documentation that proves their provenance, which is also locked away in the filing cabinet. If you do decide to sell anything, then the proceeds will keep you comfortable for many years to come.

"Now your father is no longer around to push for Coronation Terrace to be demolished, then at least everything is safe for the time being. I wouldn't leave it too long, though, to go and have a look. You'll be amazed at what you'll find. I'm just sorry I won't be able to see your face when you see it all."

Well, Nanny was a dark horse. Richard thought he knew her well, but even he had never considered she would have connections with the underworld.

After a short time, he reached for his phone and typed a short message on his family group chat.

"Just received a letter that you'll all want to see. Suggest you come around tomorrow night, around seven to discuss. R."

That gave him sufficient time in the morning to check out the lock-up before they arrived. He had no reason to disbelieve anything Nanny had written. He was simply fascinated to discover what Aladdin's cave had to offer for himself first.

Chapter 39

"Well, I'll be damned." James finished reading the letter and passed it straight to Judy to read. Rosie had already read it, Richard having handed it to her as soon as she walked through the door after returning from work.

"Well, she is a dark horse, isn't she? Who'd have thought it, Nanny Tilbury, or whatever her real name is, knocking the old man out. With a frozen leg of lamb, no less. It's bloody brilliant. Not only that, but then getting us all to eat it, to say nothing of that poor police officer, with his lamb sandwich. I suppose the police regularly get accused of losing or misplacing evidence, but I doubt there's many cases where they've been guilty of eating the murder weapon. Brilliant."

"Yes, I have to admit that bit made me smile, too," Richard agreed.

Rosie was sitting on the edge of the sofa, drinking a glass of wine. The fire was blazing away in the grate and the sitting room felt very cosy. It was lovely having the family all together, and even better now that Miranda was out of their lives.

"Do you remember, Richard, how she loved to watch those old episodes of Roald Dahl stories, what were they called *Tales of the Unexpected*, or something like that? I seem to recall one of those involved a leg of lamb being used as the murder weapon. Do you think that's where she got her inspiration?" Rosie laughed.

"I wouldn't be at all surprised, Rosie." He smiled to himself. "Although it certainly sounds as if she had a rather interesting upbringing, doesn't it? She could have got her inspiration from anywhere, especially the way she refers to some of the nefarious characters she's dealt with over the years, and by the sounds of is still in touch with. Forgers, fences and the guys who obviously shifted the gear for her. I can't imagine any of that was legal, can you? How little we actually knew about her, or her background for that matter," he added wryly.

Richard had given them all the highlights of the letter, before letting them read it. That way they were all on the same page. He had chosen, though, not to offer any opinion on the contents of the letter, until they had all read it and made up their own minds. He was clear on what he wanted to do, and if there was any argument he was prepared to fight his corner. However, he realised it was not just his decision. Regardless of the fact Nanny had entrusted him with the truth, it was too much for him to keep to himself. After all, it was not just his father, but all of theirs. They all had to decide what actions needed to be taken.

Richard also explained that he had already visited the lock-up in Coronation Terrace, mainly to confirm it was as Nanny had described and not a hoax, and was pleased to report it was exactly as the letter said.

"It really is like Aladdin's cave in there. There's all sorts of boxes and packages. I can't say I had time to rummage through everything, but there's certainly a lot of stuff that will need sorting. I'm just amazed she managed to steal it away, without Dad, or any of us ever noticing. It just shows how much we really need 'stuff', doesn't it? Although if what she says about the value of some of the items is correct, we could be sitting on a gold mine. In fact, I think some of the items pre-date our grandparents' time, so are genuine antiques. And if the paintings are originals, then they are worth serious money. I googled earlier values for a couple of the pieces and we're talking thousands, possibly hundreds of thousands. Here, look at these." Richard passed around his phone, to show them the photos he had taken from inside the lock-up.

"OMG, Rosie, look, there's racks of clothes hanging at the back, too. I wonder what they are?" Judy's eyes searched the photo. "And Jimmy, look at that antique desk. Do you remember that from years ago, from Grampa's study? I bet that would look great in the farm shop, once it's all done up. I can't wait to go and see it." Judy was getting excited. She loved rummaging around antique shops and the lock-up looked like a dream come true.

"Look, I know it's none of my business and I don't want to rain on your parade, guys, but we need to think this through," Simon cautioned. "None of these items was declared through probate, and if you start flogging them, or bringing it to people's attention, it could start to get tricky. I think we need to be careful what we say, and to whom."

"Well, to an extent that's probably not as big an issue as you think, Si. By the looks of it, Nanny put all the paperwork into my name. So technically it's all mine, not Dad's. I haven't got a clue how she managed it, or which of her contacts sorted it, but when I looked through the insurance paperwork and some of the provenance documents she mentioned, it's clear that everything is in my name, not his."

"Well, that's great. I'd still suggest we're cautious, at least until we know a bit more. And, as she suggests, you probably should get it moved pretty fast, as the developers are still sniffing around Coronation Terrace. Now Frank's gone, you never know how long it will survive. And if everything is as valuable as you suggest, it really needs some security around it, don't you think?" There was a collective nod around the room. It would not do for any of them to get complacent.

"So," James began, hesitantly. "What's everyone's views, now that we've all read the contents of the letter, in terms of whether we go to the police, or not, with what we now know? Who's in favour of keeping shtum, and who wants to come clean and turn her in?"

"I probably speak for us all when I say that turning her in won't turn the clock back, will it? And would any of us want to do that anyway? I genuinely believe she did what she thought was best to protect all of us, not just Si. She was obviously a much wiser old bird than any of us have given her credit, with all the scheming over the years."

Judy smiled over at Simon as she spoke. The thought of him being implicated in something such as fraud, by her own father, was almost indescribable. She would never forgive him for that. "I for one am happy to leave her and Wilf to live their lives in peace. I don't think she owes us anything, and I can't begin to describe what we probably owe her for everything she's done for each of us over the years."

"I'm with Judy on this." Rosie was the next to declare her hand. "Nanny Tilbury is the only real mother I've ever known, and she never once let me down. Her whole life has been dedicated to protecting us. I think it's our turn to protect her now."

"Richard, what about you? What's your view?" James asked.

"I'm with Rosie and Judy. I just wish she was here now, so that I could give her a hug, and ask her to make me a hot chocolate," he laughed. "No one makes it like she does, and I don't think I'll ever find anyone who shares my passion for it with ice-cream, now that she's gone."

"Well, that's unanimous then." James was glad they had reached a decision without a debate. "Si, Katie, I know it's not your call, and that Nanny doesn't mean the same to you as she does to us, but are you happy to keep our secret? If not, then we may have a problem."

"Mate, it was me she was trying to protect, so I'm with you guys. Your secret's safe with me." Simon took Judy's hand, as she smiled over at him, grateful for his support.

"Same here. Nanny welcomed me into the family like no other, so I'm not going to let her down now either. Although I might change my mind if I don't get first dibs on those Fabergé earrings," she added, laughing across at Rosie, who was still closely studying Richard's photos of the loot from the lock-up.

"Great, so we just need to decide what to do about Coronation Terrace, and all that lovely booty. At this rate, we might not even have to sell the house."

As they were all laughing and discussing their next moves, over a second bottle of wine, the doorbell rang.

"Who do you think that is, at this time of night?" It was seven o'clock and already pitch-black outside. Richard walked to the window and pulled back the curtains to look out.

"It's the police. I better go and answer the door." He had a worried look on his face as he stared around the room at his siblings. "I wonder what they want?"

DS Jacobs was standing on the doorstep with PC Dickson beside her, the two of them almost shivering as they waited for the door to be opened. "Officers, how can I help you?"

"Good evening, Mr Paulson. There's an update on your father's case that we would like to brief you on. I apologise that it's late, but we went around to your brother's house earlier this evening and his mother-in-law said you were all at the manor. So, I thought it would be easier to come here and talk to you all together, rather than waiting until the morning. Do you mind if we come in, it's quite cold standing here?"

"Certainly, come through, we're in the sitting room. Would you care for a drink?"

"No, thank you. A warm should be fine."

"Good evening, Officers. Is everything alright? It's a little late for a house call, isn't it?" James was curious to learn the purpose of their visit.

"Yes, as I just explained to your brother, I wanted to update you on the enquiry into your father's death. Your mother-in-law kindly told me you were all together, so I wanted to take the opportunity of killing two birds with one stone, so to speak." As soon as the words left Ruth's mouth, she regretted her turn of speech. "I apologise, that was insensitive of me."

James smiled. "There's nothing to apologise for. I'm sure we all understand what you meant."

"Well, I wanted to let you know that we have finally tracked down Mrs Cuthbert. As you're aware, when she left so suddenly and without warning, there was a concern that her departure was connected in some way with your father's death. Whilst we always treated Miss Swann's allegation with a degree of caution, we did still want to contact Mrs Cuthbert, if at all possible." Ruth noticed a few cringes at the mention of Miss Swann's name.

"As you may know, we had evidence that she had used her bank card in London. My officer called round a few months ago to let Mr Cuthbert know. I'm not sure if you were aware? Anyway, we eventually tracked her down to an address in London. A local officer called around to the property earlier today and spoke with her on our behalf. The property is owned by Mr Carl Gilbert. He has a second property in Chidlington, I understand.

"It would appear since she left here she has been living with Mr Gilbert, who you may recall was a contact of your father's, and someone who was at the house the night of the party?" They all nodded.

Neil continued. "You may also recall there was a car that was unaccounted for the morning of Mr Paulson's death? We soon realised it was Mr Gilbert's, but for some time we were unable to make contact with him, and at the time we had no idea of any connection between him and Mrs Cuthbert."

"Yes, it would appear they had been having an affair for some time. Mr Cuthbert was unaware, but assumed something along those lines, hence the reason he'd not reported his wife missing."

"Anyway, according to Mr Gilbert, who was spoken to at the same time, the vehicle wouldn't start and it had a puncture the night of the party. Something he noticed as he was leaving. That Sunday he called the garage to organise a recovery, instructing them to return it to his property in town. He was due to fly overseas on business a couple of days later. His disappearance at the time was considered unusual, however it all checks out."

"We also followed up on a couple of leads relating to allegations of bribery and corruption in the council, especially with the planning committee. Even one relating to an employee who'd had a run-in with your father, over a traffic accident. One that you were involved in Mr Paulson, I believe?" Ruth added, looking over at Richard. "There was an outstanding complaint on file. Whilst it appeared there was still a lot of ill feeling between the gentleman and your father, there was not sufficient to provide a motive for murder."

None of them said a word as they watched the game of ping-pong play out between the two officers as they updated them on their enquiries. They were all afraid what they might say if they opened their mouths, unable to trust their words, or their faces from betraying their emotions. Nanny's letter was still in James' hand, as he stood in front of the police, concentrating on what they were saying. He could almost sense their eyes drilling into it.

Katie had noticed DS Jacobs gradually walk towards the fire to warm herself as they had been speaking.

"I love a proper fire, especially at this time of the year," Katie said in an attempt to make the officer feel relaxed. "It's so cosy, isn't it, Officer?"

"Yes, I agree. I think this one's almost burned out, though. You might need to add a couple more logs, before it burns down. Do you mind if I add some, as I love stoking a real fire?"

The flames were making her feel drowsy. It had been a long day, and after this house call it would be time to go home for a hot bath, a glass of chilled wine and some good food. She was also looking forward to some cuddles on the sofa with her husband and daughter. The order they came in was almost immaterial.

"Be our guest, in fact I was just about to throw this on, so here, why don't you?" James scrunched the letter into his hand and handed over the balled paper to DS Jacobs, who promptly threw it into the grate, along with a log of firewood that Richard had handed to her.

They all watched as the flames grew. Watched as the police unwittingly burned the best piece of evidence they would ever have. A signed confession.

"Oh, thank you, Officer," Rosie said. "That appears to have got it started again."

"Yes," Ruth replied, rubbing her hands together. "So, without taking up any more of your time, we just wanted to let you know that without any other evidence to consider, we've decided to close the case. Obviously if anything else materialises in the future, then we will consider reopening it. For now, though, I believe Officer Dickson and I have exhausted all the leads."

"On balance, it probably was just an unfortunate accident," Neil offered, believing his initial view to have now been fully vindicated.

"Thank you, Officers. And as you say, with no evidence to the contrary, we must accept it was an accident and simply get on with our lives. We do however appreciate all your hard work, and especially for taking the time to come and tell us in person. That was very kind of you. Now, shall I show you out? It's late and I'm sure you both have homes to go to."

"Yes, Good night everyone."

As the front door closed, there was a collective sigh of relief from within the sitting room.

"I think I'll open another bottle of wine," Richard suggested as soon as the police car could be heard driving away. "Perversely, it feels like we suddenly have a lot to celebrate!"

The End.

Review

If you have enjoyed The Dishonourable Groom, I would love it if you could leave a positive review on Amazon, and perhaps recommend it to your family and friends.

And, if you haven't yet discovered any of my other novels, please check these out at Amazon.com or Amazon.co.uk

Finding Home *and its sequel* **Forever Home** *- both published in 2022*
After the Rain *– published in 2023*
The Godmothers *– published in 2023.*

Thank you, Angela

Printed in Great Britain
by Amazon